THE JAKE

PERSONAL DEMONS

BY GREGORY LAMBERSON

Medallion Press, Inc.
Printed in USA

DEDICATION

Dedicated to Tom Sweeney and Joseph Fusco,
with whom I experienced some of the adventures
that inspired this novel

Published 2009 by Medallion Press, Inc.

The MEDALLION PRESS LOGO
is a registered trademark of Medallion Press, Inc.

Cover Illustration by Dan Plumley and Adam Mock

Typeset in Adobe Jenson Pro
Printed in the United States of America

ISBN:978-160542072-1

10 9 8 7 6 5 4 3 2 1
First Edition

ACKNOWLEDGMENTS

Personal Demons started as a screenplay I wrote in 1987 called *The Forever Man.* About 90 percent of the material in that script survived the translation to novel form, but it comprises only half of the story you're about to read. In the wake of 9/11, while still living in New York City, I realized I had a much bigger story to tell.

This novel is dedicated to two friends, Tom Sweeney and Joseph Fusco, with whom I experienced some of the events fictionalized in this book. Drunk and impatient to reach our Bay Ridge, Brooklyn, apartment one night, Tommy and I actually made a subway tunnel trek like the one Jake Helman makes in *Personal Demons.* A train did blast through the darkness toward us and we really did survive, only because we miraculously stumbled into an empty storage cellar. Joe and I survived an even more frightening experience together: a one-year tour of duty in corporate America, in a high security office building. Two years later—and shortly before 9/11—I had another corporate gig in a building where the obsession with security reached even greater levels of paranoia.

I gratefully acknowledge the invaluable advice given to me by three authors who generously read the first draft of this manuscript: Paul G. Tremblay, Kathy Ptacek, and Nick Mamatas. They pulled no punches, which is what every aspiring writer needs. Robert Craig Sabin, the star of my first film, *Slime City*, provided me with excellent advice as well.

I wish to thank T.M. Wright, one of my favorite authors, for selecting *Personal Demons* as the winner of the Anubis Award for Horror, and Jeff Schwaner of Broken Umbrella Press for publishing the novel as a Limited Edition hardcover and small press trade paperback. I also wish to thank the readers of those obscure editions who wrote to tell me how much they enjoyed my story; your support fueled my desire to see this work reach a wider audience.

Thank you to the folks at Medallion Press for making that possible: Helen A. Rosburg, Adam Mock, James Tampa, Ali DeGray, Christy Phillippe, and Paul Ohlson. With their continued support, I hope to write additional Jake Helman Chillers.

Thanks, as always, to my wife, Tamar, for understanding how much work is required to see a novel through to publication.

And Cain talked with Abel his brother: and it came to pass, when they were in the field, that Cain rose up against Abel his brother, and slew him.

And the LORD said unto Cain, Where is Abel thy brother? And he said, I know not: Am I my brother's keeper?

And he said, What has thou done? the voice of thy brother's blood crieth unto me from the ground.

—Genesis 4:8–10, *The King James Version of the Holy Bible*

Perched on a bar stool with her legs crossed, Shannon Reynolds sipped her Tom Collins and played with the fluffy, spotted tail of her costume. Around her, young Americans in colorful getups hoisted pints of beer to their lips and threw back Jell-O shots, their loud voices giving way to drunken laughter. Jack-o'-lanterns leered at her from the lacquered bar top, the candles within them flickering whenever the front door opened, and a giant spiderweb made of orange and black crepe paper dripped from the ceiling.

In Ireland, Shannon had celebrated the festival of Samhain with her family each year on this night. The ancient Celtic and Druid ritual marked the end of summer and the start of a new year, and spirits walked the earth. Her mum cooked the traditional Colcannon dinner of broiled potato and curly kale cabbage, followed by Barnbrack cake, and at bedtime, each family member cast an ivy leaf into his personal cup of water. According to legend, those whose leaves remained unblemished at sunrise were destined to enjoy a prosperous year. But if any leaf developed spots during the night, its bearer was destined to suffer a dreadful fate.

Shannon smiled at the memory of her favorite superstitious tradition. Here in the States, Halloween had become nothing but an excuse for shop owners to sell garish costumes and candy corn, and for television stations to dust off lame sequels to bad horror films. She'd been looking forward to the exotic parade in Greenwich Village, but her employers, the Smythes, had forbidden her from exposing their children to the "sexually deviant behavior" associated with the pageant. Instead, she took her charges, Evan and Paige, trick-or-treating within the safety of their luxury apartment building on the Upper West Side. Evan had dressed up as Captain America, and Paige had gone as Wonder Woman. Later, while the kids watched black-and-white monster movies on TV—no Jason or Freddy for them—she inspected their sweets for razor blades and other signs of tampering.

Bloody insane world.

"The Monster Mash" came over the speakers for the second time since Shannon had arrived at the pub, and the costumed drunks singing along still couldn't manage to get the lyrics right. Shannon looked at her watch: midnight, the Witching Hour. Her roommate,

Meg, must have gone to the flat of her new boyfriend, Ronald or Donald or something, a cocky investment banker. Stroking the gold crucifix suspended from a chain around her neck, she gazed at its reflection in the mirror behind the bar. Orange candlelight flickered on the crucifix's polished surface.

Bollocks, she thought, draining her tall glass. *Too late to make other plans.* She pulled on her red leather jacket and tossed back her blond hair. As she slid from the stool, her eyes locked on those of a man sitting in the shadows at the far end of the bar. Sitting alone, he appeared to be in his midtwenties, clean shaven, with short, sandy brown hair. His charcoal gray business suit blended with the shadows, which explained why she had not noticed him nursing his bottle of Heineken.

But she noticed him now, and he'd obviously noticed her. How long had he been watching her? Holding her gaze, he smiled at her and then raised the green bottle to his mouth. Shannon's body tingled with nervous excitement. Raising her glass to her lips, she used her tongue to separate the maraschino cherry from half-melted ice cubes. Then she set the glass down and sucked on the cherry between her teeth. Perhaps the night would not be a waste of time after all.

With the gin in her bloodstream emboldening her, she took a deep breath, detached herself from the bar, and circled it on numb legs. Had she already had too much to drink? Clearing the costumed bodies in her path, she zeroed in on the empty seat beside her target. In the dingy glow emanating from a neon beer sign, his features appeared delicate, almost feminine, his Brooks Brothers suit tailored for his slim frame. Stepping before him, she felt his liquid blue eyes measuring the curves of her body.

"Nice costume," he said over the music and drunken chatter.

She had almost forgotten about the feline ears clipped to her hair, and the tail pinned to her miniskirt. "And what are ye supposed to be?" Following Meg's advice, she played up her brogue.

"A Hell's Angel." He said this without even a hint of irony.

She summoned an appreciative laugh.

"Actually, I'm a CPA." Smiling, he raised a black leather briefcase into view. "I had a late business dinner with a client and thought I'd have a drink before cabbing it home to Brooklyn. I completely forgot about Halloween."

Shannon leaned against the bar, offering him a glimpse of her cleavage through the flaps of her jacket. If only Meg could have seen her! "Sure ye did. I bet that's just your bag for trick-or-treating, and it's full of goodies."

His eyes dipped to where she desired them. "Just an adding machine and a worn-down Number Two pencil, I'm afraid."

"I'm Shannon." She held out her left hand instead of her right, and when he shook it she saw no wedding band on his finger.

"Byron." He paused. "What's a pretty kitty like you doing alone on a night like this?"

Shannon shrugged. "'Where's Old Nick?'" The phrase had become a common response to unanswerable questions ever since Nicholas Tower, the world-famous billionaire, had gone into self-imposed exile three years earlier.

Byron's smile widened. "Can I buy you a drink?"

"Only if I can buy the next round."

"It's a deal."

Lou Reed's "Halloween Parade" blasted over the speakers.

Inside the vestibule of Shannon's building, she and Byron rubbed their hands together for warmth, laughing as the wind howled at them from the other side of the glass door. Their footsteps echoed in the stairway as they climbed to the second floor, and Shannon felt warm anticipation rising from her thighs. She unlocked her apartment door and flipped the switch for the overhead light, and they entered the long, narrow kitchen, large by Manhattan standards.

"Nice place," Byron said as Shannon closed the door and twisted the locks. Steam hissed from a radiator in the darkness beyond the kitchen.

"It's not worth half what we're paying for it, and I'm

told we got a sweet deal. But what can ye do? This is New York City, as everyone insists on reminding us."

She led him into the darkness, the heels of her pumps clacking on the hardwood floor. She switched on a tall halogen lamp, and bright light bounced off the living room ceiling. A solitary window faced a brick wall close enough to touch, and framed photographs of smiling faces and rolling green hills obscured the titles of paperbacks nestled in a wooden bookcase.

"This is my suite," she said, sweeping her arm like a game show hostess, "and that's my bed." She pointed at the foldout sofa on the other side of a chest that served as both a dresser and a coffee table. "I must seem like an orphan in a Charles Dickens novel, but Meg moved here first, so she got the bedroom." Cocking her head to one side, she smiled. "But it's all ours tonight."

Pushing on the door beside the modest television, she led him into the dark bedroom. A white shag rug muffled Shannon's steps as she circled the queen-sized bed. Two windows on either side of the headboard overlooked the street, and drunken laughter rose on the wind. She clicked on a small lamp with a red shade, which glowed beneath her like a small fire. Returning to the spot where Byron stood, she closed the door, shutting out the living room light. The sound of his even breathing made her smile.

Stepping to one side, Shannon pressed the PLAY button on the CD player atop Meg's bureau, and Bono launched into a live rendition of "Sunday, Bloody

Sunday." She hummed along with him as she removed the cat ears from her hair and set them down. Seeing Byron's reflection in the mirror, his eyes appraising her body from behind, she felt a surge of impatient desire. "Are ye going to keep your coat on all night?"

He smiled in the dim light. "That could prove awkward."

"Spot-on." Her words came out sounding slurred. Unpinning the cat tail from her miniskirt, she twirled it as she faced him.

Byron set his briefcase down on the bureau and slipped off his coat, which he laid over the back of a padded chair. "I've never made love to a cat before."

A cat in heat, Shannon thought, suppressing a giggle as she closed in on her guest. Purring, she ran her painted fingernails up the front of his shirt and loosened his tie, leaning close to his face. His lips parted, and she teased them with the end of the tail. His nostrils flared and she dropped the tail on the floor.

"Meow," she said, closing her mouth over his. Their lips pressed against each other, their tongues meeting. She breathed in his cologne, a subtle brand she failed to recognize, and her heart beat faster. Pulling the jacket from his shoulders, she threw it on top of his coat. She circled the bed once more, swinging her hips, and faced him from the other side. Drawing the tab of her jacket zipper down inch by inch, she allowed the fringed leather to slip to the floor. Stepping out of her shoes, she watched

Byron pull his tie over his head like a noose and toss it on top of his garments. She pulled her top over her head and discarded it on the floor. Unhooking her lacy black bra and tossing it aside, she exposed her pale, freckled breasts to him, the crucifix gleaming between them. She hooked her thumbs inside her miniskirt and wiggled her hips free of the tight fabric, then stood before him in black panties, her breasts rising and falling as she waited for him to catch up to her.

Byron unbuttoned his shirt with methodic deliberation and stepped over to the bureau with his back to her. He thumbed the tabs on his briefcase and the latches snapped open.

Shannon stood on her toes, trying to see inside the case as Byron raised its lid. "What are you doing?"

"Just getting ready," he said under his breath.

She scrunched her eyebrows together. Did he carry condoms in his briefcase? American businessmen were so anal!

Byron moved his hands in the darkness, and Shannon heard the elastic snap of latex. When he turned around, she saw that he wore opaque surgical gloves. He whipped off his shirt in a fluid motion and flung it at the chair, the sudden motion causing her to flinch. Even in the dim light, she discerned the taut muscles on his wiry frame. She squinted at the colorful tattoos covering the upper half of his torso, and confusion clouded her eyes. He had seemed so straightlaced in the pub, hardly the type for such elaborate needlework. Her instincts told her this made no sense, that she had miscalculated his makeup.

Byron reached into the briefcase behind him. Raising a pocket-sized digital camera to one eye, he squeezed its shutter button. The flash made Shannon blink, spots dancing before her eyes, and she heard a whirring sound.

"What the *fuck?*"

Without making a sound, Byron returned the camera to the briefcase and took out a second object. As he moved around the corner of the bed, closing the distance between them, Shannon's mind registered the details of the tattoos on his chest and gasped. Then she saw the long blade of the knife in his hand and her eyes widened.

This isn't happening, she thought, sobering as panic coursed through her veins. She backed against the bedside table and the lamp crashed to the floor. The flickering bulb projected her shadow over the stranger she had brought home. No, wait; her real home was far away, in Ireland . . .

"Get the hell out of here right now!" The outburst strained her vocal cords as she scanned the dark room for something with which to defend herself. Why couldn't Meg suddenly walk in with Ronald or Donald, or whatever the hell his name was?

Byron raised the knife high above his head and brought it down in a broad, diagonal stroke. First the blade sliced through the darkness, then through the soft flesh of Shannon's throat, jerking her off balance. Hearing something spatter the wall to her right, she flailed her arms, struggling to maintain her balance. Blood jetted out from beneath her jaw, painting the floral bedcovers.

Sweet Lord Jesus! She gagged on hot fluid rising from within her, and she knew it was not bile.

Byron rotated the knife and slashed upward with a backswing, severing her jugular vein. More blood spattered the mirror behind him.

Shannon tried to scream, but only a strangled gurgling escaped her throat. The hot liquid filled her mouth and she saw her reflection in the spotted mirror: blood sprayed out in opposing directions from the gaping wounds in her throat, which opened and closed like small, screaming mouths.

That isn't me, she thought, collapsing onto the rug, her body tingling. She tried to support herself on her elbows but fell back. Her head rolled to one side on the rug, blood pumping out over her bare shoulders and breasts. The wet sounds of her own breathing filled her ears as she gazed up at the ceiling. The swirling pattern in the plaster inspired images of clouds in heaven, and the flickering lightbulb suggested lightning. Footsteps vibrated the floor and she dropped her gaze. Byron had returned to the bureau, his naked back to her. No tattoos there. He set the bloody knife inside his briefcase and removed something else.

Why is he doing this? He had seemed so kind—so safe—in the pub, and she had only wanted to get close to him for one night. Her head throbbed and she felt her

life ebbing away. Her feet jerked in spasms, and she wondered if they were keeping time with the beat of the U2 song fading on the boom box.

"Sunday, bloody Sunday . . ."

Byron returned to her, his movements calm and detached.

He leaned over and clasped what looked like an oxygen mask with a translucent vinyl bag attached to it over her mouth and nose. She felt his breath on her face and saw twin reflections of herself in his eyes. His lips moved rhythmically, forming unintelligible words.

Chanting—?

She wanted to pull the mask away, but her limbs refused to obey the commands from her brain. The smell of vinyl filled her nostrils and the bag attached to the mask crinkled up as she sucked in oxygen. Then it inflated as she exhaled. She felt light-headed, and as her vision turned dark, she saw Byron—what was his last name?—staring down at her, waiting for her to die.

She knew he would not have to wait long.

Darkness, followed by blinding white light.

Deprived of her senses, Shannon no longer felt the wounds in her throat. She experienced an odd sensation of ascension; it soothed her, like floating on her back in a gentle stream, naked in languid sunlight.

Where am I?

Perhaps she had only passed out, drunk, and the man with the knife had existed only in a nightmare. Or maybe he really had stabbed her, and she now lay in a coma, trapped inside her mind with nothing but her thoughts for company. She concentrated, willing herself to see again, and the world came into focus through the light: it was like staring through a veil of cottony gauze. A bright, golden glow filled the bedroom even though the only visible light source was the lamp on the floor. Her hearing returned, the sounds in the room amplified as they ricocheted around her; she went from sensory deprivation to sensory overload in an instant. She heard deep breathing and an excited heartbeat, neither of them her own. Two gigantic eyes stared down at her, blue and crystalline. She felt like an insect trapped in a jar before—

God?

No—Byron. He lifted her toward him as if she was an infant, yet she did not feel his hands on her. His lips split open like a fissure, revealing his teeth, snowcapped mountains. She tried to pull away, but her body refused to respond. Then her peripheral vision expanded, opening up as if her eyeballs had been turned inside out, and she saw around her in every direction at once.

What's happening to me?

Her body lay bloody and motionless on the floor

below her, an empty shell, and she stared into her own unblinking eyes. The gold crucifix between her breasts shimmered in the light, the blood around it rippling. Could all of that blood have come from her?

Dead. No use denying it. The bastard had murdered her! How would Meg react when she discovered her corpse? How would her parents cope with the news? She felt a gentle tide tugging at her and sensed she belonged elsewhere, that Byron's attention was somehow keeping her from her natural destination. Again she tried to break free of his grasp, but it was like trying to awaken from a nightmare that would not release her. Her thoughts scattered like dust in a windstorm, and when they re-formed, she realized that her disembodied essence had been trapped within the vinyl bag affixed to the oxygen mask.

Now I lay me down to sleep, I pray the Lord my soul to keep . . .

Byron turned toward the bureau, and Shannon saw his reflection in the blood-spattered mirror: he held the inflated oxygen bag between his palms like a basketball. The bright light emanated from inside the bag—from *her*—but Byron seemed blind to it. He stepped toward the bureau as if carrying a fragile antique. Shannon focused on the briefcase as they approached it: inside it she saw the bloody knife and the camera. Her panic multiplied a thousandfold.

Not in there!

Stopping at the bureau, Byron set the bag inside the case, fitting it snug in a compartment. Smiling down at her, he closed the lid like that of a coffin. The bag flattened out and Shannon sensed it expanding on the sides. Her light filled the interior of the case, spotlighting the candy-colored blood on the knife's blade. She heard two clicks as Byron latched the tabs, then felt vibrations as he thumbed the combination locks, entombing her.

A scream welled up inside her, unable to escape.

Jake Helman stood on the sidewalk of West Forty-fifth Street, in the upscale Manhattan neighborhood formerly known as Hell's Kitchen. The current residents preferred to call the area Clinton or Restaurant Row, but to Jake it would always be Midtown North, one of the precincts below Fifty-ninth Street that comprised Manhattan South. He lit his second consecutive Marlboro to steady his nerves, but the nicotine only added to his edge. Less than one hour into his shift, the rising sun restored color to the faded urine and vomit stains on the gray concrete, the remains of smashed pumpkins rotting near his feet.

Jake hated Mondays, especially during morning rush hour. The neighborhood yuppies moved like lemmings to the nearest subway station, casting sideways glances at the police activity on the block. Jake stood rigid in a cascading river of khaki slacks, designer sunglasses, and cell phones. Inhaling cigarette smoke, he tensed his muscles beneath his three-quarter-length black leather coat, and the tide of corporate hucksters parted around him like the Red Sea around Moses.

The pulsating strobes of three Radio Motor Patrol cars and one Emergency Services ambulance parked along the one-way street splashed garish red and blue light on the residential buildings. The doors of the white radio cars bore the NYPD's motto in sky blue lettering: COURTESY, PROFESSIONALISM, RESPECT. Jake had parked his unmarked Chevy Cavalier up the block, behind the EMS bus. Uniformed police officers stood outside the apartment building behind him and along the curb before him, controlling the crowd.

Across the street, behind a chain-link fence, schoolchildren chased each other around a playground, their joyful shouts rising above the traffic noise coming from Eleventh Avenue. Jake watched them with bleary eyes. After two years of marriage, Sheryl wanted a baby. He had shared her desire at first, but he had only been in the Special Homicide Task Force for one year then, a rising star on the prestige team. After three years in the unit, he knew firsthand that terrible things happened to children in the boroughs of New York City. Sheryl wanted to move from their one-bedroom apartment on the Upper East Side, in the One-Nine Precinct, to Long Island, where she believed the suburbs offered relative sanctuary from the city's brutality. They had begun saving money for a down payment on a house, but Jake knew that children were vulnerable to predators in even the most mundane settings. His mind reconstructed the image of a photograph he had spent countless hours studying: a school portrait of a six-year-old girl named Rhonda Kelly, whose own father had—

Stop it.

The image faded, receding into the dark corridors of his mind. His knees shook as he sucked on the cigarette; at thirty-two, he felt more like fifty.

"You Helman?" a female voice said behind him.

Jake turned toward the brick building. Two paramedics emerged behind the patrolman stationed at the front door: a Chinese man with spiky black hair and acne-scarred cheeks, and a short black woman with relaxed hair. Jake recognized them from other homicide sites, but did not know their names. He nodded in response to the woman's query.

She lit a cigarette. "Your partner says to stop procrastinating and get your ass upstairs."

Jake mustered a faint smile and took a final drag on his Marlboro, which he flicked into the gutter. "How bad is it up there?"

The Chinese man shook his head, his complexion matching his green Windbreaker.

"When are you guys gonna catch this freak?" the woman said.

Jake shrugged. "'Where's Old Nick?'"

Raising her left hand, the woman showed him a palm-sized digital camera strapped around her wrist. "I took some snaps," she said in a conspiratorial tone. "I bet I can sell copies on eBay."

Jake didn't respond. He had nothing against city employees scoring a little extra bread on the side, but he loathed serial killer memorabilia, the parasites who bought it, and the ghouls who pushed it.

Sensing his disapproval, the woman motioned to her partner. "Have a good one," she told Jake. "If that's still possible once you see the vic."

"You, too."

The Chinese man gave Jake a grim nod and followed the woman up the sidewalk to the EMS bus. Jake debated lighting another cigarette and decided against it. He looked up at the windows on the second floor and closed his eyes, listening to the sounds of the children across the street.

I don't want to go up there, he thought. *But I've got no choice.* When he opened his eyes, he saw the patrolman at the door staring at him.

"You okay?"

"Yeah," Jake said without conviction. Taking a deep breath, he entered the building. Another day, another corpse.

The sunlight behind Jake projected his shadow across the lobby's dusty stairway. He felt pressure building at the base of his skull as he looked up at the second floor and heard muted voices beyond his field of vision. Reaching into the left-hand pocket of his coat, he removed a small jar of vapor rub. He popped the lid, dipped two fingers into the cold, gelatinous substance, and rubbed some inside each nostril. A tingling sensation awakened his senses: the poor man's fix.

He grasped the banister and climbed the stairs, unsnapping his coat and tugging at the collar of his black turtleneck. Sheryl, who worked as the buyer and manager for a fashion boutique in Soho, selected all of his clothes. His fellow detectives chided him for being the sharpest dresser in his unit, but he secretly enjoyed the attention.

He turned left at the landing. At the opposite end of the narrow hall, standing before an open doorway crisscrossed with yellow crime scene tape, a uniformed officer consoled a woman with fiery red hair. As Jake approached them, he saw that the attractive woman was in her twenties. Her open coat revealed a sheer, body-hugging costume and she twisted a pair of *Playboy* bunny ears with her hands, her knuckles turning white. She'd probably just returned home from a long night of partying, Jake reasoned. She uttered a few words between choked sobs and he recognized an Irish accent.

A sudden flash of light inside the apartment, like distant lightning or the muzzle flash of a pistol, made his heart skip a beat. He found the lack of an accompanying sound unsettling. In his decade on the Job, he had never fired a gun in a crisis, though he had pulled his Glock Nine from its shoulder holster on several occasions. The queasy feeling in his stomach clawed its way up his throat.

Keep it together, Jake.

A diminutive woman lurked in an open doorway to his left, dressed in a dirty blue robe. She had stark white hair and wrinkled, birdlike eyes. The look he shot her sent her scurrying into the bowels of her apartment. The officer nodded to him, a somber expression on his face. Jake averted his eyes to avoid the sobbing woman. He would deal with her when necessary. A second flash of light blossomed inside the apartment.

Ducking beneath the tape, he came face-to-face with another officer in the kitchen. The well-groomed PO looked fresh out of the Academy. His complexion pale, he clutched a pen in one hand and a notebook in the other.

"Detective Helman," Jake said. "That's with one *L*. You guys always get that wrong."

"Yes, sir." The Recorder noted Jake's name and the time in his log.

"That the First Officer?" Jake nodded at the patrolman in the hall.

The Recorder nodded. "Yes, sir. His name is

Wilkins. I'm Keller."

Wilkins had been the First Officer on the scene. He had contacted Dispatch Control, which had then contacted Special Homicide rather than the Detective Area Task Force for Manhattan South. Entering the living room, Jake felt a stillness hanging in the air. He turned in a complete circle, feeling like an intruder as he scanned the room for details. A tall halogen lamp—common in Manhattan apartments, which often lacked overhead lighting—had been left on. Makeup, skin care products, and framed photographs covered the shelves of a cherry wood bookcase. An open doorway led into the only bedroom.

Stepping closer to the bookcase, he noted rosary beads coiled on one shelf and he studied the photographs. In one, two teenage girls stood giggling outdoors, the wind whipping their hair. He recognized the woman in the hall as the girl on the left, and connected her accent to the green landscape in the photo's background. The girl on the right also appeared in the next photo, with her arms around the waists of a man and woman—her parents, Jake guessed—outside a Tudor-style house. The blonde had a wide smile and appeared to have lost weight between shots.

Another flash drew his attention to the sunlit bedroom. Bracing himself for the worst, he stepped through the doorway. To his left, Detective Edgar Hopkins raised a digital camera, his hands gloved in cream-colored latex. The tall black man aimed the camera at the floor on the far side of the bed, and the ensuing flash caused Jake to see spots dancing before his eyes.

Staring at the ribbons of blood radiating out from the violent splotch in the center of the bed, Jake said, "No need for Luminol here." The phosphorous chemical caused blood traces to glow in the dark.

Edgar glanced at him with one eyebrow cocked as he lowered the camera. "It's about time. I was about to call Missing Persons on your ass."

"Those jokers couldn't find me if there was only one bar in all of Manhattan." Eyeing the swirling patterns of blood that had dried on the walls in the far corner, Jake took a pair of latex gloves from his coat pocket and pulled them on. "Happy All Saints Day, by the way."

Edgar grunted. "You're not religious."

"Old habits die hard." Through the closed windows, Jake heard the voices of the children across the street fading as they filed inside their school, which meant that the 9:00 a.m. bell had rung. He nodded in the direction of the hidden corpse. "Number six?"

Edgar nodded. "Cipher: six; Murder Police: zero. This asshole's making us look like chumps."

Stepping over a spotted costume tail, Jake moved around the foot of the bed. A matching pair of cat ears rested on the bureau, beside a silent boom box with a glowing red LED light. He glimpsed his reflection through streaks of blood on the bureau's mirror, then joined Edgar and swallowed. The corpse of a young blond woman lay on the floor, nude except for her black panties. He recognized her from the photos in the living room. Her discarded shoes and clothing lay around her in disarray. Two slits, approximately two inches long, opened her throat, and clotted blood had matted her hair to the sides of her neck. More blood, thick and syrupy, covered her torso and the white shag rug beneath her, and a gold crucifix lay caked in red between her breasts. She stared at the ceiling with glazed eyes, her lips parted. Her flesh had turned blue, laced with ghastly streaks of purple, and she had soiled herself. Jake felt grateful that the vapor rub in his nostrils blocked the odors. A fly buzzed somewhere in the room, and he admired its tenacity for surviving out of season; maggots would soon follow.

"'I could not stop for Death, so He gladly stopped for me.'"

Now Jake cocked one eyebrow at Edgar.

"Emily Dickinson."

"I knew that," Jake said with a straight face. "You're not the only one who graduated from college."

"She was a pretty girl. Our boy's first nude. Looks like she performed a striptease for him. No telling what else she did just yet. But this is different from the others. It was no home invasion. Something consensual happened here before things turned ugly." Edgar raised the camera and squeezed off another shot.

The close flash made Jake flinch and lingered in the pupils of the dead woman's eyes. "Can't you say 'fire in the hole' before you do that?"

Edgar pocketed the camera and took out a notebook. "Do I tell you how to do your job?"

"Every damned day."

"That's why you've made it this far." He opened the notebook. "Meet Shannon Reynolds, age twenty-two. Moved here from Leprechaun Land two months ago."

"Watch it . . ."

"Don't get your Irish up."

Jake snorted. His father had been German-Irish, his mother pure Irish.

"Shannon worked as a nanny for a family on West End Avenue. The young lady in the hall is her roommate, Meg Foley. Similar stats—you know how these foreign nannies like to stick together. Meg saw Shannon at breakfast yesterday morning, spent last night with her boyfriend in Williamsburg, and came home to this at 0730. This is her bedroom; Shannon slept on the sofa, at least until last night. Meg's too broken up to tell us if anything's missing."

Jake frowned. He knew what the result would be once Meg had calmed down enough to inventory the apartment's contents. Unlike many serial killers, the Cipher did not collect souvenirs from his victims, making it more difficult for the detectives to construct a psychological profile. Jake stared at Shannon's crucifix.

Souvenirs . . .

An image formed in his mind. "There are rosary

beads in the living room."

Edgar shrugged. "Yeah, I noticed."

"She was Catholic."

"Uh-huh."

"Jerez and Yee were Catholic, too."

"So? Bass was Methodist. Rosenthal was Jewish. I don't remember what Williams was."

"Presbyterian."

"What's your point? Three out of six vics were Catholic and three weren't. That's no pattern."

"None of them were atheists."

Edgar narrowed his eyes.

Jake pointed at the crucifix. "We've been beating ourselves up searching for a common link between the vics, and this might be it. Each one was religious, or at least subscribed to a nominal religion."

Edgar stroked the ends of his mustache. "You think our boy has it in for the righteous? I see blood on the walls, not pentagrams."

"I didn't say anything about satanic rites. But look at her wounds. They're exactly like the others: precision cuts to the jugular and carotid. No deviation."

"Jack the Ripper was supposedly a surgeon."

"He's not just killing them; he's *bleeding* them."

"So what are you saying, that the Cipher's been committing human sacrifices? That will go over big at the next press briefing. It will also get your ass sent back to Alphabet City."

Recalling the frustrating two years he had served as a plainclothes detective in the Street Narcotics Apprehension Program on Avenues A, B, C, and D, Jake sighed. "These murders are orderly, possibly ritualistic."

"How would you know? The only ritual you ever perform is kneeling at the toilet after a night of heavy drinking."

Jake said nothing and Edgar offered him the end of a measuring tape. They measured the distances from Shannon's corpse to the various bloodstains around the room, with Edgar recording the measurements.

"According to Meg, Shannon didn't have any boyfriends since moving here, and she wasn't the type to sleep around."

Jake stepped closer to the body, a knot twisting in his stomach. "Yeah? Then she made an exception last night. She didn't dress up like a cat just to curl up at the foot of her roommate's bed. She went out and partied, and she brought home the wrong guy. Trick or treat."

Edgar gestured at the corpse. "We've got rigor mortis and lividity, and the body's cold. Given the room temperature and her size, I'd say she's been dead for six hours."

Jake nodded. "That would put her murder shortly after the bars closed." He narrowed his eyes. "If she and our boy hooked up at a bar or club—"

"We might actually get our first description of this guy." Edgar looked at his watch. "The bars open at noon, which gives us three hours. Give me the car keys so I can go back to the squad room and brief L.T. You interview Meg and work up a list of Shannon's hangouts, then canvass the building."

Fishing for the keys in his pockets, Jake pictured himself going from door to door in the building, interviewing tenants while Edgar sat in Lieutenant Mauceri's office. "You want me to pick up your laundry while I'm at it?"

"After I interview Shannon's employers, I have to call the next of kin. You want to trade?"

Jake tossed the keys to Edgar. "Nah, you're better at that than I am." He felt mucus trickle out of his nostrils and snorted it back into his head. Shoving one hand into a pants pocket, he pulled out a tissue and blew his nose.

Edgar gave him a suspicious and disapproving look.

"Allergies," Jake said, sniffing.

Marc Gorman awoke from a deep sleep with sunlight shining in his eyes. He had stayed out late the night before and his body did not process alcohol well. Rising from bed, he pulled on a terry-cloth robe and tied its belt. He had not yet grown accustomed to the blank white walls of the room, which reminded him of a hospital's stark interior. Sitting at the hutch in the corner, he awakened his computer from its slumber and opened five of his e-mail accounts, each with a different user name.

It's Monday, he thought as he selected the account for "Robby" and one dozen fresh messages appeared. Thank God his digital hookup prevented spam from cluttering his system. He sifted through the messages from various chat group friends. Gary on AOL wanted to know if Robby had read his college thesis on therapeutic cloning yet. Wanda on Yahoo wondered if Robby wanted to meet her in person sometime, since they both lived in New York City. And Chet on Earthlink asked Robby for his views on the recent political turmoil in the Philippines.

After replying to each of them, Marc entered the bathroom, dropped his robe on the cold tiled floor, and showered. The prickly hot water soothed his muscles, and the steam unclogged his pores. He stepped out of the tub feeling purified. Using a hand towel, he wiped the mirror over the sink, but his features remained obscured in the steamed glass. Drying himself off, he returned to the bedroom, leaving a trail of wet footprints on the gleaming, hardwood floor. He opened the closet door and stood naked before his wardrobe, the garments inside arranged by color, fashion, and personality. He debated what Robby would wear on a day like this, and chose casual slacks and a sweater.

In the all-white kitchen, he fixed a power shake for breakfast. Then he sat on the living room sofa and used a remote control to activate his brand-new LCD television. He zipped through the channels to his favorite morning talk show. The hosts, a perky young woman with blond hair and a boob job, and an older man with gray curls, wore identical grins. Marc enjoyed their mindless banter and looked forward to breakfast with them each weekday. Studying their outfits, he shook his head. He saw the same styles on their show day after day.

How boring, he thought. If he had his own TV series,

he would alter his wardrobe style every episode. Finished with his shake, he set the empty glass on a coaster. His stomach felt better with something in it. He went into the bathroom again, listening to the show while he flossed his teeth. The hosts discussed an experimental drug that supposedly prolonged the human lifespan. Aging did not concern Marc, who had just celebrated his twenty-fifth birthday. The woman told the man that he needed to use the drug, and he asked if he could borrow some of hers. The studio audience—housewives, mostly—laughed, and Marc had to join them. He pictured the woman's reaction, which he had seen many times before: her face red, her open mouth forming a perfect, indignant O as she slapped her cohost's arm.

Marc traded his floss for a toothbrush, and he laughed again when a commercial came on for the same brand of whitening paste that he had just applied to the bristles. Ah, the power of advertising! He brushed up and down, as he had been taught at the Payne Institute. When he finished, he glanced at his watch, then went to the front closet and took his cell phone out of his coat pocket. He did not have a landline. Stepping before the bedroom window, he peered through the slats of its blinds at the concrete buildings separating his apartment from the West Side Highway. His chest swelled with love for New York City.

Tearing his eyes away from the skyline, he activated his cell phone. He had only programmed one contact number into its memory, and he pressed the auto-dial button now. After a series of electronic beeps, a phone rang on the other end and his palms turned moist.

A woman's prerecorded voice answered after the second ring. Marc's nostrils flared, as if he could smell her fragrance through the phone.

"I need to make a delivery," he said, glancing over his shoulder at the briefcase on his computer stand.

Robby boarded the downtown Number 2 train, standing room only, and gripped the metal pole near the doors with one hand and the handle of his briefcase with the other. He avoided making eye contact with his fellow commuters, so they ignored him. He disembarked at Fourteenth Street, where a female National Guard clutching an M16 stood near the token booth, scrutinizing the departing passengers with girlish eyes. She did not even look at Robby, who followed the flow of bodies up the concrete steps leading to the street level. A tall man in a suit smiled and shook hands with the exiting commuters, pressing campaign buttons into their palms. Robby passed the politician undisturbed and crossed the street.

Heading toward Broadway, he spotted a woman in a nun's habit sitting on a milk crate. She played "Amazing Grace" on a portable electric keyboard and scabs covered her bare feet, which rested on a ragged piece of cardboard. Robby narrowed his eyes as a portly man deposited a coin into her paper cup. As the man moved on, Robby made eye contact with the woman, something he rarely did with strangers. Reading the glassy haze in her eyes, he saw through her habit. She stared past him with a blank expression, and he knew that she had not even noticed him.

Smiling to himself, he turned right at the southeast corner of University Place. On Broadway, his body turned rigid as he approached a bulky Chinese man in a police uniform. His muscles relaxed as soon as he passed the officer without incident. He studied the tall, dirty windows of a used bookstore across the street. Glancing at his watch, he saw that he had arrived five minutes early, and punctuality mattered to him. He idled near a hot dog vendor, his face registering disgust. With so many fine restaurants in Manhattan, why would anyone spend money on processed animal waste? He looked from side to side, observing people as usual, studying their mannerisms and ticks.

At 11:59, he crossed the street and entered the bookstore, which reeked of old newsprint and musty cardboard. A paunchy black man wearing a red T-shirt sat on a raised stool like a lifeguard, looking down on the customers who prowled the disorganized stacks of books. Robby frowned. He disapproved of security guards who did not wear uniforms. Where was their pride? The man did not ask him to check his briefcase in at the counter. Good thing; if he had, Robby would have left the store, which would have caused complications.

Navigating the cluttered space, he noted the intense expressions on the faces of the people hunting for rare books. He did not care for the smell that the books gave off; he preferred new things. He wandered the aisles until he located the tome he sought: *The Devil and Daniel Webster*, by Stephen Vincent Benét. He did not remove the volume from its space on the crowded shelf, but looked several shelves below it. In the shadowy recess on the bottom shelf rested a black briefcase identical to the one in his hand. He looked around, making sure that no one was observing him, then switched the briefcases.

As he hurried to the exit, a deep voice made him recoil: "Check your bag?"

Robby turned to the security guard and blinked. "Excuse me?"

The guard leaned forward on his stool, and Robby saw that he had a lazy right eye. "I need to check your bag."

Robby swallowed. "There's nothing in it." He held the briefcase out to the guard and shook it. "See? It's empty."

The guard hopped off his stool. Standing a foot shorter than Robby, he puffed out his chest. "Just open the bag, okay, Chief?"

Robby's mouth turned to cotton and he felt the eyes of the browsers in the store on him. For an instant, he became Marc Gorman again, surrounded by bullies at the playground of his grade school, and he felt himself turning red.

My name is Robby.

"You want me to call the cops?"

Staring into the guard's eyes, Robby hesitated. The Chinese cop he had seen across the street could respond to a 911 call in seconds. Bowing his head, he rotated the briefcase in his arms and thumbed its combination dials. He prayed that the Widow had set the right combination. If she hadn't, this situation would become even more embarrassing. The tabs snapped open and he raised the lid.

The guard peered down into the case, and Robby held his breath. "I thought you said it was empty?" The guard reached in and removed an oxygen mask with a deflated vinyl bag attached to it.

Robby heard someone snicker behind him, and he felt as he had in the corridors of Red Hill High School when girls had whispered behind his back.

Those are Marc Gorman's memories. Concentrate!

The guard turned the mask over in his hands. "What's this?"

"An oxygen mask," Robby said. "My job issued one to every person in the company in case of an attack on our building."

Shaking his head, the guard returned the mask to its compartment. "Don't see what good a mouthful of air is gonna do if a building falls on your ass."

"I hear you." Robby closed the briefcase.

The guard resumed his post and Robby exited the store. Outside, he imagined what the guard's reaction would be if he also stopped whoever left the bookstore with Robby's original briefcase.

Marc hurried into the cool lobby of his building, his fingers twitching. Sweat soaked his armpits and trickled down his back, and he just wanted to get into his apartment and change his clothes. Why had that guard singled him out? He disliked being noticed. Wiping his brow on the back of one hand, he unlocked his mailbox and took out his mail. Other than the bills, the envelopes had been addressed to "Dear Friend," "NAME or Resident," or simply "Occupant."

Moving up the wide stairway, he came to an abrupt stop. An old woman gripping the railing in one arthritic claw and a cane in the other descended the stairs: Mrs. Callister, who lived on the third floor. He had seen her several times before and she had always failed to acknowledge his presence. For a moment, he feared she might speak to him, but she passed without comment, her breathing dry and labored.

That's better, he thought.

Inside his apartment, he slid the briefcase onto the top shelf of his closet. Then he went into his bedroom and stripped off his outfit, allowing his clothes to accumulate at his feet. Posing nude before the tall mirror on the closet door, he flexed his muscles. He liked the way his rail-thin body bulged and rippled on command. Still shaking, he pulled on a long, baggy sweatshirt, knee-length shorts, and dirty sneakers.

Hurry, he thought, shaping his hair into bangs. He pulled a knit cap over his head, then shouldered a knapsack that he had purchased at an Army surplus store. Knapsack Johnny always blended in with the young people in the East Village. He would have looked perfect if he had allowed stubble to grow on his chin; unfortunately, Byron never left the apartment without shaving.

In the bathroom, Marc selected a pair of green contact lenses, but as he tried to insert them his hands trembled.

He needed to see the Needle Man.

Jake slipped his NYPD calling card into the last door on the ground floor of Shannon's apartment building. He had started at the top and worked his way down, and had conducted eighteen interviews. Few of the tenants knew Shannon or Meg, and they offered only ambivalent comments about them. He glanced at his watch: 11:30 a.m. Edgar would not be back for another hour. Snapping his coat shut, Jake stepped outside. The temperature had risen with the sun, which cast long shadows over the empty playground across the street.

"I have to run an errand," he told the patrolman stationed outside the door. "If Detective Hopkins shows up, tell him I'll be right back. Keep the press out."

"Yes, sir."

He lit a cigarette and headed up the sidewalk toward

Eleventh Avenue. Passing the parked white van used by the Crime Scene Unit, he pictured the forensic team, dressed in blue jumpsuits and yellow latex gloves, combing through the crime scene behind him. So far, the DNA detectives had been as befuddled by the lack of evidence left behind by the Cipher as Special Homicide had been.

As he turned the corner, the smell of burnt toast and coffee filled his nostrils. He passed a bagel shop and Kearny's Tavern, a popular cop hangout owned by a retired arson squad detective, and crossed the street. As he neared Twelfth Avenue and Forty-sixth Street, the cacophony of traffic sounds faded behind him.

A black prostitute stood on a shadowy stoop ahead of him, gyrating her hips as she balanced on high pumps. Clad in a tight, one-piece bathing suit the color of midnight, she ran her large hands between her muscular thighs and shook her taut ass for him. She wore a wig with straight black hair, and gold hoop earrings.

"My pussy itches," she said in a deep voice. "My big pussy."

Jake smirked. "You can't scratch what you ain't got, darlin'."

The transvestite placed his hands on his hips. "You cold."

"I gotta call them how I see them, and I see baggage where I shouldn't. The Halloween Parade was yesterday."

"Suit yourself." The transvestite scanned the sidewalk for another mark. "You don't know what you're missing."

"I think I do. Aren't you out a little early?"

"You Vice?"

"Nope. Homicide."

"You never heard of overtime? I like working the lunch crowd."

Chuckling, Jake took a final drag on his cigarette, flicked it at a rusty trash can tied to a low, black metal fence, and walked on. He reached his destination a few doors later, a brick building painted battleship gray, with a fire escape crisscrossing its white trimmed windows. Through the front door he saw a brunette flight attendant struggling to get her rolling suitcase through the vestibule. Darting up the steps, he held the outer door open for her.

"Thank you," the woman said in a friendly Texas accent. "It's nice to encounter a gentleman."

Jake caught the inner door behind her before it could latch. "You're welcome." The overpowering stench of her hairspray and perfume made him dizzy.

"Have a nice day—"

Jake slipped into the bright lobby without answering. The door shut behind him, terminating their conversation. He took the carpeted stairs two at a time, and when he reached the second floor, he heard the dull throb of rap music above him. He followed the cacophony to the third door on the third floor and pushed the doorbell.

The gray metal door opened and a heroin-chic

girl with glassy eyes peered across the chain lock. She had skin as pale as a fish's belly, and her long, straight blond hair needed washing. Jake estimated her age to be eighteen—barely.

"Yeah?" she said in a groggy voice. The music throbbed behind her.

"Tell AK he's got company."

She looked him up and down and he could tell she smelled cop. "Who wants him?"

Her accent betrayed her midwestern origins, but if she had ever possessed any wholesome appeal, she had shed it like snakeskin. A green football jersey with the number thirty-two emblazoned on its front reached midway down her naked thighs, and Jake zeroed in on a pink heart tattooed on the inside of her right ankle.

"Tell him it's the IRS." He projected restrained anger at the girl, hoping to unnerve her.

"Just a minute."

She closed the door and Jake glared at the peephole. When the door reopened, minus the chain lock, a brown face stared out. AK wore baggy jeans with a white muscle shirt that made his skin appear darker than its true shade. The whites of his eyes had turned yellow and a grin cracked his face.

"Jake!" AK embraced him in what Jake liked to call the Bronx Brothers' Hug. "The fuck is up?"

Stepping past AK, Jake entered the apartment, which reeked of stale marijuana smoke. "The tax man cometh."

"That goddamned tax man." Shaking his head, AK closed the door and locked it. "He just won't cut a working brother any slack."

They entered the living room of the one-bedroom apartment. The girl sat coiled on the sofa, a half-smoked Newport burning in an ashtray on the coffee table. She stared at the plasma screen television with unblinking eyes as Scooby Doo and Shaggy fled from a spectral figure with flaming hair, its shrieks punctuating the rap music coming from the MP3 system by the window. Over the speakers, a deep voice described a shoot-out that left "three pigs drowning in their own blue blood" while a monotonous beat hammered at Jake's synapses. AK lowered the music.

"This is Karen," he said, gesturing at the girl.

Jake offered the girl a strained smile. "How do you do?"

"Hi." Karen's eyes remained focused on the screen.

"You remember me telling you about Jake, don't you? He's my main man with NYPD."

"Yeah." She seemed unimpressed.

AK stepped over to the couch. "Go watch TV in the room so Jake and I can talk business."

Sighing, Karen picked up the pack of Newports and shuffled toward the bedroom. AK swatted her ass as she passed him and she closed the bedroom door behind her.

AK flopped down on the black leather sofa and propped one leg on the coffee table. Admiring his spotless white sneaker, he picked up a remote control and switched off the television. "Fucking cartoons, can you believe it?" He set the remote down. "But with titties like those, who needs the Discovery Channel?"

Saying nothing, Jake sat in a chair perpendicular to the sofa.

AK took the cigarette from the ashtray, flicked away its long ash, took a single drag, and stabbed it out. "She from Minnesota," he said, smoke shooting through his nostrils. "Land of milk and honeys. Her pops would have her ass on a plane back to the heartland yestidday if he knew a brother was all up in that. She gonna be a model."

She gonna be strung out before she's twenty, Jake thought.

AK leaned closer. "You wanna fuck her?"

"I only fuck my wife."

AK nodded at the bedroom door. "She's good. Do you like a pro as long as she's flying."

Jake didn't smile. "I guess we just have different tastes, Lester."

AK cocked his head. "How you gonna diss me like that, Jake? You know I don't go by no slave name."

"I thought your moms named you, and I don't remember any Mandingo warrior named 'AK' in *Roots*."

AK burst into exaggerated laughter. "True, true."

Jake stared at the young man. "I missed you on Friday."

AK's eyes did not blink. "Oh, on Friday?" He sat

up, clapped his hands, and aimed a finger at Jake. "You know what? Check this out. I had to make a buy from my wholesaler."

"You forget my cell phone number?"

"Ah, come on, Jake. You know I'd never do you like that. Matter of fact, I was gonna call you tonight."

Jake gave him a subtle nod. "I'm real glad to hear that. Makes me feel like I'm an important part of your life."

"You my man, Jake. I need you watching my back."

Let him pretend that's what's going on, Jake thought. Lester had been his snitch back in Alphabet City. "Then we still have an understanding."

"'Course we do. Whatchoo think?"

"I think you should give me what I came for so I can get back to work."

"Oh, yeh-yeh-yeh," AK said as he stood up. "How you want it?"

"Half-and-half."

"Coming right up." AK strutted across the room, stopping at the bedroom door. "I've got all the serial numbers on this shit written down, so don't make me call Five-Oh on your ass." He laughed at his own joke, then entered the bedroom and closed the door.

Jake leaned back in the chair and wondered how Edgar was faring on the case. Another song about thug life in the projects came on. AK returned before it ended, carrying a plastic baggie filled with cocaine in one hand and a wad of cash in the other.

"Fucking bitch is a human vacuum cleaner." He sat down with a beleaguered sigh. "I don't know which one of you is costing me more."

"Haven't you heard? It's expensive doing business in Manhattan."

"Tell me about it." AK tossed the coke to Jake, who caught the baggie with his left hand. "Check it out, baby. That's Fish Gill."

Jake didn't believe AK had ever even seen Fish Gill, the street term for cocaine before greedy hands along the food chain diluted it to increase profits, and he flicked the baggie with one finger. The stuff looked potent, all right. He tucked it into the inside pocket of his coat, his heart already beating faster.

AK counted out twenty-five twenty dollar bills and handed them over to Jake, who recounted the cash before slipping it into another pocket.

"You're doing okay for yourself," Jake said.

"So are you."

Jake stood up. "I'll see you on Friday."

AK blew air out of his cheeks. "No doubt."

Pulling the glass paned door open, Jake entered the cool darkness of Kearny's Tavern.

Hurry, he thought, his pulse quickening as the aroma

of beer-soaked wood filled his nostrils. He heard the deep voice of a television newscaster ahead of him. Tom Kearny stood behind the bar, polishing its nicked surface with a soiled rag. He looked up as Jake passed the picture window facing the street, its stained glass defusing the sunlight.

"Well," Kearny said, drawing the word out. "Look who's here: the hotshot Homicide detective. What are you doing in Midtown?"

"I caught a stiff over on Forty-Five." Jake surveyed the empty bar stools and pool tables. "Where are your degenerate customers?"

"Out making arrests. What's your excuse?"

"I'm chasing a ghost."

"The Cipher?"

Nodding, Jake glanced up at the television mounted on the brick wall behind Kearny. The broadcast showed shaky images of police in riot gear patrolling a crowd of demonstrators outside an office building.

"The Anti-Cloning Creationist League staged a demonstration outside the headquarters of Tower International this morning," a newsman said offscreen. "The ACCL opposes Tower's use of human stem cells for therapeutic cloning and genetic enhancement. A spokesperson for Tower International stated that stem cell research has helped combat diseases such as diabetes, Parkinson's, and Alzheimer's."

"These chromophobes are getting out of hand,"

Kearny said.

Jake agreed but didn't say so.

The camera cut to the anchor at his desk in the newsroom: perfect skin, coiffed hair, zero personality. "In a related story, the Food and Drug Administration has postponed its decision on whether or not to approve the sale of Deceleroxyn-21, the controversial drug developed by Tower International to decelerate the aging process in humans by as much as thirteen percent." A graphic of a medicine bottle with a blue DCL-21 label appeared beside the man. "While results in test subjects have been encouraging, critics of the genetic drug maintain it will be decades before potential side effects are known. Tower International is owned by reclusive billionaire Nicholas Tower."

"'Where's Old Nick?'" Kearny said with a grin.

"I have to make a pit stop," Jake said, turning and crossing the empty floor. "I'll let you know if I see him."

"Hey, that bathroom's for paying customers!"

Jake waved a hand. "Set me up with a shot and a beer." The men's room reeked of Pine-Sol disinfectant. He inspected the stalls, all of them empty. Sliding the metal bolt on the door into the locked position, he stepped before the sink and gazed at the cloudy mirror on the wall. Instead of his own reflection, he saw the discolored face of Shannon Reynolds staring back at him with dead eyes.

Reaching into his inside coat pocket with trembling fingers, Jake withdrew the bag of cocaine. With shortened breaths, he dipped his right pinkie into the bag and scooped coke up his right nostril. Closing his eyes, he shuddered as the powder worked its way into his system. Opening them, he snorted the drug deeper into his skull, then scooped a hit up his left nostril.

Waiting . . .

Blast off.

His mind turned numb and the world around him softened. Shannon's countenance faded away, replaced by his bloodshot eyes. Perhaps she disapproved of his habit.

I'll see ya when I see ya. Dipping his pinkie back into the bag, he massaged coke into his gums and dabbed some on his tongue, which lost all sensation. The shit was potent, all right. AK must have dipped into his personal stash to make amends for dodging him. Jake closed the baggie and returned it to his pocket. Outside, voices rose above the television broadcast as customers arrived. White ooze trickled from his sinuses, and he snorted it back up his septum. He unlocked the door and returned to the bar, tasting the nasal drip in the back of his throat.

Then he froze.

Kearny had turned to the cash register, his back to Jake and two men standing between them: one tall and lanky, with dirty orange dreadlocks spilling midway down the back of his bleached denim jacket; the other short and stocky, with a head as smooth and shiny as a cue ball. Jake felt a prickling sensation as the hair on the back of his neck stood on end: Perp Fever.

The register drawer sprang open, coins rattling

inside it. Jake saw Kearny's reflection in the long mirror behind the register and recognized fear in his eyes. Reaching inside his coat with his right hand, he curled his fingers around the grip of his Glock Nine in its shoulder holster. The sound of his sleeve rubbing against his coat flap caused his heart to skip a beat.

The man with the dreadlocks spun around, his face fringed with orange fuzz and his eyes flaring with alarm. He swung the .32 revolver clutched in his left hand in Jake's direction, its short barrel narrowly missing his partner's bald head. Baldy stepped to one side, revealing the shotgun in his hands as he turned his body. Both men had pallid skin and wore predatory scowls.

Shit! Jake's heart launched into overdrive. Pulling the Glock free, he gripped it in both hands as he assumed the stance drilled into his head back at the Academy. No fool, Kearny dove for cover behind the bar.

Dread's .32 made a *pop* and Jake heard a bullet whiz past his ear and chew into the wall behind him. Baldy raised the shotgun to his shoulder, leveling it at Jake. Seeing Baldy as the greater threat, Jake aimed his Glock at the center of the Harley-Davidson T-shirt the man wore beneath his long, dark coat and squeezed the trigger. The weapon kicked in his hands, the ear-splitting gunshot reverberating against liquor bottles behind the bar and bouncing back at him like a radar signal. Blood erupted above Baldy's left collarbone and his body jerked sideways, his face twisting into a scarlet grimace. He triggered the shotgun, blasting a pool table to Jake's left.

Dread fired the .32 again, his dreadlocks trailing the motion of his head like the tail of a cat doused in gasoline and set on fire. Hearing plaster explode to his right, Jake dropped to one knee and returned fire. His bullet missed its mark, shattering the mirror behind the bar. He fired twice more, blasting Dread against the bar stools. Blood spurted from the robber's face and chest and he crumpled to the floor.

Unleashing a primal scream, Baldy pumped his shotgun. Jake leapt to his feet, aimed the Glock, and squeezed its trigger. This time he kept the trigger depressed, the sharp reports of semiautomatic gunfire ringing in his ears. He lost count of how many rounds he fired, and how many hit their target, as the Glock spat out empty shell casings and bottles exploded.

Blood blossomed across Baldy's chest and he staggered back, firing the shotgun at the ceiling. Debris rained down on him and he hit the floor with a protracted scream. Dark blood gushing over his fingers, he clutched at his chest and kicked out, the heels of his motorcycle boots smearing crimson over the green- and pink-tiled floor. Then he quivered and stilled.

The Glock stopped kicking in Jake's hands, and he felt, rather than heard, the empty clicking. He released the trigger, his heart slamming against his chest as he gasped for breath. On the floor, Dread moved his mouth, the gaping hole in his left cheek revealing bloody gums and missing teeth. Then his eyes glazed over and he stopped moving.

Liquor rained down from shattered bottles behind the bar and pooled on the floor. Kearny raised his head and peered at Jake with unblinking eyes, then crept around the bar and gaped at the bodies lying side by side on the floor. Jake had never shot anyone before, let alone killed someone. Dread's bloodied outfit included camouflaged cargo pants and combat boots.

Jake estimated that a maximum of thirty seconds had passed since he had exited the bathroom. Spilled blood rippled on the floor and he stepped back to prevent the spreading puddles from staining his shoes. The air reeked of gunpowder and the Glock felt hot in his hand. His knees wobbled and his gun hand shook as he holstered his weapon. He saw Kearny speaking to him but heard only a ringing sound. Kearny pointed at Jake's feet and Jake looked down. Droplets of blood spattered the floor between his shoes. Panic surged through him and he patted his torso with both hands, searching for bullet wounds. A drop of blood landed on his left thumb, and he realized where it had come from. He brushed a finger beneath his nose and it came away red and sticky.

Goddamn it!

The distant siren of an approaching RMP car rose above the ringing in his ear. Jake shot one hand into his pants pocket, fumbling for the crumpled tissue he had put there earlier. Heart rate accelerating, his knees shook and he felt the blood rushing from his head. The bar spun around him, its multicolored bottles blurring into streaks. The tissue fell from his hand before he could use it, and he reached out for something with which to steady himself, his hand clawing at empty air.

Jesus Christ, no! Not an overdose! Not now!

His mind tried to outrace his pounding heart, and he toppled to the floor and felt blood soaking through his pants as darkness overtook him. Like most drug addicts and atheists facing death, he prayed to God for help.

Knapsack Johnny snaked between the hipsters crowding Saint Mark's Place. Leather motorcycle jackets crinkled around him, and clouds of cigarette smoke lingered in the air. A girl with pink hair relaxed in the doorway of a vintage clothing store; a boy carried a skateboard into a comic book store; two college students exiting a video store debated the aesthetic subtleties of a foreign film playing at the New Angelika. At the corner ahead, a middle-aged black man with horn-rimmed glasses and a black suit shouted at disinterested Villagers:

"Sinners! You'll all burn in hell!"

Knapsack Johnny crossed the street and descended a half flight of steps leading to a bloodred door. He used an old-fashioned knocker to announce his arrival. Moments later, a security window in the door slid open and paranoid eyes peered out from between black bars.

"Who is it?" the man on the other side of the door said in a hoarse voice.

"It's just me, Professor. Knapsack Johnny."

The man squinted and closed the window. Heavy locks turned and the door swung open. Professor Severn stood in the doorway, staring past Johnny at the pedestrians clogging the sidewalk, his craggy face slick with sweat. Wild, iron-gray hair mixed with long, unkempt whiskers. Wrinkles crisscrossed his black garments like varicose veins and a cloud of pipe smoke swirled in the air behind him. He would have looked equally at home hoisting beers in a biker bar or reading poetry aloud in a café.

"Hurry up," he said, pulling Knapsack Johnny inside. "You'll let the noise in." He slammed the door shut and secured its bolts. "I didn't know you were coming tonight."

"You don't have a phone, Professor. Or a computer to receive e-mail." Nor did Severn own a television or radio.

"You're damn right, I don't. And I never will, either. Too many damn spies. The government is cataloguing everything we do. I should let strangers in here? Their eyes, their thoughts, their voices?"

"You're right to be cautious."

As Severn turned, Knapsack Johnny caught a whiff of pungent body odor mixed with tobacco. He followed the Professor into the living room and swooned from the overpowering paint smell. The barred windows had been covered with wax paper, which allowed sunlight entry while maintaining privacy. Plastic tarps smeared with oil paint covered the floor, and canvases hung on the peeling walls. Looking at the unfinished paintings, Johnny saw one recurring image: distorted human eyeballs stared out from the swirling splotches of color on each canvas.

"A new series?"

"I started it two days ago," Severn said, gazing at his artwork.

"I bet you haven't slept yet, either."

"Of course not. Who has time to sleep?"

Knapsack Johnny waded through the bunched-up tarps, Severn leading him into a smaller room. A dentist chair, no doubt scavenged from a Dumpster, sat next to a table with a boxlike tattoo machine atop it. Johnny slid the knapsack from his shoulders and pulled off his sweat-shirt, leaving the knit cap on his head.

"What did you bring me?" Severn said.

Johnny reached into his knapsack and took out a photo, which he handed to the Professor.

"Ahhh," Severn said as he examined the photo. He had stubby fingers for an artist. Professor Aldous Severn, the Needle Man, had achieved legendary status among the denizens of lower Manhattan and tattoo artists worldwide. Specialty magazines featured photos of his elaborate body art, but Severn never granted interviews or allowed himself to be photographed. Johnny had first heard of the mad artist in a bar on Avenue B during his first week in Manhattan. Severn's nearly mythic reputation intrigued him, and he made locating the eccentric tattooist a priority. When he succeeded, he had to press the Professor to accept his commission. Reclining in the dentist chair now, he gazed at the designs and patterns pinned to the walls.

Severn studied the photo as he arranged his pigments on a tray. "I don't like working from photos, but yours are different. You've got a good eye. Your work shows passion and immediacy."

Johnny smiled. "Thanks, Professor."

"I never allow my photograph to be taken." He loaded the pigments into the tattoo machine. "Crazy Horse and his Sioux warriors believed that cameras robbed their subjects of their souls."

Johnny's smile faded. "Do you believe that?"

"No. If my photo were taken, my soul would live on in my work." Severn unwrapped the plastic from a fresh pack of tattoo needles, then pulled on a pair of latex gloves.

Don't be so certain, Johnny thought. The sight of Severn's gloves reminded him of his own work and his heart beat faster.

The Professor inserted the needles into the tattoo machine. "You keep your chest shaved," he said, looking over Johnny's torso. "Good." Using a spray gun, he applied a coat of rubbing alcohol on Johnny's torso and Johnny shivered. "Shall we begin?"

Johnny nodded. "Please."

Holding the photo in one hand, Severn lowered the tattoo machine.

Johnny held his breath, anticipating pain and blood.

Grateful that Kearny had gotten him back on his feet before the emergency response teams had arrived, Jake sat on a stool, gnashing his teeth as police personnel swarmed through the bar. His heart continued to slam against his ribs and he still tasted coke in the back of his throat. He raised a glass of water to his lips, ice cubes rattling as his hand shook. The cold water made his throat feel swollen. His sweaty shirt clung to his flesh, his own body odor repelling him. Hand radios crackled around him, and shadows moved across the masonry he had exposed by shooting out the mirror. He could only wonder if he looked as bad as he felt. For some reason, the image of Shannon's rosary beads filled his mind. His thoughts turned to Sheryl. How would she react upon learning that he had almost been killed, and that he killed two men? Someone triggered a camera, and the flash ricocheted off scattered shards of glass, causing him to flinch. After ten years on the Job, he had become the star attraction at a crime scene.

Two uniformed officers—the First Officer on the scene and the Recorder—stood at the door, outlined in red and blue glare from the revolving strobes of emergency vehicles parked at the curb. Otherwise, darkness coated the interior like industrial soot. Gesticulating, Kearny spoke to a wiry-looking man from the Detective Area Task Force for Midtown North while the detective's partner counted shell casings on the floor. The two paramedics who had proclaimed Dread and Baldy dead now approached Jake. Shaking his head, he waved them off. Exchanging suspicious glances, they shrugged and turned to leave. Exiting the bar, they separated as two men in matching black coats entered between them.

The Rat Patrol, Jake thought.

Internal Affairs Bureau superseded all other investigative branches of the department in police-related shootings. Jake recognized the taller IAB Inspector, Gary Hammerman, who had busted some of his former colleagues in the SNAP, the Street Narcotics Apprehension Program, for dealing on the side. He had never seen Hammerman's partner, a squat man whose black hair and five o'clock shadow made him resemble Fred Flinstone. As the Inspectors consulted with the Recorder, Jake narrowed his bulging eyes, which threatened to explode from their sockets. His heart skipped a beat as Hammerman looked up at him from the Recorder's log. Snorting mucus high into his nose, he straightened his posture.

With their hands shoved deep in their coat pockets, the Inspectors circled the corpses, their expressions grim as they sidestepped the pools of blood. Hammerman spoke to the DATF detectives in a tone too low for Jake to hear. Nodding and pointing around the bar, they answered his questions in the same manner. Hammerman stepped closer to Jake. "Detective Helman."

"Hammerman." Jake's voice sounded hoarse, and he swallowed as Fred Flinstone joined Hammerman. Cognizant that he still had shakedown cash and cocaine in his pocket, he wondered if they heard his heart pounding in his chest.

"This is Inspector Klein," Hammerman said, gesturing to his partner.

Jake nodded at Klein, who stared at him with his game face on.

Thump-thump-thump . . .

"Do you need to see a doctor?" Hammerman said.

Jake felt sweat trickling down his temples. "No, I'm good."

"Then how about walking us through this?"

"Sure." Jake slid off the bar stool, the walls tilting around him. He teetered to one side and regained his balance, his chest tightening. The smell of copper rose from the bodies on the floor and he fought the urge to vomit. As he told his story, he pointed at the spots on the floor from which he and the robbers had exchanged gunfire. The Inspectors listened without taking notes or interrupting. When Jake had finished, Hammerman took a plastic bag from his coat pocket and held it out to him.

"You know the drill, Helman. We need your gun."

With a trembling hand, Jake eased his Glock from its holster. The gun felt heavier empty than it had loaded. Ejecting its spent magazine, he showed Hammerman the gun's vacant chamber, then deposited both pieces into the bag, which Hammerman sealed.

"Are you ready to give us your statement?"

"Sure," Jake said without conviction.

Handing the evidence bag to Klein, Hammerman reached into the breast pocket of his suit jacket.

"Jake!"

All heads turned as Edgar hurried away from the Recorder with a concerned expression on his face. His gait slowed as he gazed at the bloody corpses on the floor, but he did not stop to gawk. Stepping before Jake, he gave his partner's shoulder a reassuring squeeze.

"You okay?"

Jake nodded. "Yeah, but you look as white as a ghost."

"At least with me it's only a temporary condition." Edgar fired a sideways glance at the Inspectors. "They confiscate your gun?"

"It's procedure," Hammerman said, handing his card to Jake. "Meet us at IAB at 1430 hours."

Two-thirty, Jake thought, focusing on the card. He had less than two hours to pull himself together.

As Hammerman and Klein circled the corpses in opposite directions, Edgar surveyed the damage behind the bar. "You don't play. It looks like the O.K. Corral in here."

Jake took his notepad out of his pocket and tore out a page, which he handed to Edgar.

"What's this?"

"The rundown on Shannon Reynolds's hangouts. The roommate even wrote down some of the bartenders' names."

Edgar skimmed the list, then glanced at his watch. "The bars have been open for half an hour. I need to move on this."

"Sorry I won't be able to help."

Edgar pocketed the list. "You'll do anything to get out of a little legwork, won't you?"

Jake grunted. "Does L.T. know I'm jammed up?"

Edgar nodded. "I was in his office when the call came in."

Jake looked at Dread and Baldy. Their skin had turned purplish gray. He needed a cigarette.

After Edgar had departed, Jake ducked beneath the crime scene tape stretched across the entrance. The crisp air revived his senses, and in the afternoon sunlight he winced at the crowd of spectators gathered on the sidewalk: hard-bodied men and women, many of them wearing police uniforms.

The lunch crowd, he thought, taking a deep breath. Only a few of the intense faces looked familiar. Their silent attention caused his stomach to knot up. Were they pissed that they had to drink somewhere else on their breaks? A patrolwoman with a ponytail brought her hands together, and the others joined her. The applause grew louder and Jake felt himself turning red. Offering them a weak smile, he wondered if their support would have been as strong if they'd known he had snorted cocaine only thirty minutes earlier.

Across the street, a Crime Scene Unit vehicle and a news van competed for a parking space. Jake had no desire to be in the spotlight. Lighting a cigarette, he turned his back on the cops and strode uptown, the clapping fading behind him. Nicotine soothed his nerves but did nothing to decelerate his heartbeat. Pedestrians moved toward him in jerky starts and stops, like figures in a silent film. Traffic noise intensified, and he flinched at a honking car horn. After two blocks, he flicked his cigarette at a storm drain and hailed a taxi. Inside the car, he rolled down the window and took several deep breaths. Closing his eyes and willing his stomach to settle, he tapped one foot on the floor. Five minutes later, as the taxi crossed Central Park, he still saw Dread and Baldy lying dead on the floor, covered in blood.

I killed two men, he thought. *I had no choice.*

The Metropolitan Museum of Art came into view as the park opened onto the Upper East Side. Jake had never been much of a museum-goer, but Sheryl had made it one of her missions in life to civilize him, and he had grown to appreciate the treasures within the sturdy structure. The cab turned left on Museum Mile and he gazed at the people sitting on the Met's front steps and alongside the decorative water fountains outside the museum, stagnant in the wake of water restrictions. Turning right, the cab cruised the congested shopping district on Eighty-sixth Street, in the One-Nine Precinct. Another right turn and Jake got out at the corner of First Avenue and Eighty-fourth Street, his muscles uncoiling in the still air of the quiet neighborhood. He entered his building, a five-story walk-up, and climbed the stairs to the fourth floor, pulling himself along the railing. By the time he reached the door to his apartment, his heart had started hammering again and he felt winded.

Wiping his forehead on his coat sleeve, he dropped his keys. He scooped them up from the welcome mat and let himself inside. Sunlight flooded the silent living room, silhouetting the plants hanging before the windows. He closed the door and locked it. As much as he wanted to hold Sheryl in his arms, he needed privacy more. Opening the front closet door, he reached up to the shelf and took down an aluminum attaché case. Kneeling on the floor, he thumbed the dials on the combination locks and the tabs sprang open.

His personal Glock lay within its foam rubber compartment in the case, along with two magazines of ammunition and a silencer. He had bought the weapon for home protection only, and the silencer had been a gag gift from his colleagues in Special Homicide after he had put down his first case as Primary Detective. Sliding his fingers between the edge of the foam padding and the metal rim, he removed the false bottom containing the gun and its accessories. A rubber-banded bundle of twenty-dollar bills lay at the bottom of the case, nearly ten thousand dollars the last time he had counted it. He removed the cash and cocaine from his coat pocket and added them to the cache. Then he set the false bottom in place and locked the case, which he returned to its spot on the closet shelf. He hung up his coat, went into the eat-in kitchen, and guzzled a glass of water. Only ninety minutes before his IAB interview, and he needed to shower and brush his teeth.

His mouth tasted like death.

Jake had been sitting in the waiting area of Internal Affairs Bureau, located on the sixth floor of 315 Hudson Street, for forty-five minutes. The carpeted room resembled the reception area of a doctor's office more than an entry to a branch of the NYPD. The buttoned-down investigators passing through projected the professional demeanor of lawyers rather than the urban grittiness of cops. Jake's heart rate had decelerated, but sweat continued to dampen his forehead. He felt like an errant schoolboy summoned to the principal's office whenever the civilian receptionist glanced in his direction. Her medium-length dark hair and horn-rimmed glasses reminded him of Sheryl, but she lacked his wife's natural beauty.

Fidgeting in his seat, he dug into a pile of wrinkled magazines. A *Sports Illustrated* cover featured the Yankees dousing themselves with champagne following their latest World Series victory. Jake always rooted for the underdog, which made him a Mets fan. Tossing the magazine aside, he unearthed a Time magazine from the bottom of the pile. Seeing the cover, dated two years earlier, he grunted. The paranoid eyes of a pale face, framed by a mane of unruly white hair, stared back at him. Lampooned on late-night talk shows and humor magazines, the painting had become iconic. The headline that spawned a thousand jokes read, Time's *Person of the Year: Exploiting the Genetic Frontier*—"Where's Old Nick?" Jake leafed through the issue, glancing at photos pertaining to the article: third-world citizens reaping the benefits of genetically enhanced food crops; a paraplegic taking his first steps following therapeutic cloning; and a low angle shot of the Manhattan headquarters of Tower

International.

The front door opened and Hammerman and Klein entered, their coats folded over their arms. Hammerman wore a black suit with razor-sharp creases, but Klein's taste ran strictly off the rack, his sports jacket at least one size too small for his girth. They wore identical smiles, as if they had just shared a joke.

"Sorry to keep you waiting, Jake," Hammerman said. "We had to follow up some loose threads."

"No problem," Jake said, setting the magazine down and sitting up. *What loose threads?*

"We'll just be another few minutes. Would you like some coffee?"

"No, thanks." Jake tried to hide his indignation. He had plied countless suspects with caffeine to get their mouths running. Did Hammerman suspect him of something other than killing Dread and Baldy in self-defense?

Hammerman and Klein entered a side corridor lined with office doors. Sighing, Jake leaned back and waited. The Inspectors returned five minutes later, having traded their coats for file folders.

Hammerman turned to the receptionist. "Carol, which room's available?"

The woman checked a log on her desk. "Number Four."

"Thanks. This way, Jake."

Jake rose and followed the Inspectors into a wide, wood-paneled room with tan carpeting and a low drop ceiling. Hammerman gestured to the digital audio recorder at one end of the conference table, next to an old rotary telephone with a thick rubber connection cable. "Take off your coat and stay a while."

Jake peeled off his leather coat, draped it over the back of a padded chair, and sat. Hammerman positioned himself at the head of the table, with Jake on his left and Klein on his right. The informal arrangement put Jake's mind at ease; with open space to his right, he did not feel surrounded. The overhead florescent lights hummed as the Inspectors spread their folders and notes before them on the table.

"This is the nicest interrogation room I've ever seen," Jake said, looking around.

Hammerman smiled. "We prefer to call it an interview room. We keep it comfortable because we deal with cops here, not criminals."

Sure you do, Jake thought. "I notice there aren't any windows, though."

Hammerman looked up from his notes. "Well, you never know, do you?"

"I guess not." Jake recalled his elevator ride to the sixth floor.

Klein opened a piece of nicotine chewing gum and stuck it into his mouth. "Feel free to smoke."

"I'm good."

"Ready to do this?" Hammerman said.

"Fire away."

Hammerman switched on the digital recorder and announced the date. "Internal Affairs Bureau Inspectors Hammerman, Gary, and Klein, Richard, interviewing Helman, Jake, Detective First Grade, Special Homicide Task Force, Case Number Four-Seven-Seven-Five. Detective Helman, are you aware of your rights in this matter?"

"Yes," Jake said, drawing out the word.

Hammerman opened a folder and scanned its contents. "I see that you're a Ten."

My file, Jake thought. "That's right. I'm halfway there." He had put ten years into the Job, with ten more to go before he could collect his pension.

"And you're second generation."

"Yeah, my father was a sergeant at the One-Seven-Five." He steeled his nerves, expecting Hammerman to ask about his father's suicide.

"How long have you been chasing the Cipher?"

"Five months. We consulted on the second murder, then took over the investigation after Number Three."

Hammerman set down his pen. "Okay, describe this morning's events in as much detail as you're able to recall."

Because he had used the same tactic in numerous interviews, the sudden shift in conversation did not disarm Jake. Sitting forward, he cleared his throat and recounted his morning from his arrival at the Special Homicide Task Force squad room to the gunfight at Kearny's—leaving out a few key details. Careful to adhere to his earlier description, he spoke as he had been coached to address courtroom juries: in clear, concise sentences, just the facts, ma'am.

Six minutes later, Hammerman consulted his notes. "You say you stopped at Kearny's to use the bathroom?"

"That's right. CSU would have thrown a fit if I'd contaminated the one in the vic's apartment."

"Did you have anything to drink while you were there?"

Jake shook his head. "Nope."

Hammerman made a check mark next to one of his notes. "Did you go anywhere between leaving the Reynolds homicide site and going to the bar?"

Jake's heart skipped a beat. "No."

"Did you tell anyone you were leaving the scene?"

"Sure. A PO stationed outside the building."

"Officer Delgatto?"

"Yeah, I guess. I didn't notice his name."

"Officer Delgatto says you told him that you had an errand to run."

Jake hesitated. Hammerman had done his homework in record time. He and Klein must have visited Shannon's building right after leaving Kearny's. No wonder they had kept him waiting. "No errand. I just didn't feel like telling a uniform that I needed to take a leak, is all."

Klein said, "Did you identify yourself as a police officer before you opened fire on the perps?"

This time, the sudden shift in questioning did cause Jake to blink. "There wasn't time. The guy with the dreadlocks popped off a round from his .32 before I could say anything, and Baldy trained his shotgun on me. I had to take immediate action to defend myself."

"You're lucky to be alive," Klein said. The gloss in his eyes and the tone in his voice suggested he thought otherwise.

Hammerman opened a second folder. "Both perps were repeat offenders." He showed Jake a mug shot of Baldy, clipped inside the folder's cover. When the picture had been taken, fine brown hair had circled the lower half of Baldy's head. The steely eyes glared at Jake, who could not help but shudder.

"Oscar Soot served time upstate for armed robbery, narcotics possession, and attempted rape. Before that, he was arrested for spousal abuse, petty theft, and intent to distribute narcotics." Opening a third folder, Hammerman showed Jake a mug shot of Dread smirking at the prospect of prison time. "Kevin Creed was just released from Ryker's yesterday, if you can believe it. Served one year on an aggravated assault charge, pleaded down from attempted rape. Couple of real sweethearts. They both had crack pipes on them, so you can imagine what they were up to. I don't see the public crying over their deaths. Not only were these losers dumb enough to rob a bar that had just opened, but they chose a cop joint."

Jake nodded but thought, *Not that you two would ever be welcome there.* "If they'd had a brain between them, they'd have become florists instead of stickup men."

A shrill ringing filled the room, and all three men examined their cell phones.

"It's my partner," Jake said, checking his phone's display screen. "This might be important. Do you mind?"

Hammerman switched off the recorder. "Go ahead."

Jake pressed the phone against his ear. "Yeah, Edgar?"

Edgar's voice crackled through the receiver. "How's it going with those cheese eaters?"

Jake turned away from his inquisitors. "Peachy. What's the word?"

"Jackpot. Bartender named Teddy Kanaley works at McGinney's on West Forty-Ninth. He remembers seeing Shannon with a guy at closing last night and thinks they left together. I'm taking him to a sketch artist now."

"So my hunch paid off. Even when I'm not working, I'm working."

"And vice versa."

"What's our guy look like?"

"White boy, mid-twenties, professional looking."

"Keep me in the loop."

"You got it."

Jake switched off his phone and returned it to his pocket. "We may have just gotten our first lead on the Cipher."

Hammerman closed his folders. "Congratulations. I think we're finished here. We'll contact your CO tomorrow with our findings."

Jake rose to his feet. "You want to tip your hand just a little?"

Hammerman smiled. "Don't lose any sleep, Detective. This is a clear case of self-defense. According to Tom Kearny, you're a hero."

Jake pulled on his coat. "Tom used to be a hell of a cop."

"I think he relished getting back into the game today. You'll get a citation for this."

Jake snapped his coat up. "When do I get my weapon back?"

Hammerman stood. "Ten days after you submit your report to the Firearms Review Board. Bring a pillow to work, 'cause you're going to serve time at your desk."

Damn, Jake thought. He had hoped to help collar the Cipher if the bartender's description paid off. The biggest case of his career and he had to warm the bench. "I guess I can't complain."

"We're not quite finished here," Klein said, and Jake and Hammerman looked down at him. He removed a paper evidence envelope from a blue folder in a small leather case.

Hammerman snapped his fingers. "That's right, I almost forgot. We need a lock of your hair for a genetic follicle test."

Jake felt his heart plummet in his chest. "What for?"

Hammerman shrugged. "The city requires the

Department to cover its ass whenever a cop kills a citizen. Since you didn't have anything to drink at Kearny's, you've got nothing to worry about. Right?"

Jake stood frozen as Klein removed miniature scissors from the case and snipped at the air with them.

"These guys weren't citizens," Jake said. "They were perps who tried to take me out."

Hammerman cocked his head to one side. "Sure. I already said it was a clean shoot. This is just a formality."

Jake clenched his jaw. A genetic follicle test would reveal if he had used narcotics any time during the preceding six months, about the length of time that he had been getting high. He had to stall long enough to find a way out of this. "I put my life on the line for this city every day for ten years, and my number almost came up this morning. I don't deserve to be treated like a suspect."

Hammerman and Klein did not look at each other, but their faces assumed identical, stony expressions.

"Take it easy," Hammerman said. "Why don't you sit back down?"

Jake's eyes darted to the door. He wanted to make a run for it. Instead, he returned to his seat, as did Hammerman. Both Inspectors stared at him and the room seemed smaller now.

"Look, fellas," Jake said. "This has been the worst day of my life. I'm going to have to live with what happened for the rest of my life. Let me skip the test for now and I'll bring you a hair sample tomorrow."

Hammerman seemed unimpressed. "No dice. We have to extract the sample ourselves."

Jake closed his hands into fists. When he had first joined the force, a cop who tested positive for drugs might be sent to an upstate rehab under the guise of alcoholism treatment. But the Department's new "zero tolerance" policy precluded such maneuvering. He stood to lose his job and pension, and could face criminal prosecution if IAB sought to crucify him. He'd be humiliated before his colleagues. Worse, he'd lose Sheryl's respect. She knew nothing of his habit or extracurricular activities. If his cocaine use became public knowledge, the families of Oscar Soot and Kevin Creed would file wrongful death suits against the city and the Department. He could even face prosecution and jail time. His temples throbbed and his heartbeat quickened.

"We need that sample," Hammerman said, his voice taking on an authoritarian tone.

Jake stared back. "You can't make me do this."

"As long as you're a member of this Department, we can." Hammerman pushed the phone across the table. "Call the Detectives Endowment Association if you don't believe me."

Jake ignored the phone. "What if I refuse to cooperate?"

Hammerman leaned back in his chair. "Then we'll have you suspended and commence a full investigation. One way or the other, we'll get what we need."

Jake felt his chest tightening. "As long as I'm a member of the Department?"

"That's right."

Swallowing, Jake rose on wobbling knees. The Inspectors looked at him with puzzled expressions. He removed his shield from his belt and gazed at it. How long had it been since he had last polished it? He rubbed the tarnished gold with one thumb. Taking a deep breath, he let out a tremulous sigh and laid the shield on the table.

"That's it?" Hammerman said, his voice incredulous. "You're resigning?"

Jake circled the table without answering and opened the door.

"Wait a minute, you have to schedule an exit interview with your—"

Stepping free of the interview room, Jake pulled the door shut behind him.

Jake sat on a wooden bench bolted to the esplanade separating Carl Schurz Park from the East River. Around him, bicyclists and joggers passed couples strolling hand in hand and women pushing baby strollers. Ignoring them, Jake gazed at the factories and housing projects on the far side of the gray water. Smokestacks and unlit neon signs rose to the dark, billowy clouds that filled the sky, and a towboat struggled against choppy waves.

He had come here countless times with Sheryl, who preferred the secluded viaduct, gardens, and fenced-in dog runs to the grand expanse of Central Park. Pain seared two fingers on his right hand, and he flung away his cigarette, which had burned down to its filter. The sudden movement startled a pigeon bobbing along the bulkhead and the bird shot past his head with a frantic flapping of wings. He replayed the events of the day in his mind, cursing at himself for leaving Shannon Reynolds's apartment building to make his drug run. Why had he been so careless?

Because you needed a fix.

He'd never considered himself an addict. Out of curiosity, he had lifted a bag of cocaine from the site of a particularly grisly homicide. After sampling the powder, he discovered that the vivid images of the scene no longer lingered in his thoughts. He soon found it easier to get through his workdays high, and once he had ingested the entire bag, he tracked down AK. But he had only gotten high on the job, never at home, and he had managed to keep his habit a secret from Sheryl. How could he explain to her the reason behind his resignation? Would she believe that he had quit out of remorse over killing Dread and Baldy, or fear of getting into another gun battle? He doubted it. All he'd ever wanted to be was a good cop and Sheryl knew it.

The ringing of his cell phone pierced his concentration and he fished the device from his pocket. Edgar's number appeared on the display screen. Was his partner calling about the Cipher, or about Jake's sudden resignation? Staring at the number, Jake allowed the phone to continue ringing. Curiosity about the Cipher's identity gnawed at him, but he felt too humiliated to speak to Edgar. Switching off the ringer, he pocketed the phone and lit another cigarette. Exhaling smoke, he shivered as darkness laced the sky.

Jake's stomach clenched when he saw the light outlining his apartment's front door. He felt Sheryl's presence as soon as he opened the door, and his eyes settled on the open closet. Something about it seemed different, triggering a mental alarm. Something was missing. Then he realized that his gun case had been removed from the shelf, and nausea spread through him. Shutting the door behind him, he followed the light into the living room, illuminated by a single lamp on one of the end tables.

Sheryl sat waiting for him on the sofa, dressed in black slacks and a matching T-shirt, her arms crossed over her breasts. She had tied her hair back, and the lamp cast soft shadows across her oval face. She glared at Jake through swollen eyelids streaked with mascara. Jake wanted to take her into his arms, but the anger radiating from her held him at bay. Jake's gun case rested on the wicker chest that doubled as their coffee table. His body turned numb.

"Edgar called," Sheryl said in a monotone. "He told me about the shooting, which also made the news." Pausing, she sniffled. "I'm glad you're okay."

He stood waiting for her to continue.

"Edgar told me you resigned."

News travels fast. He did not know what to say, even though he had spent the last hour rehearsing various scenarios in his head.

"Under normal circumstances, that would make me happier than you could possibly know."

He didn't need to ask what made these circumstances different.

"Is it true you refused to take a drug test?"

Thanks, partner.

"Don't be angry with Edgar. He was worried about you and I dragged it out of him. Is it true?"

He opened his mouth to speak, but nothing came out.

"What's in the case, Jake?"

He swallowed. "My personal weapon. You know that."

"What else?"

He bit his lower lip.

"Open it."

He saw no point in delaying the inevitable. With a deep sigh, he sat down beside Sheryl and thumbed the combination dials on the case. Popping the tabs, he rotated the case toward her, then sat back. Sheryl raised the lid and stared at the Glock nestled within its compartment. She pressed the foam rubber with two fingers, feeling along the inside edges, and removed the false bottom. Setting the gun and padding beside her, she gazed at the bundled cash and the bag of cocaine. Tears formed in her eyes and rolled down her cheeks.

"So—how dirty are you?"

Jake's vision blurred. Why was this happening?

Sheryl leapt to her feet. "I believed in you!"

His vision cleared as tears escaped from his eyelids. "I'm sorry . . ."

"What are you? A drug dealer? An addict? *I don't know you!*"

He slumped his shoulders. "All I can say is that the Job was eating me alive."

"So you took drugs? Did it ever occur to you to transfer to another unit? Or to get a different job?"

He stared at the case. "Homicide was such a choice assignment."

"I see. You wanted your star to shine."

"No. I wanted a promotion so we could afford to get a house like you wanted, start a family . . ."

She leaned over him. "Don't you dare turn this back on me."

"I'm not. I'm just trying to explain—"

She snatched the bundled cash from the case. "Explain this! Were you going to use drug money to buy me a house?"

He did not answer.

She hurled the cash at the wall behind him and it thudded on the floor. "I don't want it. Do you hear me? I don't want it!"

He focused his eyes on the bag of coke.

"But I can see what you want." She seized the bag

and held it out to him. "Do you need a fix? Do you want me to get high with you?"

He shook his head.

"Because we can both ruin our lives and throw away everything that we've worked for."

He snatched the bag from her and stomped into the bathroom. Standing over the toilet, he tore the bag apart with his hands and dumped the coke into the bowl. The water turned milky and his nostrils opened and closed like fish gills. With trembling fingers, he flushed the toilet, then returned to the living room.

Sheryl stood before him, red faced and teary eyed. "Very good, Jake. Very dramatic. But that doesn't solve anything."

"I swear I'll never touch that stuff again."

"I want to believe you, but I can't. You've already lied to me. And I understand. Really. You couldn't help yourself. Because drug addicts say and do whatever it takes to get what they need."

"I'm no addict."

"I feel sorry for you, Jake. For both of us. We had something special."

"Sheryl—"

"I need time to think. And I can't do that with you here. I want you to pack your bags and leave."

"Don't do this to me."

"You've done it to yourself."

"I *love* you."

"We must have different definitions of love."

"I need you, damn it!"

"You need to get your act together."

"Please . . ."

She shook her head. "One of us has to be strong."

He paused, debating what tact to use. "How long do you want me to stay away?"

Despite the tears in her eyes, Sheryl's expression cooled. "'Where's Old Nick?'"

After he had returned to his apartment and had shed Knapsack Johnny's attire and identity, Marc Gorman's flesh continued to tingle where Professor Severn had worked his magic on it. Marc wanted to rip the bandage from his chest to admire the intricate artwork, but he reminded himself that the dyes would fade if exposed to light at this early stage. Changing into nylon gym shorts, he pulled his exercise mat from beneath the sofa and arranged his weights around it. He selected a CD from the rack and inserted it into his player. The soothing sounds of Verdi surrounded him.

He spent ninety minutes working out, supplementing his push-ups, sit-ups, and weight training with isometrics and yoga. He performed multiple reps with lighter weights because he desired strength, not bulk; too much mass would limit the number of roles he could play.

He worked his muscles, stretching them, tearing them. Sweat beaded on his forehead and his heart raced. Pushing his body to its limits, he recalled how frail he had been as a youth. His own father had told him that he looked more like a girl than a boy.

"You look just like that crazy bitch," Gary Gorman had said more than once. "You'll never grow up to be a man. I don't know why I even bother with you."

Sara Gorman, Marc's mother, had been a slender woman with delicate features and pale skin, and she had done her best to draw her only child out of his shell. In stark contrast to her generous demeanor, Marc's father had been a source of tremendous fear in his life. The burly truck driver with a taste for cheap beer never addressed Marc by his name; instead he called his son "Little Bastard" with the same degree of contempt as when he called Sara "Crazy Bitch." They lived in a trailer park in Redkill, a rural village in upstate New York, where the sole ambition of young men was to drive shiny pickup trucks. The old-timers who sat watching the traffic on Main Street from the safety of park benches joked that the town should have been called "Roadkill."

The memory of his parents' last fight burned within him again. Gary had returned to the double-wide one afternoon after a two-day absence, and Sara had smelled beer on his breath and perfume on his collar. While Marc cowered behind the living room sofa, his mother screamed at his father in their bedroom. Marc heard his mother grunting as she slapped his father, who only laughed at her feeble attempts to hurt him. In the end, his father had strode by him with nothing but his toolbox, left the trailer, climbed into his truck, and drove off without saying good-bye. Marc ran to his parents' bedroom, where he found his mother crying on the bed. He went to her and she clung to him. In that moment, he realized that she depended on him as much as he depended on her.

Sara sold the trailer and saved enough money to put a down payment on a home in which to raise her son: a dilapidated ranch house at the end of a dead end street. The roof leaked, the faucets dripped, and the fireplace had been filled in with cement. Ashamed of the peeling gray paint on the house's exterior, Marc walked home from the bus stop with his back turned to the other kids who lived on Hunt Road. He blamed his father for the impoverished lifestyle that he and his mother had been forced to endure, but he felt glad to be free of the Big Bastard.

He had no friends except for his mother. His junior high classmates taunted him with nicknames: *geek, nerd,* and *spaz*. They mocked the secondhand clothes that his mother bought for him at yard sales. His first bloody nose at the hands of a bully had terrified him, but he grew accustomed to them. Following his instincts, he learned to fade into the background of the school corridors to escape humiliation. Hiding became the primary activity in his life.

He knew that his mother sympathized with his

plight. She had been ostracized by her father for marrying outside the Jewish faith, only to be rejected by her husband, who had not been worth the trouble. She bought Marc a computer to show him that there was a larger world beyond Redkill, and soon he spent all of his free time online. The used computer had been an extravagant gift, considering their budget: their sole means of income had been disability pay that Sara received from the government each month.

At thirteen, Marc discovered that his mother suffered from "spells," during which she forgot her name and his. He blamed the Big Bastard for the gradual erosion of her mental faculties. She locked herself in her bedroom for hours at a time, raging at the walls. He kept her deterioration a secret while finishing high school, but her condition worsened. Eventually, she stopped leaving her room altogether, and he had to bathe her and prepare her meals.

She paced her room at all hours, wringing her hands and calling out for her husband and her father. Marc learned to pacify her through role-playing games; sometimes he portrayed the Big Bastard, and sometimes he played the Old Bastard, whom he had never even met. He remembered the Big Bastard's drunken roar well enough, and he imagined that the Old Bastard had been equally bullheaded. If his acting ability failed to convince Sara, she never let on. He forged her checks and deposited them into her meager bank account, withdrawing funds for their survival. Because he retained more of her memories than she did, it seemed logical to him that he should be the one to preserve her identity. And so Sara joined the canon of roles in his repertoire.

Marc liked to pretend.

Seeking refuge from his tortured existence in cyberspace, he created multiple identities to use in online chat rooms, each with a unique history and personality. He developed a flair for drama, but only within the confines of his isolated world. Outwardly, he craved normalcy and hoped to become an accountant one day. But he had no idea how to pay for his college tuition or achieve that goal. The demands that his mother's growing insanity placed on his time made it impossible for him to get even a part-time job to supplement their income. He won a full scholarship to a local community college but was unable to accept it. By then Sara had been prone to fits of violence, and he dared not leave her alone, or entrust her care to a paid companion, even if he had been able to afford one. A nurse would have seen that his father had been correct: Sara really was a crazy bitch, and Marc feared she would spend the rest of her life in an institution. He resented her hold on him, but what could he do? She had been his only friend.

He had been unprepared for the effect her death had on him. His grief had been so overpowering he had been unable to function. Free at last to live his life as he saw fit, without the burden of responsibility for someone else, he suffered an emotional breakdown. The doctors at Stonehaven had treated him with the same disdain as they had their other patients, and he had been grateful for his transfer to the Payne Institute. There he met the Widow, who filled the void in his life and inspired him to rejoin the world.

Enough.

Marc collapsed on the exercise mat, his chest heaving. Climbing to his feet, he staggered into the bathroom and stripped off his clothes. He showered, changed into his evening clothes, and cooked dinner: skinless chicken, asparagus, and salad without dressing. Setting his food on the coffee table, he sat facing the TV and turned on the news. Chewing on his lemon-soaked chicken, he felt giddy with anticipation. He relished hearing the local newscasters describe his exploits with melodramatic flair. On the screen, a female Asian reporter stood outside a familiar-looking apartment building, the wind wrapping her hair across her face.

This is it, he thought, raising the volume with the remote control. Setting down his fork, he leaned forward with the TV image reflected in his eyes. His pulse quickened when he saw that he had made the lead story. A photograph of Shannon Reynolds filled the screen, and Marc felt grim satisfaction. In his mind, he saw her standing at the bar, drawing his attention to her breasts. If only she'd known that it had been her crucifix that had attracted him to her. His blood turned cold as a drawing took over the screen: a black-and-white sketch of a white male with short hair. The food in his stomach churned as he stared at the police sketch of the Cipher.

Marc rose to his feet and staggered around the coffee table. Unable to concentrate on the reporter's words, he fell to his knees before the TV. With trembling fingers, he touched the screen, tracing his likeness.

It's me, he thought, his lower lip quivering. His picture would soon be on display all over the city. He sank his teeth into the knuckles of his left fist. Choosing a soul from a crowded bar had been a careless mistake, he knew, but Shannon had been too tempting a target for him to resist.

The Widow would be displeased.

He needed to change his appearance immediately, destroy the persona of Byron, and do what he was best at: fade into the background like a chameleon, biding his time.

I want my mother, he thought. *I never should have killed her.*

The ringing shattered his dream like a softball hurtled through a window.

No! I don't want to wake up! Not yet . . .

His cell phone dragged Jake back to reality, away from Sheryl. He awakened in darkness, tears in his eyes, alone in a queen-sized bed. His head throbbed, his senses dulled.

Where am I?

It didn't matter. Nothing mattered anymore. He covered his head with a pillow until the ringing stopped, then descended into a half sleep. Sheryl did not return to him, but faces did hover in his mind: Dread and Baldy. He shut them out. Then someone knocked on the door to his left.

Who—?

Removing the pillow, he propped himself up on his elbows. Gray light outlined the blinds to his right, reflected in the bureau mirror across the room.

Hotel, he thought. *The Lexington.*

The unseen door swung open, and a column of light sliced through the darkness. The door's chain lock jerked it back and the light shrank to a narrow blade.

"Sorry," a woman with a heavy Hispanic accent said.

The maid. He must have forgotten to hang the DO NOT DISTURB sign outside the door. "Not today," he called out, his voice hoarse. "Come back tomorrow."

"Ho-kay." The woman closed the door.

Darkness again.

He laid back and groaned, the throbbing in his head intensifying into outright pain. Attempting to recall what he had done after checking into the hotel the night before, he drew a blank. Touching denim fabric on his thighs, he wiggled his toes inside sneakers. His sweater reeked of cigarette smoke, and vague impressions of a seedy bar clouded his mind. His insides felt as if they had been coated in black tar. Pressing a button on his watch, he narrowed his eyes at the luminous display: 11:58 a.m. on Tuesday, November 2nd.

Twenty-four hours without cocaine.

Twenty-four hours without Sheryl.

His body yearned for something stronger than the alcohol flowing through his veins. Rolling out of bed, he opened the blinds and squinted in the dull sunlight. From the sixth floor, Lexington Avenue appeared cold and gray, its sidewalks crowded with people scurrying on their lunch breaks. People with jobs; people with lives. Turning from the window, he sighted his gun case on top of the cherry wood desk on the far side of the television, gleaming beside his cell phone. Swallowing, he staggered into the bathroom, flicked on the lights, and emptied his bladder. Returning to the main room, he spotted his coat lying on the floor at the foot of the bed. Picking it up, he searched its pockets until he found the Marlboro pack. It felt light, and when he shook it, tobacco flakes rattled inside it.

Figures, he thought, discarding the empty pack. He sat at the desk and stared at the gun case. He slid his hands over its aluminum surface and then thumbed the combination dials. The sound of the tabs popping pierced his brain like a scalpel. Raising the lid, he gazed at the black Glock, his heart beating faster. He reached down and removed the gun, its grip cold. He plucked a fresh magazine from the case, slapped it into the grip, and pulled back the slide, chambering a bullet. Did he have the guts to—

Do it.

Sliding the barrel of the gun into his mouth, he tasted metal. His trembling hand caused the barrel to rattle against his teeth. Rotating his wrist, he aimed the gun at the roof of his mouth. One squeeze of the trigger, one bullet through the brain, and his pain would end forever.

Like father, like son.

Good-bye, Sheryl.

He squeezed the trigger.

The cell phone rang again, making him flinch.

Who the hell—?

Maybe Sheryl had changed her mind.

His finger froze on the trigger, and for an instant he thought the gun would discharge anyway. When nothing happened, he set the gun down, seized the phone, and opened it. TOWER INTERNATIONAL flashed on the display screen.

Goddamned telemarketers.

Anger flushed through him as he jabbed the TALK button. "Hello?"

"Mr. Helman?" A cool, feminine voice.

The hair on his neck rose. "Yeah?"

"My name is Kira Thorn. I work for Tower International and I'm calling regarding an opening in our internal security firm."

Resisting the urge to say, *Where's Old Nick?* Jake narrowed his eyes. "What makes you think that I'm looking for work?"

"Today's Post mentioned your resignation in a story on yesterday's gunfight."

I'm a star. "How did you get this number?"

"It's on your home answering machine."

Sheryl had wasted no time recording a new message.

His eyes moved back to the Glock. "Sorry, but I'm not interested in being a toy cop."

"You misunderstand me. I wish to discuss a management position with you. A lucrative one. Are you available for an interview at the Tower this afternoon?"

His eyes widened. This had to be some kind of practical joke. But the display screen on his cell phone confirmed Kira Thorn's legitimacy. "Sure. What time is good for you?"

"Three o'clock. Do you know the address?"

"Of course." Everyone in Manhattan knew Tower International's headquarters.

"Use the Madison Avenue entrance and ask for me." She repeated her name and hung up.

Jake stared at the cell phone and blinked.

Tower International!

He had been out of work for less than twenty-four hours, and a representative for a major corporation had expressed interest in meeting him, all because of a newspaper story. *Gunplay equals media play.* It occurred to him that he had no résumé. Big deal. After all, Kira Thorn had contacted him. Feeling a sense of excitement and optimism for the first time in months, he showered and shaved. Then he unpacked a royal blue shirt and a navy blue suit—dress blues—and ironed them. Thorn had to be interested in his police background, so he intended to play up that image. He wore a red tie that Sheryl had bought him with a gold clip. Pulling on his trench coat, he took an elevator downstairs. Outside, the temperature had dropped to the midfifties. He bought a pack of smokes at a corner newsstand and polluted his lungs, then entered a nearby coffee shop. Too nervous to eat, he sipped a cup of black coffee while he skimmed the *Post*. The police sketch of the Cipher made the cover. Staring at the blank face, he felt nothing. Inside the tabloid, he found the story he wanted, beneath the caption, "HERO COP IN DEADLY SHOOT-OUT." Mug shots of Dread and Baldy appeared next to a photo of Jake taken at his graduation from the Academy.

Hailing a taxi, he instructed the driver to take the FDR Drive downtown to Twenty-third Street. The cab stank of body odor, and he rolled down his window as he gazed at the East River. In the last decade, Nicholas Tower, the so-called Pharmaceutical King, had acquired numerous high-profile genetics companies with names like DNAtomy, Genutrition, and Genometry. Their success in developing genetically enhanced agriculture and breakthrough drugs propelled Tower International to the top of the financial reports. Tower had no wife or children, just a reputation as a fierce businessman: the "Power of Tower" influenced legislators to repeal the president's Anti-Cloning Act. And then, at the height of his notoriety, the billionaire vanished from the public eye.

Jake's taxi drove west, through the afternoon traffic congesting East Twenty-third Street. The Tower rose into view several blocks ahead, dwarfing other buildings in the neighborhood, such as the Flatiron Building. The black structure loomed sixty stories into the sky, blocking Jake's view of the Empire State Building. The glass and steel cylinder, along with its parking garage, plaza, and tree-lined lawn, took up an entire city block of land that had once been the southern third of Madison Square Park. The sale of the park land—supposedly protected—proved as controversial as its new owner, who appeased many of his critics by pouring millions of dollars into the beautification of other parks in the city. The objections subsided, and the Tower became a fixture of the New York City landscape.

The taxi passed Madison Avenue, and Jake spotted the entrance Kira had told him to use. This portion of the avenue looked more like a side street, its sidewalk deserted. Gray, skeletal trees surrounded the building, and two police vans and two Radio Motor Patrol cars flanked the property on Twenty-third Street. The taxi pulled over to the curb at the corner of Broadway, and Jake paid the driver. Getting out, he studied the Tower's main entrance: wooden police barricades held back a crowd of demonstrators, and two dozen patrolmen in riot gear stood between them and the Tower. A twenty-foot-tall letter T, constructed of black marble, shadowed the entrance. The fountains in front of the building had been shut off due to a citywide water shortage stemming from yet another drought attributed to global warming.

A man with a bullhorn paced the sidewalk between

the police and the demonstrators. Approximately thirty years old, clean cut and professional looking, he wore a long black coat over his suit, and black leather gloves. He held the hand of a woman roughly the same age. Her sculpted hair did not move in the wind. They resembled his-and-hers department store mannequins and their audience looked more like PTA members than protesters. The picket signs rising into the air bore illustrated DNA strands with flaming red crosses over them, with "GOD CREATES LIFE, SCIENCE SHOULDN'T!" and "STOP STEM CELL ATROCITIES NOW" as their slogans.

The Anti-Cloning Creationist League, Jake thought. The grassroots movement had recently relocated to New York City from the Midwest and their ranks had swelled: Jake estimated the crowd to number at least five hundred strong.

The man with the bullhorn pointed at the top of the building. "Up there, in that Tower of Babel"—his comment inspired scattered applause and snickers—"a demagogue and his corporate minions are altering the nature of life on this planet."

The crowd jeered, and the speaker grew more animated, the woman beside him nodding. Jake walked a safe distance behind the demonstrators, measuring the intensity of their fervor. He had no use for mob mentality.

"It started with a tadpole, then progressed to a sheep. Remember Dolly?"

"Yes!" the demonstrators yelled as one.

"It continued with rhesus monkeys and pigs. Now

we have designer babies, cloned pets, 'therapeutic cloning,' and DCL-21. Where will it end?"

Lighting a cigarette, Jake circled the Tower. Deceleroxyn-21 was supposed to extend the human life span by as much as fifteen percent, but he didn't believe it. Behind him, the man continued preaching to the converted.

"Genetically enhanced food, genetically enhanced medicines, genetically enhanced people. DNA? How about G-O-D?" The crowd roared its approval. "Is it God's plan for the rich to live longer than the poor simply because they can afford Tower's new wonder drug? Of course not!"

Jake turned right on Twenty-first Street, the man's sermon and the ensuing applause fading from his ears. Prior to the Tower's construction, Twenty-fourth Street had ended at the park and resumed on its other side. Now the street continued unbroken, separating the Tower from the park's remains. A twenty-four-hour diner, an upscale Italian restaurant, and a jazz bar all faced the park from the Tower's ground level. Jake stopped at the corner of Madison Avenue and finished his cigarette in the cool shadow of the mammoth art deco buildings across the street. He popped a breath mint into his mouth, glanced at his watch, and took a deep breath.

Time to enter the lions' den.

The tinted glass doors made it impossible for Jake to see inside. Entering the lobby, he faced a security station manned by two guards, one African American and the other Caucasian. The door closed behind him, and he stepped forward, his rubber-soled shoes squeaking on the polished granite floor. His shadow skimmed a marble wall as he glanced up at the high, vaulted ceiling. The guards wore matching black shoes, gray slacks, and dark blue blazers with burgundy-colored ties. The black man sat at the console, his photo ID identifying him as "Birch, Barry." His colleague, "Laddock, James," stood beside him with his arms folded behind his back, like a Secret Service agent. Jake saw the slight bulge of a gun beneath Laddock's blazer, and each man wore a discreet listening device in his left ear. Both gave off a hard military vibe. Three sets of golden elevator doors gleamed twenty feet behind the station.

Jake removed his wallet and presented his driver's license to Birch. "I have an appointment with Kira Thorn."

Birch examined the license, then swiveled his chair so that he faced a computer monitor recessed within the wall. He keyed in Jake's name, then scanned the driver's license and printed out a visitor's pass, which he handed to Jake with the license. "Please stick that on your coat, Mr. Helman."

Jake put his license away and inspected the pass: the photo from his license had been duplicated, his name and a security number appearing beneath it. He peeled off the backing and adhered the pass to the front of his coat.

Laddock slid an electronic clipboard across the countertop. "Sign in, please."

Jake picked up the pen attached to the clipboard and signed the screen. He guessed the lobby served as a private entrance for the company's top executives.

"Take any one of those elevators to the top," Laddock said, gesturing at the gold doors behind him with a cocked thumb.

Jake moved around the security station and thumbed a call button on the wall. An elevator chimed to his left. Stepping before it, he aimed the pass on his coat at a laser scanner mounted on the wall. The elevator's doors whispered open, admitting him into a spacious car. He faced two buttons on the wall: one with an UP arrow and the other with a DOWN arrow. Pressing the top button, he raised his eyes to a shiny black dot above the doors. Recognizing it as a security camera, he lowered his gaze as the doors shut and the elevator surged upward. His stomach lurched, and he reached out to steady himself. His ears popped, and he swallowed saliva. Then the high-speed elevator decelerated and stopped, and his stomach settled.

Stepping off the elevator, he entered a marble corridor with dim lighting. The corridor led to a glass door, through which he saw another security station, this one circular and stacked high with monitors. As he approached the door, he noticed a hand scanner mounted on the wall to his right. A lone guard at the station reached across the console and toggled a switch, and a hollow-sounding click emanated from the door. The guard appeared to be Jake's age, except that his short, curly hair had already turned gray. Jake pulled the door open and entered the receiving area.

The guard stood as the door closed behind Jake. "Mr. Helman?" He had a British accent and a solid physique.

"Yes."

"Welcome to Tower International. I'm Simon Graham, the security coordinator here. Ms. Thorn will be right with you."

"Thanks." Jake looked around the space, which had no chairs. Glass doors on either side of him led to corridors that curved along the building's outer contour. Behind the security station, a glass-faced office sat dark and empty next to a pair of lacquered doors. Seeing no windows, he felt a twinge of disappointment.

"May I take your coat?" Graham held out his hand.

"Thanks." Jake removed his coat and handed it over. Graham took it to a wall on the right-hand side of the station and opened a seamless closet door. He hung the coat and returned to his seat.

The double doors behind the station swung out, and a woman stepped through them, silhouetted by sunlight flooding the space behind her. Standing the same height as Jake in her high heels, she stepped into the overhead light, her dark eyes and smooth skin coming into view. She approached Jake with catlike poise and a *Mona Lisa* smile. She could not have been more than twenty-five years old, and she wore her raven black hair pulled back. Her black jacket matched her skirt, which reached mid-way down her thighs, and she had unbuttoned her silk blouse just enough to allow a hint of cleavage.

"Mr. Helman? I'm Kira Thorn. Thank you for coming on such short notice."

She extended her right hand and Jake saw that she had sharp red fingernails and no wedding ring. He caught a whiff of her perfume, subtle yet provocative, and when he shook her hand a tremor ran through his body. His instant attraction to her caught him by surprise. "Pleased to meet you."

Without moving her head, her dark eyes appraised him. Then her full red lips parted and she gestured to the doors she had come through. "This way, please."

Jake found himself staring at her hips as he followed her into the sunlit office, but he quickly turned his attention to his surroundings. He had never been in such a large office in his life: forty feet wide and half as deep, with a ceiling fifteen feet high and floor-to-ceiling windows overlooking Manhattan.

This is more like it, he thought.

"Go ahead," Kira said, closing the door behind him. "Take a look."

Jake crossed over to the windows and looked out at the cityscape. The shadow of an immense cloud spread over the neighboring structures, scale models in comparison to the Empire State Building behind them. Although the afternoon had been cold and gray, this high up he had to squint in the warm sunlight. He took a deep breath.

"Have a seat whenever you're ready."

Jake turned from the windows as Kira sat in a soft leather chair behind a black marble desk devoid of personal items or knickknacks. He had been so taken with the view that he had failed to notice the layout of the office, which included an informal conference area with chairs arranged around a low glass table. A modern kitchenette blended into the rear wall, next to a bank of security monitors. Jake moved to the desk and sat opposite Kira, who crossed her legs.

Reaching across her desk, she handed him a folder. "I need you to sign these documents before we can proceed."

Jake saw that his name and the number on his visitor's pass had been stamped on the edge of the folder, which he opened. Gazing down at single-spaced documents, he said, "What are these?"

"Two copies of our standard confidentiality agreement."

"For what? I haven't even been interviewed yet."

In the sunlight, Kira's eyes no longer appeared dark, but dazzling green. "Mr. Helman, you're about to meet an intensely private man who insists on absolute secrecy in all of his dealings. If you're unwilling to sign the agreement, then we've reached an impasse and you may leave."

My God, I'm meeting Old Nick! Jake tried to contain his excitement as he scanned the document, six pages of legalese, with a second copy beneath it. He removed a Lexington Hotel pen from his shirt pocket, signed and dated both copies, then returned the folder to Kira.

She laid it down. "You understand that by signing this, you agree not to discuss any individual you see or speak to today, that you may not reveal the substance of any conversations you have while inside the Tower, and you are restrained from describing the physical layout of any part of this building."

Jake nodded. "I understand: no discussing, no revealing, no describing."

Standing, Kira handed him a business card. "I'm Nicholas Tower's executive assistant, by the way; his personal liaison to the outside world." She circled her desk and crossed the room. Jake pocketed the card and followed her to a metal door perpendicular to the entrance. Leaning close to the wall, Kira pressed her right eye against a rubber cup. A moment later, Jake heard a metallic click as the door unlocked.

Retinal security scan, he thought.

Kira pushed the door open and Jake followed her into an anteroom with a padded banquette facing steel doors. Kira placed the palm of her right hand on the opaque surface of a hand scanner, and a red laser beam passed beneath the glass, analyzing her fingerprints with a gentle hum. Jake heard a sound that reminded him of a time clock punching a card and Kira removed her hand.

"This is the only way to meet Nicholas Tower," she said. "You might say that you have to go through me to get to him." The doors separated, each one a foot thick, with intersecting steel rods. They retracted into the walls, a faint blue glow illuminating the dark space beyond them.

This is really happening.

Kira stepped aside. "Good luck."

Jake crossed the threshold, his shadow stretching before him in a narrow rectangle of light on the floor. Then the doors closed behind him, and both his shadow and the light disappeared.

Lockdown.

Scores of recessed security monitors illuminated the windowless space, which seemed twice as large as Kira's office. As his eyes adjusted to the peculiar lighting, he observed that the monitors displayed digital-sharp, color images of various locations within the Tower. At the far end of the space, the silhouette of a tall man rose from behind an immense desk and Jake felt a shudder of anticipation.

"Over here," a commanding voice said.

Jake approached the man, his footsteps silent on the carpet. As he closed the distance between them, a column of soft white light illuminated the desk area. He passed a dais upon which had been erected a three-foot-tall model of the Tower. At last he reached the desk, made of polished obsidian.

Where's Old Nick?

Right here.

Nicholas Tower stood over six feet tall and the seventy-six-year-old man appeared to be in remarkable condition. His white hair, parted at the side, may have needed a trim, but it bore no resemblance to the unruly mane depicted on the infamous *Time* magazine cover. He wore a polyester suit identical to the uniforms of his security guards.

"I'm Nicholas Tower." The old man's voice radiated confidence as he offered his right hand.

"Jake Helman." Jake shook the hand, as surprised by the old man's strength as he was by the smooth texture of his flesh. A pale film covered Tower's left eye, so Jake focused on his right eye, which reflected the blue light of the monitors. "It's an honor."

Tower released Jake's hand and gestured to the single chair before his desk. "Have a seat."

Jake eased himself into the chair and Tower sat across from him, a flat computer screen to his right. The black surface of the volcanic glass desk reflected the images from the monitors behind Jake, and a pair of gold doors gleamed in the darkness behind Tower.

Why aren't there any windows? Jake wondered, crossing his legs. The old man didn't need to worry about sniper fire this high up. Was his bad eye sensitive to sunlight?

"The Tower is the hub of my empire," Tower said without a trace of irony. "I'm changing the course of the world from right here." He tapped the desktop with one finger. "You saw the chromophobes downstairs?"

Jake nodded. "They're hard to miss."

"The media dismiss the Anti-Cloning Creationist League as some harmless, grassroots organization exercising its right to free speech. I know better. Have you heard of RAGE?"

Jake narrowed his eyes. "The Righteous against Genetic Engineering. A secret, quasi-terrorist organization operating from somewhere in the Bible Belt."

Tower smiled with one side of his mouth. "The ACCL is the legitimate, fund-raising arm of RAGE, and RAGE wishes to destroy me and this company. They've made several threats against this building and they're camped right outside its front doors."

Jake had never heard of a link between the ACCL and RAGE before. "Sounds like a job for the FBI or Homeland Security."

Tower leaned back in his seat. "In retaliation against me for opposing the Anti-Cloning Act, the president's ordered his attorney general to file anti-trust charges against me. They don't like that I dominate the market I helped create. So I can hardly turn to the federal government for protection. I prefer to handle my security needs internally, which is why I've called you here today. I fired my last director of security for sympathizing with those Luddites downstairs and now I need to replace him. I think you fit the bill."

Jack set his foot back on the floor. "I don't have any experience in executive protection."

Tapping the keyboard before him, Tower glanced at the computer screen. "You've had antiterrorist training, haven't you?"

Jake nodded. "I served on the HERCULES assault team for six months before I was assigned to the Street Narcotics Apprehension Program. I also took mandatory refresher courses every three years."

"And you spent another six months on the previous mayor's security detail."

"True."

"I see you were orphaned as an infant."

Jake's body tensed. Just how deeply had Tower researched his background? "Yes."

"Tragic." Tower reached into a drawer and tossed a copy of the *Post* onto the desk. Jake avoided looking at the police sketch of the Cipher on the front page. "Were those cretins your first kills?"

Jake's stomach muscles tightened. "Yes."

"Did you resign because you got squeamish at the prospect of killing again?"

"No. I quit because of departmental politics."

"Bureaucrats," Tower said with a look of disgust. "Let me be direct, Jake. I need a man of action, a man who's not afraid to pull a trigger if my life depends on it. I think you proved yourself to be that man yesterday. The position I'm offering pays three hundred thousand dollars a year, plus excellent benefits. Are you interested?"

Jake gripped his chair's armrests to keep from falling over. *Three hundred thousand dollars!* He had never dreamed such a salary would ever be within his reach. With an income like that, he could buy Sheryl the house she wanted and set his life back on course. "Definitely."

"Ms. Thorn performed a preliminary background check on you as soon as she read of your availability. If I hire you, you'll report directly to her."

Jake pictured Kira Thorn and for some reason his heartbeat quickened. "That won't be a problem."

"My living quarters are beyond the doors behind me. Both the media and my enemies would pay a great deal of money to know that, so you can see why confidentiality is a priority. Ms. Thorn lives on this floor as well, and until the FDA approves the sale of DCL-21, and the climate outside changes, you'll be required to stay here, too. You'll be on call twenty-four hours a day, seven days a week."

Jake had already made up his mind. "I'm your man, Mr. Tower."

"I think so, too." Rising to his feet, Tower offered his hand again. "Then we have a deal?"

Jake stood, as well. "Deal," he said, grasping Tower's hand.

Jake stepped through the entrance of *La Petit Mort*, on the corner of Lafayette and Houston, with a dozen long-stemmed roses in one hand and his new employment manual and insurance booklet in the other. He had not been to the fashion boutique for six months, and it looked like a different store: ebony mannequins customized with Day-Glo tattoos and graffiti modeled chic women's garments. He made eye contact with Carol, the young saleswoman at the counter, who preferred to be called Carl. She had cropped her red hair into a crew cut and her waist had expanded quite a bit. Her features registered disdain upon seeing him and he assumed she disliked him because he had a cock and she didn't.

"Sheryl in?"

Without acknowledging him, Carol picked up the

house phone and pressed a button. "Jake's here," she said, the stud in the center of her tongue glinting. A moment later she hung up. "She'll be out in a minute." She returned her attention to the catalogue on the counter.

"Thanks." Jake wandered around the store, examining the selection. He had met Sheryl DeCosta not far from here, when they had both been waiting in line to see *The Maltese Falcon* at the Film Forum, one of the few cinemas that still projected film prints. At the time, he had been assigned to SNAP in Alphabet City and she had worked as a costume designer on independent films.

Sheryl emerged from her back office and Jake's heart clenched. He had to bite his tongue to keep from gasping. She wore a fashionable black suit and the horn-rimmed glasses that he liked, but she had cut her hair short, something he had always discouraged.

That didn't take long, he thought, trying to suppress his bitterness. Expressionless, Sheryl took his arm and guided him to one corner. "The place looks great," he said, trying not to stare at her haircut.

"You promised me you wouldn't do this," she said in a low voice.

"Here." He offered her the roses. "These are for you."

"Thank you." She took them, her demeanor remaining cool.

"Your hair looks nice."

"I think so, but I doubt you do."

"No, really—I like it."

"Jake, you can't just show up at my job like this. It isn't fair. I told you, I need time to think things through. And I don't want the people I work with to know what's going on between us."

Jake feigned innocence. "My stopping by to see you is telling them something?"

"When did you ever bring me flowers before? When was the last time you even picked me up here? When—"

"All right," he said, glancing around. "I just came by to let you know that I got a new job."

She glanced at his suit. "Doing what?"

"You're looking at the new director of security for the Tower."

"Uh-huh. Halloween was three days ago, and April Fool's Day isn't for six more months."

"I'm serious." He held up his employee manual, embossed with Tower International's logo, and she narrowed her eyes.

"How on earth did you swing that?"

"They came to me. Apparently Old Nick is a true-crime buff and wants a real gunslinger to protect him from those chromophobes outside the Tower."

"You mean you *met* him?"

He smiled. "I'm contractually prohibited from saying."

Her eyes lit up. "My God, how does he look?"

"Like Mr. Magoo crossed with Dracula, or a

demented Jimmy Stewart."

"I don't believe this. What are your responsibilities?"

"I'll be in charge of the entire internal security outfit. That means supervising surveillance, running background checks on potential employees, and implementing counterindustrial espionage procedures."

"How much are they paying you?"

He grasped her shoulders to steady her. "Three hundred Gs."

Her jaw dropped. "You've got to be kidding me."

Jake shook his head. "I'm on the level."

"That's incredible! My God, congratulations! I'm really happy for you. I always knew you were meant for better things than the Department."

He let go of her. "It's not entirely a perfect situation. I have to live in the Tower until this DCL-21 craziness blows over."

"We all have to make sacrifices to get ahead."

"I'm doing this for us."

"Do it for yourself."

"I don't want us to live apart."

Her face cooled. "We're already doing that."

"And I don't like it."

"We've only just separated. You have to think about yourself right now, and I have to think about myself."

"I am thinking about myself. I want you back."

She sighed. "I know you do. If we're meant to work

things out, we will."

"I swear I'll never touch that stuff again."

"You made that clear last night. What about the booze?"

"I'll give that up, too."

"We're going around in circles. You can make all the promises you want, but the only thing that's going to convince me that you mean business is time."

He stared at her, careful not to glare.

"I don't want to argue. When do you start this job?"

"Tomorrow morning."

"So soon? You always manage to land on your feet, don't you?"

"I wanted to wait until Monday, but they need someone right away. They're paying me a ten-thousand-dollar signing bonus to see things their way."

She whistled. "Good luck, then. I mean it. This will be a fresh start for you."

He glanced around the shop. "Can we have dinner next week?"

She looked into his eyes. "I'll think about it. That's all I'm willing to commit to right now. Call me over the weekend and let me know how the job's going, and we'll discuss it then." Her hand brushed his arm. "I have to get back to work. Thanks again for the flowers."

He watched her return to her office, sniffing the roses as she closed the door behind her. His heart swelled and he felt like a sap.

I love you.

Jake charged three new suits to his credit card before returning to the Lexington. Treating himself to a steak dinner in the hotel's restaurant, he resisted the urge to have a celebratory glass of wine. He knew that if he started drinking, he would be unable to stop and that would lead to greater trouble. He needed to be clearheaded in the morning. While eating, he pondered his good fortune. He had done more than just land on his feet, as Sheryl had suggested. He had climbed from the ashes of his police job to a full-fledged position in the private sector, all because Nicholas Tower acted on impulse.

Upstairs in his room, he ironed his shirts and repacked them, then sat at the desk and pored over the documents Kira had given him. His hand shook as he signed his employment contract. He filled out his insurance forms, considered his 401K options, and studied the company's regulations.

At 11:00 p.m., he pushed the manuals aside. Thirsting for alcohol, he smoked a cigarette, then showered and went to bed. Lying on his back, he went over his interview with Tower. It had gone exceptionally well, much better than he had expected. Thank God his new employers had not insisted that he take a drug test. The only awkward moment had been Tower's comment about him being an orphan. Jake disliked discussing the events that had deprived him of natural parents.

He had been raised by his Aunt Rose, his father's sister. Rose, a devout Catholic, had put her nursing career on hold to take care of him. She had never married, nor had children of her own, which Jake partly blamed on himself. As a boy, he had been incapable of grasping the toll that his father's death had taken on Rose. She kept her medicine cabinet stocked with vials of antidepressants and her face occasionally took on a blue pallor. She kept the circumstances of his parents' deaths a secret from him until his sixteenth birthday, when she deemed him mature enough to cope with the truth.

Jake's mother, Mary, had hemorrhaged to death while giving birth to him. His father, Sergeant Neal Helman, had been overwhelmed with grief. One week to the day after his wife's passing, he parked his Ford in the parking lot of the 175th Precinct in Queens and blew his brains out with his police revolver.

After those revelations, Jake had romanticized the notion of police work. Rose encouraged him to become a lawyer and he studied pre-law at John Jay College of Criminal Law. But the urge to follow in his father's footsteps had been too great, and after obtaining his bachelor's degree, he enrolled at the Police Academy. Three weeks after his graduation, he discovered Rose's corpse on the sofa of the apartment in which she had raised him.

The coroner ruled her death the result of an accidental overdose of antidepressants, but Jake knew better. His personal investigation revealed that his aunt had put her beloved cats to sleep the day before her death. Suicide ran in the family.

The craving for cocaine gripped him and he could not sleep. The inside of his nose felt dry and sore, and his stomach cramped. He tossed and turned, soaking the bedsheets with his sweat. Christ, he needed a drink.

The minibar . . .

No!

He got up, switched on a light, paced the floor, smoked another cigarette.

The clock read 1:09 a.m.

He opened the door to the minibar and gazed at the miniature glass bottles inside. Picturing Sheryl's face, he slammed the door shut.

He wrung his hands, pulled his hair, struck the mattress with his fists.

I won't break.

He awoke with spiders crawling over his face. He slapped his cheeks and forehead with both hands, but the spiders had disappeared. Opening his eyes, he saw Sheryl standing before him, her nude body glowing in the moonlight that shone through the windows.

Sitting up, he attempted to control his breathing. Sheryl's hair had grown long again, the way he liked it.

"I miss you, Jake."

He swallowed. "I miss you, too."

She drifted closer to him, her movement liquid. "Do you believe in true love?"

He nodded. "You know I do."

"Are you my soul mate?"

"Yes."

"I want you." Standing before him, she slid her hands over her breasts and the flat of her stomach. "I need you."

Tears formed in his eyes.

She sat on the edge of the bed and arched her back so the moonbeams highlighted her erect nipples. Turning her face toward his, her lips parted. "Please come back to me."

He felt himself growing hard.

She leaned even closer, her breath moist on his face. "Kiss me."

He embraced her. "Sheryl . . ."

He pulled her closer to him, sliding his hands up her belly and over her breasts, around her back and along her neck. He kissed her with desperation, enjoying the warm taste of her tongue. Then he opened his eyes and stared into the elliptical pupils of a reptile framed within feminine features.

His heart beat faster, and he tried to pull his hands away from her neck. Sheryl seized his wrists and dug her fingernails into them so hard that she drew blood. Her flesh turned rough and sandpapery, like sharkskin, and her tongue writhed inside his mouth like a snake. He twisted his head, pulling his mouth free of hers, and saw that he had been kissing Kira, not Sheryl. How had he confused them? A forked tongue darted at him from her gaping jaws.

Crying out, he threw her from the bed, leapt to his feet, and reached for the bedside lamp. He heard her body thump on the carpet and roll away in the darkness, heard her crawling on hands and knees as he fumbled with the light switch. The shaded lamp came on, and out of the corner of one eye he glimpsed her malformed shadow disappearing around the corner of the bed.

Jake sat up wild-eyed in the darkness, gasping for breath, the hair on the back of his neck standing on end. He reached over and turned on the lamp, then relaxed, reassured that he alone occupied the room. The nightmare had been so vivid that he had kicked the damp covers over the edge of the bed. He looked at the clock: 4:27 a.m. Sighing, he reached for the pack of Marlboros and lit a cigarette. Then he gazed at the ceiling and waited for the sun to rise.

The Tower came into view as the limousine crept through morning rush hour traffic. Wearing his trench coat over a dark, olive-colored suit, Jake sat in the backseat, tapping his foot on the floor. While suiting up for his civilian job, he had felt strange strapping on his holstered Glock. The driver turned onto Madison Avenue and pulled over to the curb, where a dozen men and women stood loitering outside the glass doors of the building. Jake paid the driver, collected a receipt, and got out, the lingering scent of urine on the sidewalk greeting him. Circling the limo as the driver removed his luggage from the trunk, he noticed that the people on the sidewalk stood gazing at the sky. With a sick feeling growing in the pit of his stomach, he raised his expectant eyes to where the Tower met the overcast sky. He saw no flames shooting through the windows, no black smoke billowing from the rooftop, no jumper perched on a ledge; just the structure, silhouetted against a gray canvas. He dropped his gaze to the motionless people before him. What the hell did they see?

"Have a good day, sir."

He turned to the driver, who had balanced his luggage on the edge of the trunk. "Thanks; you, too." Tucking the gun case under his left arm, he grabbed the handle of the suitcase with his left hand and swung the carrying bag with his suits over his right shoulder. Stepping onto the sidewalk, he passed between the sky gazers, who stood so still he felt as though he had somehow entered a photograph. He stopped beside a black man with graying hair and a trimmed beard.

"Excuse me?"

The man turned to him with a confused expression on his face. As a cop, Jake would have labeled the man an EDP: an Emotionally Disturbed Person.

"What's going on?"

Knitting his eyebrows together, the man squinted at Jake as if struggling to remember him from somewhere. Then his facial muscles relaxed and he turned back to the Tower without saying anything. Shaking his head, Jake glanced at the other people and moved to the glass doors. They all looked like EDPs to him. He struggled with a door and carried his luggage into the lobby. Laddock sat at the security station with Birch standing beside him, their positions reversed from the previous morning.

"Good morning, Mr. Helman," Laddock said.

"Good morning, sir," Birch echoed.

"Good morning." Jake set his gun case on top of the station and his suitcase on the floor.

Laddock handed him a stick-on visitor's pass. "You won't need one of these after today."

Jake peeled off the backing and affixed the pass to the front of his coat. Nodding at the front doors, he said, "Who are those people?"

Laddock shrugged. "I think they live down the street at a group home for the mentally disabled. As long as they're not demonstrators or terrorists, I don't care."

"Maybe we should call Dispatch—I mean, the police—just to be safe. I'm sure they can spare one of those uniforms out front to keep an eye on these folks."

Laddock shook his head. "Ms. Thorn's ordered us to ignore them."

Jake raised his eyebrows.

"She doesn't want any unnecessary public relations problems," Birch said.

Jake faced the doors. The EDPs continued to stare at the skyscraper's peak. Considering the PR concerns, he shrugged. "Okay, if that's what she wants." He carried his luggage to the elevators, summoned a car, and boarded it. When the doors opened on the sixtieth floor, he entered the corridor and saw Graham standing behind the glass door. Another guard sat behind the security station. Graham palmed a lock release and held the door open.

"Good morning," Graham said.

Entering the receiving area, Jake repeated the greeting. At least by living on-site he would be spared this small talk every morning.

Graham gestured to the burly guard at his station. "This is Pulaski. He has seniority after me. I'll be giving you the grand tour. and he's cleared to cover for me."

Jake glanced at the guard's name tag: Pulaski, Robert. The man's lopsided mustache divided his sour face, and he reminded Jake of several firefighters he had tangled with over the years. "How are you?"

Pulaski nodded without smiling. "Fine."

Prick, Jake thought.

"That's your office." Graham pointed at the dark, glass-faced office behind them, and it dawned on Jake that he'd be on permanent desk duty. "We're standing in the security bay. I'll show you to your unit now. Let me take that." He eased the suitcase from Jake's hand and led him to the glass door to the right of the entrance. Pulaski pressed a button at the console and the door unlocked with a metal click. Jake followed Graham into a curved corridor with cones of subdued light descending from circular ceiling fixtures. The carpet muffled their footsteps as they passed closed doors on their left and a mirrored surface on their right.

"This is the residential corridor," Graham said. "These first four units are guest rooms. Sometimes Mr. Tower's physicians stay here and sometimes I do if I'm pulling a double shift." They stopped at the fifth door. "This one is yours." He gestured at the sixth and final door. "Ms. Thorn lives there." The corridor ended twenty feet beyond Kira's door. "There are no cameras here, so you can relax." Graham aimed his ID badge at the door scanner. A red light turned green and the door unlocked. Graham opened it and stepped back, allowing Jake to enter first. "Welcome to your new home."

Jake entered the bright unit. An office area with a computer and eight security monitors opened into a furnished living room with a large picture window overlooking the city. A black leather sofa faced an LCD TV screen and tan carpeting covered the floor.

"As soon as we get you a security card, I'll have the scanner reprogrammed with your code," Graham said.

Jake moved to the living room window. Sixty stories below, a police car raced up Broadway with its strobes flashing, its siren inaudible at this height. Wondering what crisis the uniforms in the Radio Motor Patrol faced, he entered the kitchen and opened numerous cupboard doors.

"You're fully stocked," Graham said, "and your grocery expenses are covered. We don't allow deliveries on this floor, but the downstairs lobby is okay."

Jake set his belongings down in the bedroom, which reminded him of his room at the Lexington. He inspected the spacious bathroom, complete with a Jacuzzi. Returning to the living room, he hoped his new digs would impress Sheryl.

"I'll give you half an hour to unpack," Graham said, "and then we'll get on with the tour. I just need to give your contract to Ms. Thorn."

"Oh, right." Jake removed a folded copy of the contract from his inside coat pocket and handed it to Graham. He had hidden his own copy in the false bottom of his gun case. "Signed in blood," he said with a smile.

After unpacking his clothes, Jake rejoined Graham in the security bay. Pulaski stared at the monitors, ignoring him. Graham removed a compact walkie-talkie from a charger beneath the console and handed it to Jake, who admired the high-end device.

"Never go anywhere in the building without one of these," Graham said. "The charge is good for twenty-four hours, so just exchange it for another one first thing in the morning."

Jake switched on the walkie-talkie and clipped it to his belt.

Graham stepped before the front door and rapped on the glass. "Bulletproof," he said, palming the release button. He led Jake to the elevators and thumbed a call button.

"We maintain a rotating force of one hundred armed men, but only a quarter of them are cleared to work the top floor. That's not counting our unarmed force. Only you and Ms. Thorn and I know that Old Nick is in the building."

They boarded an elevator, and Graham pressed a button in the control panel marked *B*. The doors closed and the elevator plummeted. Then it slowed to a stop and its doors opened. Jake followed Graham through a windowless basement level with gray, cinder-block walls, and they stopped at a steel door with a wire-mesh window. Jake glanced at the camera peering down at them from above the door like an electronic gargoyle. Graham aimed his badge at a scanner, and they entered a wide room with a drop ceiling and paneled walls.

"This is Tower Security," Graham said. "We call it the 'Dungeon.'"

Behind a counter to their left stood a tall man with a crew cut, his badge identifying him as Thomas, Paul. He looked at Jake with alert eyes.

Graham said, "Paul, I'd like you to meet Jake Helman, the new DS."

Paul shook Jake's hand. "Sir."

"Jake. Mr. Helman, if you must."

"We thrive on formality here," Graham said. "This way, Mr. Helman, sir." Graham led Jake to another door. "We're parallel to the parking garage, but we're separated by ten feet of solid concrete. If the chromophobes hit us with a car bomb, we're safe."

In the next room, a half-dozen uniformed men and women with perfect posture sat behind a long console.

Wearing headsets, they faced scores of monitors recessed in the wall, each feeding a digital recorder. Some of the screens displayed as many as nine images at once; others cut from location to location. Jake felt as if he had wandered into a massive electronics store or an air traffic control center. A woman observing the central lobby moved her trackball, and a camera zoomed in on a man in a suit as he passed the security counter without signing in.

"Unauthorized person in Sector Alpha," she said into her microphone.

On another monitor, two guards stopped the man, who raised his hands as if to say, *What did I do?*

"There are almost two hundred cameras in the building, plus infrareds and motion detectors," Graham said before guiding Jake toward yet another door.

They entered a pale yellow cinder-block corridor and Jake peered through an open doorway on his left: shower steam obscured his view of scores of blue metal lockers. Graham unlocked a black metal door and they entered a dark chamber that reminded Jake of a bowling alley. Six booths faced fifty-foot lanes with paper targets at their ends.

"You've got to be kidding," Jake said, his voice deadened by soundproofing.

"Every guard on this force is required to log in an hour of target practice each week. Anyone who misses a session is barred from working the following week."

"Who enforces that rule?"

"You do."

Jake entered a booth and gazed ahead. The snarling faces on the illustrated targets stared back at him.

Blood erupted from Dread's torso as he flew back against the liquor store counter . . .

Jake swallowed.

Baldy's chest opened up in three spots and he fired his shotgun at the ceiling . . .

He needed a cigarette.

"Mr. Tower prefers old-school paper targets to digital projections," Graham said. "He also prefers live ammo to laser simulators. Says you need to feel the real thing kicking in your hand."

Jake stepped out of the booth. "You've spoken to him?"

Graham shook his head. "Never met the man. All of my info comes from Ms. Thorn."

On the walk back to the elevator, Jake said, "Who held this job before me?"

"Dick Drewniak, a retired fed. Drew was okay, but I'm working double shifts because he resigned without giving proper notice." They boarded the elevator. "The building's on Yellow Alert right now because of the demonstrations outside. We work on the standard color-coded system: Yellow, Orange, and Red."

"What happens on Red?"

"All hell breaks loose."

"That's reassuring. At what stage do we call nine-one-one?"

A puzzled expression passed over Graham's face. "The guidelines for emergency responses are on your desk, but we try to minimize police involvement here. You might say that's our goal."

Sunlight streamed through the central lobby's thirty-foot-high glass facade, which overlooked the police officers and demonstrators outside. A rotating sculpture of a DNA molecule reached the ceiling. People in business attire entered through revolving doors and stopped at a long counter manned by guards acting as concierges. Twenty elevators and an escalator transported professionals to their destinations. Jake took it all in with wondrous eyes.

He had arrived.

The elevator doors parted on the fiftieth floor, the words TOWER INTERNATIONAL emblazoned on the opposite wall in letters six feet high. Graham unlocked double doors with his badge and they entered a maze of intersecting corridors honeycombing the floor. High ceilings, stark white walls, and metallic carpet created an industrial effect while overhead florescent lights hummed and massive windows offered awesome views of lower midtown Manhattan. They passed recessed glass offices, conference rooms, kitchen areas, and a sea of cubicles occupied by intense-looking junior executives. Some ate at their desks while juggling multiple phone calls. Jake actually felt sorry for the poor bastards.

"All of the big shots and their peons work here," Graham whispered. "As far as they're concerned, this is the top of the food chain. Mr. Tower tells Ms. Thorn what he wants done and she relays his orders to Daryl Klemmer, the CEO."

Jake's ankles throbbed and he knew that he would be unable to find his way back to the elevators on his own. Impressed by the size of the circular floor, he realized that he had only seen a fraction of the equivalent space on Sixty. They approached a giant glass cube in the center of the floor.

"This is the Corporate Security Office," Graham said. They entered the cube, and Jake took in the desk, chairs, computer, and security monitors. "We run background checks from here and meet with department heads who aren't allowed upstairs. That means everyone but Klemmer."

Jake gazed through the glass at the harried workers. The pervasive sense of fear felt palpable.

Graham took a digital camera out of a metal cabinet and raised it to one eye. "Smile for posterity . . ."

Jake forced a smile and the camera flashed.

"I'll download this upstairs." Graham removed a memory card from the camera. On their way back to the elevator he said, "Life Support is on Fifty-Nine. That's Mr. Tower's personal ER. His food is prepared on the same floor. There's a separate kitchen for each meal of the day, and they're sterilized after every use."

"No food tasters?"

"Not of the human variety, but the meals are tested in a lab next to the galleys."

When they returned to the sixtieth floor, Graham pointed at the hand scanner next to the glass door. "Enter your Social Security number on the keypad and put your right hand on the scanner, palm down."

Jake punched in his Social Security number and placed his palm on the scanner's cool, opaque surface.

"Hold still."

Jake held his breath, and a red laser beam beneath the glass scanned his hand, moving up and down like a copy machine.

Graham pressed a button on the keypad and the scanner beeped. "You're part of the system now. Take your hand off the scanner, then put it back on."

Jake obeyed. After the scanner verified his handprint, the door unlocked.

"Every employee's security card is custom programmed. Yours will admit you to every area below Fifty-Nine, and most of the areas up here. But only a hand scan will admit you beyond this point."

Jake opened the door for Graham and then followed him into the security bay. Pulaski glowered as they passed two black lacquered doors with gold handles; even the bathrooms had scanners. Graham used his badge to unlock the glass door to the left of the entrance.

"This is the utility corridor," Graham said as they crossed the marble floor of the wide corridor, which followed the same curve as the residential corridor. He identified the doors that they passed: "Maintenance, Custodial, Electrical . . . this one is ours." He unlocked a door near the end of the corridor, and Jake followed him into a windowless space divided into three sections by gray metal shelves. The far wall housed multiple security monitors with split-screen images, digital recorders, and a viewing station. "Our Control Room. We record what the cameras see on Sixty, Fifty-Nine, and the private lobby from here; everything else is recorded in the Dungeon."

Jake moved to the metal shelves and examined the equipment stored on them: digital cameras, camcorders, electronic listening devices, locksmith kits, and night vision goggles—enough toys to give a surveillance expert wet dreams.

I'm Big Brother's little brother, he thought.

They exited the Control Room and turned to the corridor's final door. Aiming his badge at a scanner, Graham opened the wide, wooden door. "Ms. Thorn meets with high-priority clients here."

Jake peered inside the conference room. Sunlight shone through the windows onto a giant oval table surrounded by a dozen leather chairs. A RESTRICTED sign had been posted on a door across the room. "What's in there?"

"Couldn't tell you. We're not cleared to enter the Demonstration Room."

Jake grunted as Graham closed the door.

"That concludes our tour. Please come again."

Stars appeared one by one in the black background of the computer screen and an animated graphic of the earth rotated into view. A DNA strand enveloped the globe and golden lettering formed beneath it: TOWER INTERNATIONAL—BUILDING BETTER LIFE.

Jake sat back in his chair. He had seen the graphic before, in a TV commercial narrated by a movie star. Debbie Brown, the IT manager, had helped him set up his password and activate his voice mail. The scent of her perfume lingered in the air long after her departure, sickly and sweet, like flowers in a funeral parlor.

Security monitors surrounded Jake's curved desk, and the glass face of his rectangular office provided a view of the security bay and the corridor leading to the elevators. He opened his e-mail and scrolled down the page. Forty-five messages had been copied to him. Was this how yuppies spent their days? He opened the first message, a company-wide memo from Kira introducing him as the new director of security. He closed the message and opened the next one. And the one after that.

His telephone rang just before noon and he saw Kira's name on the display. He glanced at a framed photo of Sheryl, looking luminous at a resort in the Poconos, as he pressed the speaker phone button. "Helman."

"Come to my office."

Kira hung up before Jake could respond. Leaving his office, he stood outside her double doors. Their locks clicked and he stepped inside. Kira rose from behind her desk and circled it, and Jake felt his body temperature rise. She wore knee-high black leather boots and a short black skirt with a matching jacket, her long hair loose around her shoulders. He caught a whiff of her perfume, and an image of her naked legs wrapping around his bare back flashed through his mind. He dug his fingernails into his palms, suppressing the fantasy.

"How is your day going so far?" Kira said.

"Good." Jake studied her mouth.

Kira held out a business envelope to him. "Here you are." Her red lips revealed perfect white teeth but no forked tongue.

"What's this?" he said, taking the sealed envelope.

"The pay stub for your signing bonus. We deposited it into an account with your name on it at our branch today."

Jake slid the envelope into the inside breast pocket of his suit jacket. "That was fast."

"We own the bank. You can take your lunch now."

"Thanks."

She handed a tiny black cell phone to him. "The company's directory has been preprogrammed and the security bay's on auto-dial. Never leave the building without notifying whoever's at that station." She sat down again as Jake pocketed the cell phone. "Do you know who Bill Russel is?"

Jake searched his memory. "No."

"He used to be a deputy director at the CIA. He designed our security systems and implemented the procedures you're paid to enforce."

A spook, Jake thought. Old Nick had recruited members of the CIA, the FBI, and the NYPD for Tower security; the alphabet soup method of executive protection.

"He still does some freelance work for us. At four o'clock, he's bringing some important clients to meet with me. They know that Dick Drewniak resigned as our DS, and it's important that we make them feel secure. Introduce yourself when they arrive."

She wants me to be window dressing, Jake thought. "You got it."

Kira turned to her computer screen, dismissing Jake.

Jake's heartbeat quickened and he pictured himself taking her right there, on top of her desk. *What's wrong with me?*

As he turned to the doors, he glanced at the security monitors recessed in the back wall. One of the screens displayed a perfect view of his office, shot from above the elevators. With the zoom function, Kira had the ability to observe every move he made.

Jake ate lunch at the Midnight Diner, located on the ground level of the Tower, off Twenty-fourth Street. Afterward, he sat on a wooden bench in Madison Square Park and smoked two cigarettes. He stared at the stub for the direct deposit made into his special account. *Ten thousand dollars.* Of course, he owed taxes on that. Still, even if the government claimed half that amount, he was in good shape. He watched squirrels gather nuts while the leader of the ACCL addressed his followers across the street and around the corner. When he reentered the security bay, Graham looked at his watch and smiled.

"You're back early."

"I'll have to eat farther from home next time."

"I've got something for you." Graham handed Jake a security card in a plastic holder with a clip. "Your keycard to the kingdom." TOWER SECURITY appeared over a dark blue stripe on the light blue card, and Jake's ID photo resembled a holographic mug shot. A twelve-digit identification code appeared over a magnetic strip on the back of the card. "Congratulations, you're a number."

"Hooray."

"We update the codes and photos every three months. We're in the beginning of a new cycle, so the next update will be in January."

"Sounds like a lot of work." Jake peeled the visitor's pass from his trench coat, crumpled it up, and tossed it into the wastebasket behind Graham's station. Graham retrieved the pass and ran it through a shredder.

Jake approached his office and saw that a narrow gold plaque with his name engraved in black lettering had been posted on the glass beside his door. On his desk, he discovered a small cardboard box. Opening it, he found hundreds of business cards. He removed one, which bore the Tower's logo in its upper left-hand corner, followed by embossed lettering: JAKE HELMAN, DIRECTOR OF SECURITY, TOWER INTERNATIONAL HEADQUARTERS. The card listed the Tower's address and Jake's extension number.

He had an identity again.

Using his browser, he opened the computer folder

tagged "Security" and studied the personnel files on the guards under his command. As he clicked from file to file, a pattern emerged: all of the men and women in Tower Security had served in the military. All had seen combat action, many of them as members of Special Forces, Navy SEALS, Rangers, or Delta Force. Graham had received three medals while serving Great Britain's force in Iraq. Most of the personnel had gone on to work as private security consultants in destabilized nations; mercenaries hired to support the U.S. military in war torn lands. Laddock and Birch had both worked for Blackwater Worldwide. For his team, Tower favored heroes with blood on their hands, and he paid them a thousand dollars a day for their skills. Although he had never served in the armed forces, Jake now understood how he had qualified for his current position.

At 4:00 p.m., he saw on one monitor that three men had entered the private lobby downstairs. Russel had to be the tall man with the bald head and mustache, because the short men with him appeared to be foreigners. They had dark complexions, darker hair, and matching black suits. Russel shook hands with Laddock and Birch at the security station, and the guards motioned the visitors beyond the checkpoint. The next monitor showed a reverse angle of the men boarding an elevator. One of the guests appeared to be fifty, like Russel, and wore glasses; the other, who may have been Jake's age, carried a wooden box between his hands. A third monitor looked down inside the elevator from its ceiling. The guests looked at each other and laughed as the car ascended at high speed.

Jake stood, straightened his tie, and joined Graham in the security bay as the elevator doors opened. Russel allowed his guests to exit first. They followed the corridor to the glass door, which Graham unlocked from his station. The men entered the security bay, the visitors looking around as if they expected to see something wondrous.

"Hello, Graham," Russel said in a deep voice as the glass door closed behind him. His expensive suit had been tailored for his muscular frame.

Graham stood beside Jake. "Good to see you again, Mr. Russel."

Russel turned to Jake. "You must be Helman."

Stepping forward, Jake extended his right hand. "Call me Jake."

Russel gave Jake's hand a hard squeeze, and Jake had no choice but to squeeze back. Russel reminded him of a circus strongman.

"I hear you were in an 'officer-related' a couple of days back."

"That's right." Jake tried to cover the surprise in his voice.

"I'd like to have lunch sometime to discuss your thoughts on how we can improve our security measures here."

"I look forward to that." Jake did not believe for one second that Russel desired to have lunch with him or listen to his ideas.

Kira emerged from her office and Russel smiled as she joined them. "Here she is," he said to his guests. "Kira . . ."

"Bill, it's been too long."

Jake watched them shake hands. He had not seen Kira turn on her charm before. Russel's guests gaped at her appearance.

"Gentlemen, this is Ms. Thorn, Mr. Tower's executive assistant. Kira, meet Mr. Fortaleza and his assistant, Mr. Villanueva."

"How do you do?" She shook each man's hand. "Welcome to Tower International."

"The pleasure is ours," Fortaleza said in a heavy accent. "Will Mr. Tower be joining us?"

"I'm afraid not," Kira said without offering an explanation for Tower's unavailability.

Fortaleza looked disappointed. "We've brought this gift for him from President Seguera."

Jake's radar went up, and Kira glanced in his direction to gauge his reaction. He didn't follow international politics, but he knew that Kimo Seguera, the president of the Philippines, had been the controversial subject of recent newspaper headlines due to human rights violations committed in his country.

Fortaleza gestured to his assistant, and Villanueva stepped forward with the hand-carved wooden box trimmed with jewels. He bowed as he offered it to Kira, who accepted it.

"How generous of President Seguera. I know that Mr. Tower will be pleased. Shall we proceed?"

Fortaleza nodded. "By all means. We're eager to see your demonstration."

Russel motioned them toward the utility corridor. "This way to your future, gentlemen." Graham unlocked the glass door from his station, and the entourage filed through it. Russel and Fortaleza walked side by side, followed by Kira and Villanueva, with Jake bringing up the rear. At the end of the corridor, Russel produced a security card and opened the conference room door. He and the Filipinos entered the sunlit room and Kira turned in the doorway, blocking Jake's path.

"Thank you, Mr. Helman. That will be all."

Jake hesitated. "Shall I wait out here?"

"That won't be necessary."

She closed the door in his face.

Bitch, he thought.

"What's this demonstration they're holding in there?" Jake asked Graham in the security bay.

Graham held his right hand over his eyes, then over his right ear, and finally over his mouth: see no evil, hear no evil, speak no evil.

Returning to his office, Jake sat at his computer and

opened an Internet search engine. In less than a minute, he found the information he wanted.

Kimo Seguera had been the president of the Philippines for six years, with Jose Fortaleza serving as his diplomatic emissary. No information turned up on Villanueva. Rocked by attacks from various terrorist factions based in its impregnable jungles, the Philippines had suffered drastic economic woes when corporations seeking exploitable territories deemed them too unstable for investment. The steps taken by Seguera to crush the terrorists had been so extreme that his own people had risen against him. To protect his position, he imposed martial law, transforming the democracy into a police state almost overnight. The terrorists continued to plague him, with the support of his oppressed subjects.

Jake sat back in his chair. No direct connection linked Seguera to Tower, but the CIA had played a pivotal role in the dictator's early campaign against terrorism, and an additional search showed that Bill Russel had worked for the CIA when Seguera had first become president. What could Seguera possibly want from Tower International? Tower had a stranglehold on genetic industries, and Seguera needed military strength.

What's inside that Demonstration Room?

He stared at two white pens that lay side by side on the desktop, like lines of cocaine. Sweat formed on his brow and his vision turned blurry. Seizing the pens, he shoved them into a drawer, which he slammed shut.

Russel and the Filipino delegation departed an hour later, and Kira summoned Jake to her office again. Through her expansive windows, Jake watched the sun dip behind the skyline and wondered when his workday would end.

"Have a seat," Kira said.

He made himself comfortable.

"According to our intelligence, RAGE intends to launch an attack on the Tower soon."

Jake tensed up. No wonder Tower had needed him to start right away. Exactly what intelligence had Russel given Kira?

"I want you to issue a company-wide memo raising our alert status to Orange immediately."

"Right." Jake rose to his feet.

So did Kira. "But I need you to do something else first." She led him to the anteroom door outside Tower's office and gestured at the black rubber eyecup of the retina scanner. "You need access to Nicholas's office in case of an emergency and this entrance can't be opened with a security card or hand scan. Swipe your card for identification."

Jake removed his badge from his jacket and swiped it through a slot on the scanner. When his security code appeared on the display window, Kira pressed a button.

"Press your right eye against the eyecup."

Jake hesitated.

"It's perfectly safe."

Stepping closer, he leaned forward and pressed his eye against the eyecup. Staring through a lens at a mirror, he saw his own bloodshot eye.

"Don't blink."

A red laser beam scanned his eye and his lids twitched, threatening to close. He heard a buzzing sound, followed by a click that reminded him of the sound made by an x-ray machine.

"Okay."

Blinking, he stepped back.

The anteroom door unlocked and Kira opened it. "There's one more step." She took him into the anteroom and pointed at the hand scanner beside the steel doors. "Place your hand on the scanner."

"I already did this with Graham."

"Do it again."

Frowning, Jake set his right palm down on the scanner. The laser scanned his hand, and his security code appeared on the display.

Kira pressed a button. "Now hold perfectly still. You're going to feel a pinch—"

Jake furrowed his eyebrows. There had been no pinch before—

Pain shot through the back of his hand, as if a needle

had pierced his skin, and his body turned rigid. He heard what sounded like an electric stapler in action as his fingers spread out. The pain and sound ebbed at the same time.

"Remove your hand."

Jake slid his hand from the scanner and examined the area of skin that had hurt. He saw no mark or blood.

"DNA scanner," Kira said. "There's no fooling this machine."

Jake disliked the idea of a genetics outfit possessing a sample of his DNA, but what could he do?

Back in her office, Kira sat at her desk and turned to her computer, ignoring him. Jake studied the way the orange light from the setting sun highlighted the contours of her face. She looked up at him with one eyebrow cocked.

"Is there something else? I need you to disseminate that memo."

Jake felt like a schoolboy who had just been caught staring at the prettiest girl in class. "I was wondering if you'd like to go out for a drink sometime? It would give us a chance to go over procedures away from all of this." He wanted to kick himself even as the words tumbled from his mouth. Why had he asked her out? He disliked her and she clearly detested him. He had no interest in being with anyone but Sheryl and had sworn off drinking.

Kira studied him for a moment with a curious expression. Then her eyes darkened. "No, thank you. I'm allergic to alcohol."

Jake's body relaxed. *Maybe you're allergic to men.*

But he doubted that very much. "I'll send that e-mail now."

Jake had dinner at Sinare's, the Italian restaurant next door to the Midnight Diner. *I'll never have to leave the block,* he thought, eyeing the bar in the rear of the restaurant. When he returned to the sixtieth floor at 8:00 p.m., he saw that Graham had been relieved by a tall young man with broad shoulders and short hair: Cutler, Barry.

"I'm Jake Helman." He offered his hand, which the guard shook.

"Pleased to meet you." Cutler possessed a Southern accent.

"I read in your dossier that you were an MP."

Cutler nodded. "Yes, sir."

"I just resigned from the police department. It's good to know that I'll have a brother in arms to depend on."

Cutler just looked at him with a blank expression.

"I'll be in my unit if you need me for anything."

"Good night, sir."

Inside his unit, Jake kicked off his shoes and set his walkie-talkie down on the computer station. On one of the monitors above the computer, he saw Cutler drum the fingers of one hand on his desk. Jake hung his suit in the bedroom closet. It felt strange living in the same building where he worked. In Homicide, he had crashed on a cot in the locker room on numerous occasions while working around the clock on major cases, but he had always made it home to Sheryl eventually. He looked around the bedroom, his home for the time being.

Stripping naked, he climbed into the Jacuzzi. As high-powered jets of water massaged his tired muscles, he allowed his mind to wander. The rising steam moistened his nostrils, and he dug his fingers into his palms. Squeezing his eyes shut, he fought off the craving for cocaine. His thoughts turned once more to Kira's clandestine meeting with the Filipinos that afternoon. What had that meeting concerned? It occurred to him that he had not seen Tower all day. The old man seemed like a prisoner in his own castle. How could he protect someone he never saw? And he had seen nothing that explained the unused floor space on the sixtieth floor. He found it hard to believe that Tower needed all that square footage for his private quarters.

When his skin had wrinkled, he drained the Jacuzzi and changed into a pair of red shorts and a blue NYPD T-shirt. He crossed the living room and turned off the lights, then stood before the picture window, gazing out at the twinkling lights of the city. Killers lurked out there. Not just psychos like the Cipher, or murderous thugs like Dread and Baldy, but organized zealots like the members of RAGE, who pulled triggers and planted bombs in God's name. He lit a cigarette and the automatic air purifier in the wall hummed.

He needed to get home to Sheryl.

Without a computer or security monitors, the bedroom felt comfortable, its natural wood decor offering welcome relief from the high-tech environment in which Jake had spent the day. Closing the door, he stripped down to his briefs and set his alarm clock for 7:00 a.m. Thinking of the ACCL and RAGE, he slipped his Glock beneath the pillow beside him, holstered so he would not accidentally pull the trigger in his sleep. He crawled beneath a blanket and switched off the bedside lamp, then rested his head on his pillow. Sleep claimed him before midnight.

A sharp noise awoke him sometime later. His body jerked upright, his eyes scanning the darkness. Had he actually heard a door close, or had that just been part of a dream? He recalled disjointed images from his sleep: locked doors, security cameras, and key cards. Listening to the darkness, he heard only the sound of his pensive breathing. The luminous numbers on the clock showed the time: 12:35. He had been asleep for less than an hour. Had he heard the door to Kira's unit closing? He smiled at his paranoia; no terrorists had stormed the Tower.

Then yellow light, as pale as an alligator's eyes, outlined the bedroom door and he held in his breath.

Someone had entered his living room.

His eyes opened wide, his heart threatening to explode through his chest.

Then he heard footsteps on the other side of the door, moving closer.

Jake reached beneath the pillow and seized the grip of his Glock. Pulling the gun free of its holster, he rolled off the bed and crouched on the floor behind it. He pulled back the Glock's slide and gripped the weapon in both hands. Across the room, the door creaked open and a shaft of light fell over him, exposing his upper body to the intruder. Squinting at the light, he aimed the Glock at the silhouette in the doorway.

Kira stood there in a sheer nightie cut midway to her thighs. Jake saw the curves of her body through the transparent fabric, even more exquisite than he had imagined. She turned to one side, allowing him to admire her profile, her features inscrutable.

He relaxed his grip on the Glock and released its slide. Rising to his feet, he dangled the gun at his side, allowing Kira to see his body as well. "I could have killed you."

She moved out of the light as she entered the room, her voice silky. "I doubt it."

He stood still as she penetrated the darkness. "What do you want?"

Stepping around the bed, she touched a clasp between her breasts and the nightie slipped to the floor. "What does it look like I want?"

She stepped into the light, her body so close to his that he felt heat emanating from it. She had the most incredible body he had ever seen, perfect in every way he could imagine. Her eyes captured a sliver of light and her moist lips parted. He smelled sweet perfume, which mingled with her body's natural scent, and felt himself hardening. He tried to picture Sheryl, but her face dissipated along with his resolve. An animal longing grew deep inside him, and he knew that he could not stop himself, even if he could have stopped her.

She reached out with one hand, her fingernails raking the flesh from his chest to his abdomen, and his cock stood at attention. She closed her fingers around the barrel of his Glock, then eased it from his hand and tossed it onto a chair. She wrapped her arms around his back and pressed her breasts against his chest, her nipples hard and erect, then pushed her tongue against his. He gathered from her flat stomach that she worked out every day. His erection poked at her mound of fine black hair as she slid her hands down to his waist, seized the band of his briefs, and twisted it in opposing directions until the fabric tore.

Before he knew it, she had freed him from the constricting material and squeezed his shaft between her thighs. Looking at the bureau mirror behind her, he saw a dark tattoo of a spider on her back, just below her left shoulder.

Pivoting on one heel, Jake pushed her down onto the bed. He climbed on top of her and spread her knees apart with his own, guiding himself into her slick opening. She wrapped her limbs around him and he felt her abdominal muscles clench. Her inner muscles squeezed him in ways he had never thought possible. He grabbed her hair and stared into her eyes, which taunted him, challenged him. He buried his tongue inside her mouth and drove himself into her with all his strength, channeling the anger and frustration that he had felt over the past few days into a desperate need for physical release. She arched her hips beneath him, encouraging him and fighting him at the same time, writhing in response to his efforts.

"Fuck me!" Kira said through clenched teeth.

I . . . thought . . . I . . . was . . .

"Harder!" Her claws raked his back and ass.

Any harder and I'll have a heart attack!

Still, he found the strength to accommodate her, and soon he felt a torrent of hot fluid gushing around his member as her body quaked beneath his.

"That's it," she cried. "That's *it!*"

She whimpered like a wounded animal and he cried out in orgasm, his heart pounding and his eyes rolling up in their sockets. He wilted over her and she pushed him off and stood without saying anything.

He felt drained. "That's it . . ."

Kira wiped his sweat from her body as she might have (had she) come into contact with some toxic chemical, then snatched her nightie from the floor and strode from the room, her departure as abrupt as her arrival. Jake heard the front door open and close, and he ran one hand over his sweat-soaked face. In only a few short minutes, Kira had given him the ride of his life. His legs shook as though she had sucked his blood like a vampire, leaving him with just enough hemoglobin to function.

What about Sheryl?

Fuck her.

The thought startled him and he felt a tide of guilt wash over him as rationality returned to his mind.

I can never do this again.

But he knew he had an addictive personality and sex with Kira felt like a new drug. He wondered if he had the strength to resist her if she visited him again. Still smelling her fragrance, he went into the bathroom and showered. Returning to the bedroom, he saw something glossy on the floor, near the foot of the bed. Stepping closer, he picked it up: Kira's security card. She must have dropped it while shedding the nightie.

Then why hadn't she come back for it?

Perhaps she had tried to do so while he had been in the shower.

He went into the office space and checked the security monitors above his computer. Cutler sat alone in the security bay. The monitors didn't show the two corridors beside the elevators, but he assumed Kira had gotten into her unit by entering her security code into the keypad of her door scanner. He turned the card over in his hand, considering his options.

Cutler looked up from his console with raised eyebrows.

"I need to check something in the Control Room," Jake said as he passed the security station. He wore blue jeans and hi-top sneakers, with no shirt beneath his V-neck sweater. His walkie-talkie hung from his belt and he held his security card in one hand. "Stay alert."

"I will," Cutler said.

Jake waved his card at the door scanner, entered the utility corridor, and approached the Control Room. He waved his card again and pushed the door open. Monitors flickered in the darkness as he stepped inside and closed the door. He had clearance to be there so he wouldn't need to justify his presence to Kira if she caught him. He sat at the viewing station below the monitors, his watch ticking off seconds while Cutler patrolled the security bay. Satisfied the guard seemed intent on remaining in his assigned territory, Jake stood and crossed the room. Opening the door, he leaned his head out. The curvature of the corridor made it impossible for him to see Cutler—or for Cutler to see him. He stepped out, closed the door, and crept to the far end of the corridor. Looking over his shoulder one last time, he waved his card at the final scanner, unlocked the conference room door, and slipped inside.

The glow of the city outside outlined the furniture in the dark room. Half of the empty chairs around the conference table faced Jake, and the windows reflected his image over the vista of the nighttime cityscape. He flicked on the overhead lights and his reflection flickered away like a ghost. Across the room, the RESTRICTED sign on the Demonstration Room door beckoned to him.

This is insane, he thought.

But he moved forward anyway, staring at the door, his right hand maneuvering Kira's security card over his own.

I could be fired for this.

Was it worth it?

Of course not. But the cop inside him had to know what Kira, Russel, and the Filipino men were up to. Why all the secrecy? His instincts told him he had stumbled onto something illegal, possibly even something with international repercussions. He waved Kira's card at the scanner, half-hoping it wouldn't work.

The door unlocked.

Standing rigid, he took a deep breath. Then he reached out and his fingertips brushed the metal door, which creaked open. Machinery hummed in the darkness, like a swimming pool filter, and escaping air chilled him. Reaching inside and groping along the wall, he located a light switch and slipped inside as they flickered on. The deep room contained no furniture. Twenty feet ahead, in the room's center, a giant glass globe, ten feet in diameter, sat upon an octagonal metal base. Green in color, it stared at him like an unblinking, cyclopean eye.

He pulled the door behind him, careful to leave it unlatched; he didn't want to risk locking himself in overnight. He approached the globe, his footsteps slow and his reflection in the curved glass growing larger. The green color did not come from the glass, but from the globe's contents; the liquid inside resembled murky green water. Why would an island nation need seawater?

He stopped before the globe. Plastic hoses and metal coils ran from it into the metal base, which had drainage holes similar to those he had seen in autopsy tables. The humming sound came from a motor in the base. He saw no safety gloves or oxygen masks lying around, so he felt safe as he reached out and pressed his right palm against the glass. He felt the vibration of the filter through the cool, smooth surface and his body shivered.

A shadow darted through the green liquid and Jake blinked. Two bulbous red eyes and dozens of razor-sharp teeth smashed against the glass where his hand rested. Recoiling with a startled cry, he snatched his hand away, backpedaling until he fell on his ass. Inside the globe, the creature bashed its head against the glass over and over, striking where Jake's hand had left a condensation print.

What in God's name is that?

The creature stared at him with anger blazing in its hungry eyes, its head the size of a fist. A wide gash beneath its eyes exposed rows of piranha teeth receding into fleshy darkness. Its body, three inches in diameter and two feet long, writhed like a snake, its scales silvery green. It could have been a mutated eel with a shrunken human head and the mouth of a shark. It gave Jake a hateful look and retreated into the murky green water.

Jake remained sitting on the floor for a moment, unable to budge. Then he managed to rise to his feet but his eyes remained locked on the giant globe. He knew he had just seen a creature that had never existed until the scientists at Tower International had created it, and the presence of the demonstrators downstairs suddenly made total sense to him. Stepping forward, he peered into the globe again. A half dozen of the shadowy things swam within it, the machine in its base simulating the current of a stream or river.

Jake staggered back to the door, too frightened to take his eyes off the globe. He backed into the conference room, closed the Demonstration Room door, then fled into the corridor. His feet pounded the floor as he sprinted through the corridor, the glass door to the security bay coming into view around the curved wall. He palmed the release button, threw the door open, and rushed toward the security station, startling Cutler, who leapt to his feet. Jake skidded to a stop on the marble floor and the guard stared at him with bulging eyes.

"What's wrong?"

Jake could only imagine how he must have looked: pale as a ghost and shaken to his core. He looked behind him at the empty corridor. "Nothing." Not caring whether or not his explanation had satisfied the guard, he waved his card at the scanner for the residential corridor and hurried along the curved wall, moving in and out of the light. Praying that Kira would not suddenly emerge from her unit ahead of him, he unlocked his door, stumbled inside, and slammed the door, locking it behind him. He rushed across the room to the windows, seized his pack of Marlboros, and lit a cigarette with trembling fingers. He took a deep drag, exhaling as he gazed at his troubled reflection in the window.

What am I going to do?

Nothing. Keep your mouth shut.

For all he cared, the creatures in the globe didn't exist. He took another drag on the cigarette, searing his lungs. His adrenaline surging, he knew he would be unable to sleep. He finished the cigarette in silence and carried the pack into the bedroom with him.

Tower International?

That's where they make the monsters.

15

Jake chain-smoked through the night, emptying the pack. Streaks of orange split the sky when he finally succumbed to exhaustion, and he snapped awake when the alarm went off thirty minutes later. His eyeballs throbbed, his scalp felt prickly, and he wished he had forced himself to stay awake. Sitting up, he gazed out the window, midtown Manhattan coming into focus. He craved another cigarette even though his throat felt raw. After a shower and breakfast, he put on his black suit and took his trench coat from the closet.

Graham had returned to his post in the security bay. "Good morning. Sleep all right last night?"

"Not exactly." Glancing at Kira's office doors, Jake handed his walkie-talkie to Graham. "Ms. Thorn around?"

Graham set the walkie-talkie into a charger and

offered Jake a fresh one. "She's always in her office by seven-thirty."

Jake waved off the walkie-talkie. "I'm stepping out for a few. I'll take that when I get back."

"No sweat."

Jake entered the elevator bay and pressed a call button. Having slept little the previous two nights, he felt stiff and disoriented as he boarded an elevator.

Descending . . .

His stomach lurched. He did not look forward to seeing Kira and he didn't wish to trip himself up with a lie if she asked him about her security card. The elevator doors opened, and he joined Laddock and Birch at their security station.

"Right on schedule," Birch said from his seat.

Jake blinked. "Excuse me—?"

Birch looked up at him. "Not you—*them*." He nodded at the front doors. "They rise with the sun."

Jake followed Birch's gaze to the dozen men and women gathered outside the doors. At first he failed to recognize them through the glare on the glass, but then he realized they stood gazing up at the Tower, as still as statues. "Jesus. What are they looking for?"

Laddock shrugged. "God?"

"Do they ever come inside?"

"Sometimes. But it doesn't take much to get rid of them." Laddock reached behind the security station and picked up a wooden nightstick that reminded Jake of the baton he had carried as a patrolman. Laddock slapped it into the palm of his other hand, and the fleshy-sounding echo made Jake wince.

"That seems a little extreme."

"We've got orders not to touch them with our hands," Laddock said.

Jake remembered the caution he had shown as a uniform when handling homeless people, who were potential carriers of disease.

"Are you going somewhere, Mr. Helman?"

Jake spun at the icy sound of Kira's voice. She stood in the open doorway of an elevator, dressed in another dark miniskirt and blazer combo with knee-high leather boots. The lady liked black. Her disposition toward him seemed no warmer since their tryst.

Good morning to you, too, Jake thought. *I almost didn't recognize you with your clothes on.* "I was just stepping out for some fresh air."

"I want to see you in my office as soon as you get back."

Here it comes. "Sure."

Kira gave him a hard look before the elevator doors closed and he felt himself turning red. Did she know he had sneaked into the Demonstration Room, or was she just upset that he had not returned her security card to her yet?

"Uh-oh," Laddock said.

Turning back, Jake saw one of the Emotionally

Disturbed Persons detach herself from the crowd outside. The young woman, dressed in a black miniskirt, a satin top, and no coat, staggered toward the doors in a daze. Cupping her hands around her eyes, she pressed her face close to the glass and stared into the lobby. Behind her, the others remained focused on the Tower.

Grinning at Jake, Laddock slapped the nightstick in his hand again. "We're going to have to break her in."

The woman shook the door closest to her, rattling it. She looked up at the top of its frame, then down at its brass handle.

"Don't do it," Birch said, rising. "Keep your ass *out* there."

"They never make the same mistake twice," Laddock said in a conspiratorial tone.

The woman pulled the door open, allowing cold air to precede her. She stepped inside, her eyes wide and unblinking.

Her face, Jake thought, narrowing his eyes. Something about it looked familiar . . .

"I need it," the woman said as she approached the security station. "Give it back to me."

An Irish accent? Jake stared at the gold crucifix hanging around her neck, and the image of rosary beads formed in his mind.

Laddock stepped around him and raised the nightstick over his head. "Crazy bitch . . ."

The woman continued forward, oblivious to the

threat Laddock posed to her. Jake's right hand shot out and seized Laddock's wrist, preventing the nightstick from crashing down on the woman's skull. Laddock turned to him with a surprised look and Jake shook his head.

Laddock jerked his arm free. "Have it your way," he said through clenched teeth. His snarl transformed into a smirk as he stepped back, giving Jake free reign over the situation.

Birch pointed past them. "Look out!"

The woman stepped closer to Jake, her face taut. "*Give me back my soul!*"

Jake saw his reflection in her eyes and realized he had seen it in them before.

Impossible.

He had not recognized Shannon Reynolds because he had only seen her previously as a bloody corpse lying tits-up on a bedroom floor in Hell's Kitchen. He raised his hands to hold her back.

Birch raised his voice: "*Don't touch her, man!*"

Too late.

Shannon walked into Jake's hands and Jake flinched as an electric current jolted him. Unable to bow his head, he lowered his eyes and gasped. His hands had been absorbed into Shannon's sternum. His arms simply stopped after his wrists, which pressed against her satin top. He opened and closed the fingers that he could no longer see, but the current made it impossible for him to feel anything but fear. He tried to jerk his arms free, but they did not respond to his will. Over the top of Shannon's head, he saw the other EDPs outside turn their heads toward him in unison. All of them stared at him, wide-eyed and unblinking.

Birch said, "Ho-ly shit . . ."

Staring into Shannon's eyes, Jake saw undiluted terror. Her lips trembled, and when her quivering mouth opened as wide as possible, she unleashed a scream that caused him to shudder. A gurgling sound rose from deep within her, and the flesh on her face drew taut. Her features collapsed, as if her skull had caved in on itself, and her liquefied eyes ran over her cheekbones like runny eggs. Beams of intense white light shot out of her gaping sockets and open mouth. Jake watched in mute horror as the energy dissolved her flesh and a stench like that of rotten fruit filled his nostrils. He felt Shannon's guts gushing over his hands like warm gelatin, and her flesh and clothing swirled together like mixing paints, absorbing her crucifix. Her scream elongated into an agonized wail unlike anything he had ever heard, and her liquefying body splattered the floor at his feet. Steam rose as the flesh-pink liquid evaporated and the light from her core intensified like a sun going supernova. Jake clamped his eyes shut and did not reopen them until the light on his eyelids had faded. No trace of Shannon remained.

Bile rose in Jake's throat and he fought it down. His hands jerked open and closed, translucent slime dripping from his fingers like long strands of saliva. The electric current had cut off, but his body continued to shake. He turned to the guards, who stared past him, and the hair on the back of his neck stood on end.

"Good Lord," Birch said in awe.

Now what?

Facing the entrance again, Jake nearly lost his balance. The EDPs stood shoulder to shoulder, blocking the doors with their bodies as they peered in at him and the guards. He focused on the bearded black man he had spoken to the previous morning, and his heart beat faster as he recognized him: Luther Bass, the Cipher's second victim. Swallowing, Jake studied the other faces. All of the Cipher's known victims stood before him: Abigail Williams, Miguel Jerez, Sung Yee, and Rachel Rosenthal. He did not recognize the other five figures, but in any serial killer investigation, detectives anticipated a number of undiscovered victims.

Dead people stood on the other side of the glass doors.

Murder victims stared at him with glassy eyes.

Ghosts.

Jake stepped back. He wanted to flee, to run and keep running, but the doors offered the only means of escape and he had no intention of going through the dead things outside. Had they come to the Tower because of him?

No, they're not here for me.

What had Shannon said?

They want their souls back.

Laddock and Birch had already recovered from

Shannon's meltdown, and Jake's gut told him they had witnessed similar light shows before. An edge crept into his voice. "Do you guys think you can handle things down here?"

Birch nodded. "It's not like they can hurt us."

Jake glared at Laddock. *Thanks for warning me, you prick.* "I'm going upstairs. If you need backup, call Graham."

Shaking his hands, he boarded an elevator. The slime had evaporated. As the doors closed, he took another look at the things outside and they looked back at him. He felt a sense of relief as the elevator surged upward, but his brain felt like scrambled eggs.

Not possible, not possible, not possible!

What linked Old Nick to the Cipher?

He had to know.

When the elevator doors opened, Graham rose from his seat with an alarmed expression on his face.

He saw the whole thing on the monitors, Jake thought as he entered the security bay. *They all know what's going on.*

"Are you all right?" Graham said.

"Do I look all right?" His body tingled, his legs ready to buckle as he approached Kira's office. Graham did not answer. Jake pushed the buzzer and waited. No response. He glared at the camera looking down at him from above the doors. Still no answer. He turned to Graham, who sat with his back to him. *Pretending he's not watching me on those monitors.* "Where is she?"

Graham swiveled his seat, an innocent expression on his face. "She must be with Mr. Tower."

"I need to get in there right now."

Graham's expression turned helpless.

"You saw what happened down there. This is a goddamned emergency!"

Graham swallowed. "She'll have my head."

"You're under my command. I'll take responsibility."

Sighing, Graham turned to his console and flipped a switch. Jake heard the doors before him unlock, and he pushed them open. He entered the office and closed the doors, the silence in the immense space unnerving him. Glancing at the security monitors, he saw Laddock and Birch standing at their station with nightsticks drawn. Kira must have witnessed the scene and then ran to warn Tower. Jake turned to the anteroom door, pressed his eye against the retina scanner eyecup, and waited. A flash of red light, followed by a click, and he entered the confined space. After staring at the scanner next to the double doors for a moment, he set his palm upon it. Bracing himself, he felt a needle pierce his skin. Then the immense doors separated, and he slipped between the metal rods before the doors had opened all the way.

Jake entered Tower's darkened office as the doors reversed direction, the recessed monitors providing the only source of illumination. Allowing his eyes to adjust to the LCD lighting, he saw that neither Kira nor Tower occupied the office. He passed the model of the Tower and stopped at the massive desk. The wooden box that Fortaleza had brought on behalf of President Seguera rested upon it. He reached down and opened the box: empty. The doors behind him finished closing and the reverberation caused the office to shudder.

Where had Kira and the old man gone?

His eyes moved to the double doors behind the desk.

Inside.

Circling the desk, he stepped before the doors, which had no security scanner. Anyone who made it this far had free access to Tower's inner sanctum. He grabbed the gold handles and turned them. As the doors swung open, bright light blinded him and he shaded his eyes with one hand. He stepped through the doorway and into the light—and entered paradise.

Jake found himself standing on a narrow wooden bridge spanning a narrow stream. Crossing it, he stepped onto a dirt path leading to a wooded area. A warm breeze blew in his face and sunlight shone down on him. Having solved the mystery of the missing floor space, he gazed in wonder at the landscaped park: dirt paths crisscrossed a green lawn covered with lush flowers and exotic plants; huge lights in the ceiling, three stories above, simulated sunlight, shining down on multicolored trees unlike any he had seen before; a waterfall cascaded from the third level into a pool on the first, feeding the stream that circled the entire park like a moat; a laser generator in the ceiling projected holographic birds onto the trees like shadow puppets on a wall, and hidden speakers broadcast nature sounds. At the center, thick vines crept up the brick face of a circular building with stone steps. All on the sixtieth floor of a Manhattan skyscraper.

"Welcome to my Garden of Eden."

Spinning on one heel, Jake looked up. Tower and Kira stood on a balcony fifteen feet above him. The old man had exchanged his security blazer for a khaki shirt with shoulder straps and a gauze bandage masked his pale left eye. Kira stood behind him, deferring to his authority. Jake had not seen them together before.

"This is a surprise," Tower said.

Jake's jaw tightened. "I'll say."

Tower followed the balcony to a curved stairway with no railing and trotted down the wide, Plexiglas stairs. Wearing khaki shorts and hiking boots with white, knee-high socks, he only needed a safari helmet to complete the image of a Great White Hunter.

It's November in the real world, Jake thought.

"Ms. Thorn just finished telling me about your encounter downstairs," Tower said.

Jake glanced at Kira, who glided down the stairs behind Tower, her expression inscrutable. "She's a busy beaver."

Tower let out a boisterous laugh. "Yes, she is." He joined Jake on the path and grasped his left shoulder. "Now, what can I do for you?"

Jake stared into Tower's good eye. Was he kidding? "I need to speak to you—*alone.*"

Kira joined them before Tower could answer. "I don't think that's wise, Nicholas."

Releasing Jake's shoulder, Tower turned to her. "Now, that's no way to talk, my dear. Jake's on our team. We can trust him." He turned back to Jake. "Can't we, Jake? Just hand your gun to Kira."

Kira held out her right hand but Jake hesitated. He did not wish to spend one second in the Tower unarmed.

"I don't allow weapons inside my private quarters under any circumstance," Tower said. "You'll get it back."

Sighing, Jake reached inside his jacket, removed his Glock, and set it in Kira's open palm. She gave him a patronizing look as she curled her fingers around the weapon's grip and held it with her wrist bent outward.

"Make sure everything's secure downstairs," Tower said to her.

She turned and strolled away with the Glock in her hand, crossing the bridge. Both men studied her swinging hips, and Jake wondered if Tower had fucked her, too. Kira closed the office doors behind her.

The old man faced Jake. "I'm a busy man, and my time is limited. We didn't give you emergency access to my quarters so you could just drop in uninvited whenever you please."

Jake stared into the man's good eye. "I've been here exactly twenty-four hours. During that time I've seen those—*creatures*—in your big fishbowl, and a woman whose murder I investigated on Monday just walked into your downstairs lobby and melted all over my hands!"

Tower seemed unfazed by Jake's outburst. "So you've been inside the Demonstration Room? Another surprise. How resourceful of you. But there's no need to concern yourself with my Biogens. They're just product, completely unrelated to the occurrence downstairs."

"'Biogens?'"

"Biogenetic Life Forms. Weapons made of flesh rather than steel." Tower scrunched his face into a monstrous countenance and snapped his teeth at the air, imitating the creatures in the globe. Then the snarl transformed into a smile. "'Let slip the dogs of war.' My grandfather built the family empire with munitions, you know."

"The chromophobes are right," Jake said in a tight voice. "You're screwing around with nature."

Tower rolled his eyes. "We've *destroyed* nature. Now I'm rebuilding it. Those specimens you observed are prototypes designed for a specific environment. They're incapable of reproducing, and since the only thing they crave is human flesh, the ecosystem is safe. My people engineer them with a predetermined life span, so they expire whenever we want them to. We've also integrated an Achilles' heel as a control factor."

"You're selling those things to Seguera to use on his own people."

Tower wagged one finger in the air. "Terrorists, Jake. I have what Kimo Seguera needs: a solution to his domestic crises. And he had something that I wanted in return." Reaching inside the collar of his shirt, Tower brought out an aged bronze amulet suspended on a rawhide strap. "This is an Anting-Anting, a Philippine talisman used to ward off evil spirits." The amulet bore the image of a muscular warrior slaying a scaly demon. "I refused to do business with Kimo unless he gave this to me first. The Anting-Anting only maintains its power when it's given willingly."

Jake's mouth hung open. "There are a dozen ghosts outside this building right now!"

Tower shrugged. "I call them Soul Searchers."

"Call them whatever you like. They were murdered by the Cipher and now they're knocking on your back door. I want to know *how* and *why*."

Tower smiled. "There's really no need to fear them, Jake. They're harmless enough. Nothing but excess spiritual energy."

"'Excess spiritual—?'" Jake stepped closer to the old man. "I've had enough of this bullshit, you understand? I want some straight talk and I want it now."

Tower looked amused. "Certainly. If that's what you think you want. But don't make the mistake of thinking you can intimidate me. I won't be threatened by my subordinates. We'd have brought you up to speed soon enough. Let's walk." Turning on one heel, he headed up the path, away from the stream.

Falling into step with the old man, Jake stared at the multicolored flora around them. "I've never seen plants like these."

"They don't exist anywhere else. Do you know that the first genetic experiments on Earth were conducted in 5,000 B.C.?"

"When the spacemen landed at Stonehenge?"

Tower ignored his comment. "Early Homo sapiens discovered that by planting the seeds from only their heartiest vegetables, their crops proved bountiful the following year. This was the first step in manipulating life to suit our needs, which, of course, is the goal of genetic enhancement and therapeutic cloning."

The path split in two and the men followed the trail leading to the brick structure at the park's epicenter. Jake stared at purplish, melon-sized growths hanging from the branches of the trees around them. Translucent membranes covered them. He thought he glimpsed movement inside them, like human fetuses in wombs.

"Forbidden fruit," Tower said. "At least in the eyes of the FDA. These strains were developed to produce DCL-21."

They stopped at the brick building, and Tower gestured at two black metal doors. "Dante wrote, 'Ye who enter here shall leave all hope behind.' Are you sure you want to continue?"

Jake stared at the doors. He had come too far to turn back. "I'm positive."

Tower's good eye twinkled. "Excellent! You need to fully comprehend the scope of this operation if you're going to protect me from my enemies." He thrust the doors open and motioned for Jake to enter. "After you . . ."

Darkness yawned before Jake, who wished he had not given his gun to Kira. Sweat formed on his scalp, causing it to itch. Taking a breath, he crossed the threshold. As soon as his foot touched the floor, fluorescent lights flickered above him, triggered by motion detectors, and he dropped into a fighting crouch. Tower strode by him to the floor-to-ceiling hub of the structure. Red faced, Jake stood straight. The hub, constructed of vacuum-formed plastic, had a rectangular viewing window twelve feet wide. A metal cylinder, ten feet long and three and a half feet in diameter, lay horizontally on a base near the window. Hoses and cables connected it to the wall, the apparatus resembling an oversized iron lung. Pistons hissed and monitors beeped, reminding Jake of a life support system in an emergency room.

"That's just part of the climate control system," Tower said with a dismissive wave of his hand.

Pay no attention to that man behind the curtain, Jake thought as he joined Tower at the window.

The old man nodded at the chamber's interior. "Look in there."

Jake stared through the window. The circular chamber had a mosaic floor thirty feet in diameter, with massive Roman columns rising to the ceiling. A shaft of multicolored light descended from a skylight constructed of pentagonal panes of stained glass. The panes reminded

Jake of both a church and a diagram of the sugar phosphate backbone of a DNA molecule.

"Aren't they magnificent?" Tower said in a reverent tone.

Jake followed Tower's gaze to the empty chamber. "I don't see anything."

"That's because you lack vision. But I assure you that they're here, in my Soul Chamber."

Jake stared at Tower, afraid to speak his mind.

Tower read the expression on his face. "Do you believe in God, Jake?"

Jake sighed. "Can't say that I do."

"May I ask you why not?"

"Let's just say that I have a problem with omnipotent authority figures."

"You must believe in something?"

Jake stood silent.

"How about an afterlife?"

"I don't buy into fairy tales."

"Then how do you explain the Soul Searchers downstairs?"

"I don't."

"If there's no heaven, where do you think our souls go when we die?"

Raising his eyebrows in an exaggerated manner, Jake aimed his eyes at the Soul Chamber. "There—?"

Tower leaned closer. "I'm no fanatic, but I've proven the existence of souls."

Jake glanced at the empty Soul Chamber, then back at Tower. "I find your evidence less than convincing."

"The Soul Searchers are fragments of the souls contained in this chamber. They're energy combined with memory. Through tremendous willpower, they've manifested themselves as facsimiles of their former shells. But they're unable to maintain the charade, and they want what I have."

Jake narrowed his eyes. He disbelieved the old man's claims, but he could not rationalize Shannon's miraculous reappearance and disappearance.

"I've always had a burning interest in archaeology and world religions," Tower said. "When I inherited this company from my father, I invested millions of dollars into a vast research project I hoped would prove the existence of a spiritual or supernatural afterlife. The greatest scientific and theological minds money could buy spent nearly two decades investigating religion, mythology, and the occult on my behalf. They verified the existence of human souls and discovered a method of capturing and containing them."

Jake maintained his poker face. "Oh, really? And how did they do that?"

"In Central America, one of my teams uncovered evidence of an ancient religious sect called—roughly translated—'Soul Catchers.' They were Mayan priests who believed that a man's dying breath contained his living soul. Their ritual required a priest to purify an acolyte by cutting his throat and chanting a secret verse. Then the priest sucked the acolyte's soul out at the precise moment of his death. Too soon or too late and the ritual failed. But when performed correctly, the priest absorbed the soul of the deceased. The longer he held the acolyte's breath in his own body, the more of the man's essence he absorbed: his knowledge, his wisdom, even his memories. My people found an old man who had witnessed the ritual as a boy, and he described the process and chant in detail."

"For a modest sum?"

"Naturally."

"So you spent a small fortune for some reprobate in a foreign land to regurgitate a local myth. Doesn't prove a thing."

Tower's eye gleamed. "The process works." He gestured at the Soul Chamber. "And I have modern technology to prevent the souls my Soul Catcher has captured from escaping. Of course, every system has its flaws: during the ritual, a small amount of energy inevitably escapes from each sacrifice, resulting in the creation of a Soul Searcher. We could eliminate this side effect by performing the ritual here, in a controlled environment, but the risk of discovery would be too great."

Jake eyed the Soul Chamber. "*Your* Soul Catcher." He pictured the Soul Searchers downstairs. "The Cipher works for you." Investigative instincts kicking into gear, he suppressed his excitement. "Who is he?"

Tower shrugged. "I don't know him from Adam. We outsource that."

Jake's facial muscles tightened. "So he isn't a serial killer. He's an assassin."

"Does it matter? Let me remind you that you're no longer a policeman. You're my director of security."

Jake stepped back. "Not anymore, I'm not. Get yourself another hired gun. I don't pretend to understand what happened downstairs, and I'm not buying into your mumbo jumbo. All I know is that you're having people killed, and I want nothing to do with it. Even you have to answer to someone. My former colleagues in Homicide will be happy to discuss theology with you."

Tower seemed unconcerned by Jake's abrupt resignation. "You signed an ironclad confidentiality agreement, not to mention a one-year contract." Tower held out the palm of his right hand, reminding Jake of their handshake. "A deal is a deal, after all. Besides, I just took you into my confidence. It will be difficult for me to protect you if you resign now. Your soul might end up in this chamber."

Jake's heart skipped a beat. The crazy old bastard had just threatened his life! Before he could respond, the lights went off and a deafening alarm filled the darkness, like a battle klaxon on a submarine. The overhead emergency lights came on, turning the viewing room red. Tower clutched Jake's arm, fear spreading over his gnarled features.

Red alert, Jake thought. "What's going on?"

"We're under attack," Tower said, his eye bulging in its socket. "*The Reaper* is here!"

Bathed in red light, Jake sprinted across the atrium. He charged through Tower's office, where the lights faded up and down as the alarm roared. On one of the monitors, he glimpsed Graham standing at his station, a phone clutched in one hand. Jake pulled a stainless steel lever set in the wall, and the massive doors rumbled open.

Kira met him in the anteroom, holding his Glock out to him. "Get downstairs!"

Jake snatched the gun and bolted past her. He pulled back its slide as he ran through her office, then kicked open one of the doors and rushed to the security station. No longer on the phone, Graham turned to him, fear etched on his face.

"What's happening?" Jake said over the screaming alarm.

"We've got a breach in the lobby," Graham said. "The intruder took out one camera."

Had Shannon Reynolds returned with a vengeance?

Jake focused on the two security monitors covering the private lobby. The first displayed only a field of electronic snow. The second showed Laddock and Birch moving behind their station for cover . With their blazers unbuttoned and their Glocks drawn, they fired at an off-screen target at the same time. The screen flared with hot spots from the gunfire, which reminded Jake of his battle with Dread and Badly. A moment later, a massive figure stepped into the frame, and the guards shot at it from point-blank range. Jake squinted at the monitor, trying to discern details of the statuesque intruder, but the image turned to snow. His eyes shifted to a third monitor, which had a solid black background. Red, yellow, and orange light pulsed within a humanoid silhouette closing in on two smaller silhouettes, both of them soft pink.

"What's that?" Jake said.

"Heat sensors."

"My God, he must be on fire!" Jake raced to the entrance and palmed the lock release on the door. "You stay here."

"Don't worry!" Graham unbuttoned his blazer and drew a Glock from the holster on his belt.

"And call nine-one-one!" Jake ran to the elevators and pressed a call button.

Graham looked puzzled by Jake's order, but he reached for his phone anyway. As the elevator doors closed, Jake saw Kira emerge from her office and join Graham at the security station. He doubted she would allow Graham to make the call. The alarm faded as the elevator descended to the ground floor and he took several deep breaths to calm his nerves.

Laddock and Birch ran out of ammunition within a second of each other.

"Fuck!" Laddock said, terror rising in his voice. He cocked his arm and hurled his empty Glock at the intruder, but the metal weapon bounced off a chiseled chest. He looked to his partner for help.

Birch ejected the empty cartridge from his Glock's grip, allowing it to clatter on the floor. He jammed his left hand into his blazer pocket and fished for a fresh magazine. A shadow fell over him, and he looked up into the eyes of death. Throbbing, grisly fingers closed over his hand and the Glock, fusing them together in a searing blast of pain. He screamed as black smoke curled up from his sizzling flesh.

Laddock stepped back as the intruder turned to him.

The elevator doors opened and Jake stared out at an incredible tableau: an awesome figure stood fifteen feet away, holding the guards above the floor by their faces. Fear spread through Jake like ice water, immobilizing him. The naked, humanoid creature stood seven feet tall, its frame as muscular as a bodybuilder's. A large penis hung flaccid between his powerful legs, and fiery sinew clung to his ebony skull. Two tiny pinpricks of light pulsed within dark, empty eye sockets, like miniature stars, and a pink brain throbbed beneath the glassy surface of the dark skull. Black light pulsed through the transparent organs and bones in his body, and the blood in his veins glowed like lava.

What had Tower called him?

The Reaper.

Jake recalled the Anting-Anting, with its image of a warrior slaying a demon. Sweat trickled down his face, and he realized that the temperature had climbed despite the elevator's air-conditioning.

Laddock and Birch screamed as one, their feet kicking the empty space above the floor. Dark smoke rose from between the Reaper's fingers as they dug into the guards' faces, and Jake choked on the stench of burning flesh. The men clawed at the Reaper's forearms, desperate to free themselves. Paralyzed with fear, Jake allowed the Glock to hang limp at his side. He wanted to flee upstairs, but he couldn't even raise his hand to press the necessary button, and he could not bring himself to step out of the elevator. He felt puny and insignificant before this monstrous being, and powerless to help his subordinates.

The Reaper spread his arms wide apart, swinging the guards in opposite directions like rag dolls, then swung his hands together in a thunderous clap, smashing the guards' heads against each other like watermelons. The screaming came to an abrupt stop, replaced by a wet-sounding explosion that showered Jake in blood, brain chunks, and skull fragments. Jake slid to the floor with his back against the elevator's rear wall.

The Reaper dropped the bodies to the floor, blood gushing out of their caved-in heads. Noticing Jake for the first time, the Reaper twisted his features into a hideous imitation of a grin, his gums and teeth visible through transparent lips. He stepped forward and Jake shuddered.

The monster was coming for him!

The Reaper advanced on him like some great, unstoppable behemoth. Jake felt the muscles in his neck twitch as he strained to raise his gun and failed. The Reaper's movements slowed, his body trembling as if he were walking against a mighty river's current. He pressed one shoulder against an invisible wall and tried to knock it over, his features contorting with effort. He swung his fists at the force field, thunderous blows that would have toppled a house. Jake flinched with each impact as the Reaper inched steadily closer to him. Then the Reaper stopped struggling and stepped back, surveying the space before him from floor to ceiling. He opened and closed his fists, the black light within his body pulsating faster. His chest rose and fell, and he narrowed his translucent eyelids.

Staring into the pinpricks of red light that burned within the Reaper's black eye sockets, Jake saw only death. He wanted to cry out and beg for mercy, but his vocal cords froze. The Reaper raised his right arm and aimed his pointer finger at Jake, who groaned. The monster's heart glowed fiery red, and flames rippled across his glassy skin. He became a vague outline within the concentrated inferno, then vanished, sucking the flames after him. A sulfuric odor lingered over the carnage in his wake.

Jake gaped at the bloody bodies on the floor, his eyes darting from side to side. How had he managed to escape their fate? Drenched in gore, he looked down at his trench coat, then wiped his face on his sleeves. He pulled himself into a standing position, then shifted his gun from one hand to the other. He peeled off the sticky garment and let it slip to the floor. The elevator doors started to close and he stuck out one arm, forcing them open again, his fingers flexing in the heat. Staggering into the lobby, he slipped in a crimson puddle on the floor but managed to regain his balance. He stared in awe at Birch's gun, which had become part of the dead guard's hand. Stepping around the corpses, he saw that the Soul

Searchers had departed. But how long ago? He moved forward, heart and mind racing.

Kira's voice came over the dead guards' walkie-talkies: "Stop right there, Mr. Helman."

How did she know—?

He looked up at the camera over the doors, then at the one over the elevators. Their LED lights glowed red. *They must have gone back online as soon as the Reaper disappeared.* Gritting his teeth and raising his right arm, he extended his middle finger so that both cameras picked up his action. *Fuck you,* he wanted to say, but he couldn't get the words to come out.

So he ran.

Cold air slapped Jake's face as he plowed through the doors and charged across the sidewalk, dwarfed by the towering buildings around him. He ran through the canyon of limestone, steel, and glass.

Oh, my God.

Emerging from the shadows of the massive structures, he waited until he had turned onto Twenty-third Street to jam his gun into its holster.

A demon!

Eyes wild, he dodged pedestrians on the crowded sidewalk. Some stepped out of his way with alarmed expressions, and he realized that he still had blood on his face.

He didn't care.

A fucking demon!

He ran down the concrete steps of the uptown Number Six subway station at Park Avenue and bought a Metro card at an automated dispenser. As he scooped coins from the change slot, he pictured Laddock and Birch with their heads crushed.

So much blood . . .

His shaking hands sent the coins rolling across the floor. Looking over his shoulder, he saw that no one—no *thing*—had followed him and he stumbled through a turnstile. The station tilted around him, and his stomach threatened to expel its contents. He wrapped one arm around a steel column and circled it, then paced the grimy platform, waiting for the next train. Black splotches dotted the concrete: discarded chewing gum smeared with filth.

Demon . . . blood . . . ghosts . . .

When a train pulled in and its doors opened, he boarded a car three-quarters full. He moved toward the nearest available seat, but a tiny old Chinese woman carrying four bags of groceries scurried in front of him and took it. Staring straight ahead, she ignored him. Her unblinking eyes reminded him of his first glimpse of Shannon's corpse in Hell's Kitchen. The doors chimed and closed, and he moved to the front of the car and sank into a corner seat. He buried his face in his hands as the train surged forward, rocking him from side to side. The lights blinked on and off and metal screeched against metal in the dark tunnel.

Feeling someone's eyes gazing at him, he spread his fingers and peered through the spaces between them. Two black women with wrinkled faces sat opposite him, sharing the same disgusted expression. He closed his fingers again, shutting out their holier-than-thou stares.

"Blue-eyed devil," one of them said and the other clucked her tongue.

His stomach constricted and he unleashed a maniacal laugh that would not stop.

Sitting behind his office desk, Tower stared at Kira, who stood silhouetted against the wall of monitors. With his defective eye bandaged, he had little depth perception, which made it difficult to gauge her actual distance from him.

"How did this happen?" he said. "We're supposed to be protected."

Kira did not move. On one of the monitors behind her, Pulaski mopped the lobby floor while Graham used a wet vac to suck up the gore. The corpses had already been removed.

"Either the Reaper's grown stronger," she said, "or our shield's grown weaker. I'm having it reinforced now."

Tower admired her take-charge attitude and it amused him that they thought so much alike. "Did we at least gain any useful information from this attack?"

"The new cameras temporarily shorted out—"

"Damn it!" He pounded the desktop like a petulant child. No matter how much money he poured into developing new technology, the results never met his expectations.

Kira ignored his outburst. "According to our digital thermometer system, the temperature spiked seventeen degrees, even with the air-conditioning on. There are traces of ash on the floor, and both guards suffered severe burns before they expired. It's a good thing we turned off the sprinkler system or we'd have had police and firefighters all over the Tower."

Tower smiled with half of his mouth. At least one of their measures had worked to his advantage. "And Helman?"

She circled the desk, her features coming into view. "There's only one place on earth for him to go."

Tower chuckled. "What do you make of him?"

Sitting on the edge of the desk, Kira crossed her legs. "He's a sleazy, corrupt bastard who only thinks of himself." Her lips formed a smile. "Perfect for our needs."

Tower studied the curve of her thigh, then slid his hand along it. "I agree." He looked into her eyes, green tinged with yellow. "You know what needs to be done."

Flipping her hair out of her face, Kira spread her legs apart. "Of course. I'll take care of everything."

Jake disembarked the subway train eight stops later, at Eighty-sixth Street. He bought a pack of Marlboros at a corner newsstand off Lexington Avenue and lit a cigarette with trembling fingers. Nicotine rushed through his body and his knees wobbled like rubber.

Tower knew that the Reaper existed. Did he fear the demon? Had he hired Jake to protect him from the Grim Reaper?

Jake crossed the busy intersection at Third Avenue, plowing through people too stubborn to move out of his way. He passed a movie theater, a bookstore, and two Greek diners before turning right onto a quiet stretch of First Avenue. At the far corner of Eighty-fourth Street, he waited for the traffic light to change, then crossed the avenue. It felt unreal to be back in his home neighborhood. No pedestrians in sight, just cars, a stillness hanging in the air. But he felt safe. He just needed a little time alone in the apartment to gather his thoughts and plan his next move. He stopped in midstep over the curb of the sidewalk on his block, his blood turning cold.

Oh, no.

Two men stood waiting outside his building, fifty feet ahead of him.

Oh, Christ, no!

One tall, the other bald.

Not them . . .

Kevin Creed and Oscar Soot.

Dread and Baldy.

The phantasms lurking on the front stoop looked as they had before Jake had gunned them down. They appeared to be unarmed, and no one in Manhattan would have given them a second glance, despite Dread's height and dreadlocks. The dead thugs had not yet looked in his direction.

Jake ducked behind an upright mailbox. Peeking around the metal edge at his stalkers, he reached inside his jacket and closed his fingers around the Glock's grip. Were they ghosts, like the Soul Searchers, or something else? The Cipher had not killed them; Jake had. No one had stolen their souls. He could not connect them to Old Nick, but he could not accept their presence as a coincidence, either.

A tingling sensation crawled up his right leg, sending waves of panic through him. He had experienced a similar sensation when his hands had made contact with Shannon in the Tower's lobby. Jerking his body upright, he clawed at his thigh with both hands. His right hand squeezed the source of the vibration and he dug the cell phone out of his pocket. Intending to shut the phone off, he thumbed a switch on it without reading the display. The phone rang at full volume instead.

Shit!

As he shut the phone off, Dread and Baldy turned toward him. He made eye contact with them as their faces filled with rage. Dread pointed in his direction, and both dead men sprinted toward him.

Jake hurled the cell phone at the sidewalk, experiencing fleeting satisfaction as the device shattered into pieces. Looking both ways, he saw no means of escape along First Avenue. He looked over his shoulder at the traffic light behind him, facing Eighty-fourth Street. It turned yellow, with the cars backed up on First Avenue waiting to proceed. In seconds, the traffic would strand him where he stood.

Dread and Baldy had already covered half the distance separating them from Jake. The traffic light turned green, and Jake charged headlong into the avenue, his shoes pounding the pavement. Horns honked and a car roared by him, its driver yelling out the window. Jake dove to the curb, knocking over a metal trash can, and rolled across the sidewalk. He came up crouching with his back to a corner Laundromat and saw the traffic lurching through the intersection. Dread and Baldy remained on the far side of the avenue, cursing at him from the curb. Baldy's domed head had turned bright red.

Knowing that they would be on his heels in seconds, Jake leapt to his feet and ran west along Eighty-fourth

Street. He pumped his arms and lengthened his stride, running low to the ground. He sped past a woman carrying a poodle in her arms like a baby—God, he hated that!—and closed in on Second Avenue. Fearing he might trip, he did not look behind him. What would happen if he stopped and emptied his Glock into them? If bullets stopped them again, could he be prosecuted for gunning down two men he'd already killed? The traffic ahead ground to a halt. Groaning, he saw no point in boarding a taxi stuck at a light.

He rounded the corner and headed uptown, toward the Eighty-sixth Street station on the new Second Avenue line. Facing congestion on the sidewalk, he snaked around the pedestrians blocking his way. He passed Eighty-fifth Street and sighted the subway entrance ahead. His chest ached and he tasted coppery salt in his mouth. His left hand grasped the yellow metal railing of the subway station and he pedaled his feet down the cement steps. Cool darkness greeted him as he heard the doors of subway cars opening below. Sure enough, a train had just stopped at the platform. Ignoring the Metro card dispensers, he hurdled over a turnstile.

"Pay your fare!" a female Metro worker in the surveillance booth said over the PA speaker.

Jake landed on the dirty floor and sprinted for the nearest subway car doors, but the commuters who had just exited the train blocked his path, eager to get aboveground, and Jake had difficulty fighting his way through the crowd. The doors closed just as he reached them and his body slammed against stainless steel. He looked at the conductor with pleading eyes. Leaning out a window eight feet ahead of him, the man shook his head with a half smile. Jake pounded on the plastic window of the door before him, which splintered into a white spiderweb. The train pulled away as he looked around in desperation. He could cross the tracks to the other platform, but Dread and Baldy might see him.

The crowd dispersed and he ran behind the departing train to the far end of the platform. Hunched over, his breathing ragged and his chest on fire, he watched the train recede into the dark tunnel. Looking back at the turnstiles, fifty yards away, he saw a domed head and a tall scarecrow with orange dreadlocks pass through them.

Jake took an automatic step toward the subway exit halfway between him and his pursuers and hesitated. Even if he reached the steps before Dread and Baldy reached him, they would spot him and the chase would resume. Seeing no other option, he stepped off the edge of the platform. Landing hard on the railroad ties five feet below, he rolled over gravel and under the platform so that Dread and Baldy would not see him from the edge. He smelled rust and urine and the ground still vibrated from the departing train. Getting on his hands and knees, he crawled toward the gray concrete at the tunnel's mouth. He flattened his back against the support as he crept into the clammy darkness. Ignoring the third rail, which ran along the far side of the tracks, he stood up, his trousers torn at the knees. Blackness swallowed him, making him confident that he could no longer be seen from the platform. He glanced over his shoulder, and as far as he could tell, Dread and Baldy had abandoned the station. Perhaps they had boarded a downtown train.

The light from the Ninety-sixth Street station winked at him like a twinkling star, ten city blocks ahead. He needed to rest, but dared not stop, and pushed forward. Putrid odors rose from stagnant water between the rails. Stepping from trestle to trestle in the dark, he stumbled over one, caught his balance, and tripped over another. Pitching forward, he banged his right forearm trying to protect his face. Lying across the railroad ties, he smelled rotting wood and heard rats scurrying in the darkness. He clambered to his feet, felt a breeze behind him, and turned around.

Another train had pulled into the Eighty-sixth Street station.

Fuck me, he thought. Never before had a train arrived at that platform so soon after he had just missed one. Looking ahead, he estimated that he still had the equivalent of more than nine city blocks to cover. Behind him, the train barreled forward.

There was no way he could reach the next platform before the metal juggernaut would overtake him, and a concrete wall now separated the downtown tracks from their uptown counterparts. The train entered the tunnel, gathering speed. He felt along the cold wall and found a ledge approximately one foot wide, four feet above the ground. Setting his palms on the ledge, he scrambled up the wall. He stood up just as the light from the oncoming train illuminated him. He stepped sideways along the ledge, his arms spread wide, hugging the wall. The sound of the approaching train filled the tunnel and wind chopped at him. The light intensified and the roar of the engine grew deafening. His destination remained far ahead.

I'm not going to make it.

He could not find anything to hold onto, and he knew that when the train passed him the ensuing wind would snatch him from his perch and suck him beneath the steel wheels. If he was lucky, he would die instantly; if not, he would remain conscious for at least a few minutes while black rats feasted on his bloody limbs, and then he would die alone in the dark. Other trains would pass over his remains, dicing them until they became unrecognizable. When some unfortunate Transit worker discovered him, Forensics would need a DNA comparison for identification.

Poor Sheryl. Would she be able to live with the guilt?

The train had almost reached him when his left hand groped at empty space. He lost his balance and nearly fell off the ledge, then moved before the opening in the wall.

The train bore down on him.

He dove through the opening, arms and legs flailing. Solid ground rushed up to meet him, and the palms of his hands slapped concrete a moment before his chest absorbed the brunt of the impact, which knocked the breath from his lungs. The right side of his face turned numb, and he gasped for breath as red spots flared before his eyes. The train rocketed past the opening and wind blew into the space like a cyclone, kicking up powdery dust that made him squeeze his eyelids shut and cough. The light from inside the passing train flickered around him like a strobe in a nightclub, and he glimpsed rusted metal drums and discolored boxes stacked across the wall nearest him. The sunken storage cellar must have been used while the Second Avenue line had been under construction.

The stench of decomposing rats filled his nostrils, forcing him to cover his mouth and nose with one hand. Rolling onto his back, he gazed at the open doorway six feet above him. Through it he saw the train streaking by, the backs of passengers' heads visible in the windows. The passing light revealed the silhouette of a metal ladder bolted to the wall beneath the opening. A drop of cold water splashed his forehead and he looked at the ceiling, crisscrossed with industrial pipes.

The light died as the train rumbled away, leaving him in darkness once more. He held his right hand before his face, but he could not see two inches in front of him. He had a vague impression of the opening, but he no longer saw the ladder. Sitting up with a groan, his chest aching, he probed his face. A cut on his forehead oozed sticky blood.

Something brushed against his shoulder, as if the darkness itself had taken shape, and terror gripped his heart like a cold metal vise. Whatever the thing was, it must have been big to have reached his shoulder.

Then he recognized the scent of foul human body odor.

Leaping to his feet in the suffocating darkness, he pulled his Glock free of its holster and pulled back its slide, ready to fire. He heard footsteps and shuffling all around him.

There's more than one of them.

He knew that mole people lived beneath the streets of Manhattan, and for a moment he imagined cannibals living in the tunnels, waiting for stray victims to prey upon. He had no intention of becoming anyone's lunch, and he reached into his pocket with his left hand, grasped his cigarette lighter, and sparked it to life. Turning around in a full circle, he waved the tiny flame. He still couldn't see anything, but the shuffling sounds retreated and stopped. A frustrated moan escaped the darkness. He sprinted in the general direction of the ladder, plastic crunching beneath his feet. He had heard that sound many times before, in the elevators and basements of housing projects in Alphabet City, during drug raids: the sound of feet crushing empty crack vials.

His left hand grasped a cold, rusty rung of the ladder

and the lighter's flame shut off. He scrambled up the ladder, toward the ledge of the opening, but two hands seized his right leg below the knee. Unable to see his attacker, he swung his pistol until it connected with flesh and bone, and he heard a bestial cry as the thing released him. He sprang onto the ledge, grateful to be free of the stench and the wretched creatures that survived on tunnel rats. Turning back, he gazed into the pit but heard nothing. He jumped onto the tracks and headed toward the platform ahead, glancing over his shoulder to make sure that another train had not entered the tunnel and that nothing else had followed him. When he felt safe, he holstered his gun and lit a cigarette.

Marc Gorman wiped his sweaty palms on his thighs. The Widow had called him to make certain he'd be home to receive her. She rarely visited him these days, so he knew there had to be an important reason for her to call on him. He hadn't been so excited by the prospect of a session with her since his release from the Payne Institute fifteen months earlier.

On that September afternoon, he'd taken a bus from Albany to Binghamton, and then a taxi to the Motel 6 on Front Street. He gave his real name to the desk clerk, who handed him a key. Inside his room, he flicked on the lights but left the curtains drawn. He showered, turned on the TV, paced. Someone knocked on the door, and when he opened it, the Widow glided past him. When he closed the door, she turned around and kissed him on the mouth. Minutes later, after they had stripped off their clothing, their arms and legs tangled on the bed. She had touched him in his private room at Payne, teased him really, but this was the first time they'd engaged in intercourse, and she exhausted him.

"I have a present for you," she said when they had finished. Reaching into her purse, she took out an envelope and handed it to him. He tore it open with eager fingers and pulled out a piece of paper. Tears welled up in his eyes as he read the name and address. She reached into her purse again, then handed him two thousand dollars in cash and a special care package. "This will get you started."

"I'm grateful. For everything."

She arranged their next meeting and departed.

The following morning, Marc took a bus to Allentown, Pennsylvania. He hiked to the outskirts of the steel town and followed a dirt road to his destination, which reminded him of the house he and his mother had shared in Redkill. Trees surrounded the isolated property, and the dirty blue siding of the ranch house needed replacing. The roof sagged in the middle, a tattered screen door creaked in the breeze, and cardboard filled one window frame instead of glass. Rust ate at the metal skin of a red truck parked in the driveway, and spare automobile parts littered the overgrown lawn. A stack of lumber rotted out back, near a stone well with a winch.

Studying the dwelling for an hour from the woods

across the road, he saw no one pass before the flickering television screen in the living room. He hid his bag behind some prickly bushes and approached the house. Greeted by the stench of decaying wood, he peered through the screen door at the dark living room, and listened to the laugh track of an inane sitcom on the television. Seeing no doorbell, he knocked on the screen door, its wooden frame bouncing on its hinges. A dog barked inside, a real beast by the sound of it, and he flinched.

"Shut up, Blackie!" a harsh voice said, and Marc trembled for a moment. Then he remembered why he had come in the first place. Heavy footsteps preceded a balding man with a beer belly who appeared on the other side of the door. "Yeah?"

Marc swallowed, his stomach knotting up. He recognized his father, who did not recognize him. He should have known; thirteen years had passed since they had last seen each other, with no birthday cards, Christmas greetings, or photo exchanges in the interim. His father did not know that Sara had died, or that Marc had been institutionalized for killing her. "I'm from the power company. I have a refund check for an overpayment you made."

Gary Gorman, the Big Bastard, narrowed one of his heavy eyes. "Why didn't you just mail it to me?"

"Policy. We need to get a signature before we can actually release the check."

Opening the door with one hand, Gary looked Marc

up and down. For a moment, Marc thought his father might recognize him after all. "Where's your car at?"

Nodding to his left and hiding his disappointment, Marc reached into the right-hand pocket of his jacket. "Right over there." When Gary leaned outside to search for the nonexistent vehicle, Mark took out a slim metal cylinder and sprayed tear gas into his father's eyes. Crying out, Gary staggered back. Marc caught the closing door with one elbow. Blackie unleashed a flurry of barks somewhere behind Gary, and Marc hesitated for an instant. When no dog charged at him, he stepped inside. Then he knew where the rotting smell originated from.

"God damn it!" his father yelled, and Blackie barked louder. The big black Labrador had been leashed to one leg of the kitchen table, which she now dragged across the linoleum floor. Marc shifted the canister to his other hand and took out a blackjack. His father rubbed his eyes, tears streaming down his reddened cheeks. Marc swung the blackjack at the back of Gary's head and the big man collapsed to the floor and lay still. Blackie snarled, her head now inside the living room. Marc walked straight toward the canine, who leaned back on her haunches as if to launch herself at him, her pink gums visible around her sharp teeth.

"Shut up, Blackie!" Marc had his father's voice down pat after imitating him for so many years.

Blackie skipped a bark, a quizzical look in her eyes, then started up again. Marc aimed his cylinder at her and released more gas. Blackie yelped and rolled over, pawing at her eyes. Marc pocketed his arsenal, seized his father's wrists, and dragged the Big Bastard across the living room while Blackie whimpered. He rested at the door before pulling the heavy body outside. Tears formed in his eyes, and he wondered if they had been caused by lingering gas or from the emotional weight of the reunion. He did not worry about being seen because he expected no traffic on the quiet road. He dragged the body through the overgrown grass to the backyard, passing an outdoor shed, which made him wonder what power tools his father owned. A drill? A jigsaw? A power sander? He relished the possibilities, but rejected them as too obvious; the Widow had cautioned him not to sign his work, and such an angry display might suggest revenge as a motive for the killing.

As Marc propped the Big Bastard against the stone well, the humidity caused sweat stains to appear beneath his armpits. He bent over, hoisted his father to an almost erect position, and pitched him headfirst into the cool darkness below. A long moment passed, followed by a deep, echoing splash. Peering over the edge, he saw nothing moving in the darkness. When the water settled, silence prevailed until Blackie howled inside the house. For the first time in his life, Marc felt as if he and his father had shared a special moment together.

Daddy, he thought.

Then he drew a knife from his back pocket and went

back into the house for Blackie.

The doorbell rang, drawing Marc back into the present.

The Widow had arrived.

Unable to contain his excitement, he buzzed her into the building. Darting into the bedroom, he combed his hair, which he had just cut with a straight-edge razor and dyed jet-black. He hoped she would like it. Hurrying back into the living room, he unlocked the front door and waited.

The Widow stepped off the elevator and strode toward him, her movements elegant and purposeful. She entered his apartment, and he closed the door and locked it. She removed her sunglasses as she turned to him, and he knew from her expression that she had come on business. His heart sank and she reached out and ran her fingers through his hair.

"Nice," she said.

"Thank you." Her approval meant everything to him.

"Still, we may need to take greater measures."

"Like what?"

"I'm considering plastic surgery for you."

Considering the notion, he grinned. "I'd like that."

"Good. But right now, I need you to do something

for me."

"What is it?"

She removed a photograph from her coat pocket and held it up for him to see. "I need you to catch this soul."

His shoulders slumped. "You've always let me pick my own targets."

Turning the photo over, she showed him the address printed on the back. "This is different. I need this *particular* soul."

He shifted his balance from one foot to the other. "But it isn't time yet. It's too soon . . ."

"Make an exception for me." She stepped closer and kissed him on the mouth. As her tongue probed his, Marc slid his hands around her waist. When she pulled back, his heart beat faster. He took the photo from her and studied it.

"When do you need it?"

"Immediately." She showed him a second photo. "Watch out for this man, her husband. He's dangerous, and I want you to avoid him."

Marc studied the man in the photo. "He doesn't look dangerous."

"He's a policeman."

Marc's eyes rose from the photo. Why did she want him to take such a risk? He breathed in the sweet scent of her perfume. "Anything for you."

Emerging from the tunnel, Jake surveyed the Ninety-sixth Street platform. A homeless man lay on a wooden bench near the stairs, where an overweight Hispanic girl in tight clothing bobbed her head as she listened to her iPod. Setting his palms on the dirty platform, Jake saw that the backs of his hands matched his filthy suit. He sprang onto the platform, then got to his feet and moved toward the stairs. On the upper level a locked door prevented him from entering the men's room. He went to the turnstiles to call out to the heavyset woman reading a romance novel in the surveillance booth, but no sound came out. He could not speak. Massaging his throat muscles, he glanced at a pay phone mounted on a steel column. Even if he found his voice, what would he tell anyone?

He passed through a turnstile and climbed a second

flight of stairs into the sunlight. On Ninety-sixth Street, he breathed fresh air. The temperature had risen, and pedestrians regarded him with mild curiosity. Ignoring them, he glanced at his watch: 11:15.

Forty-five minutes until the bars opened.

He walked south along the East River until noon, then located a tavern on Thirty-eighth Street. Inside, a clean-cut young man wiped down the empty joint's bar. Jake made for the men's room.

"Those bathrooms are for paying customers," the bartender said.

Jake opened up his wallet, took out a fifty dollar bill, and slapped it on the bar. The bartender nodded, suspicion in his eyes. Jake entered the men's room, which smelled of pine. He stared at the unrecognizable reflection in the mirror above the sink. Grime and blood streaked his face, and his suit, covered in chalky dust, made him look like the survivor of some catastrophe. He did not remember his name.

Shock, he thought.

Pressing a wet paper towel against the gash on his forehead, he winced at the stinging sensation. Under different circumstances, he might have gone to an emergency room for stitches. As he scrubbed his face and hands, his visage came into view, and with it his memory.

Demon-blood-demon . . .

He gulped cold water from the faucet, relieved himself, then did his best to make his suit presentable. Five minutes later, he emerged from the bathroom and sat on the stool before his fifty dollar bill. The bartender stepped over to him with an unimpressed look on his face.

Say something, Jake thought.

The bartender waited.

Speak.

"Double bourbon," Jake said at last.

After the Widow had left, Gorman returned to his bedroom and opened the closet door. Unable to go out in public wearing a suit again, he selected a pair of faded jeans and a black T-shirt from a rock concert he had never attended. After he had dressed, he rubbed grease in his hair, which he plastered to his scalp. The change in hair color made his flesh look even paler than usual, and he inserted green contact lenses before stepping into steel-toed motorcycle boots. A black leather jacket completed the ensemble. Now he needed to create a new identity for himself.

Ryan Coulter, he thought.

Once he had a name, the rest of the pieces fell into place. Ryan's friends called him Python because they did not trust him. He had lived alone in Boston and currently resided at a YMCA in New York City while hoping to land a job at a recording studio. He had no real musical talent, but he sure dug rock 'n' roll.

With his new identity set, he tucked the tools of his trade into a ratty-looking backpack—not the one that belonged to Knapsack Johnny. A screwed-up kid like Ryan Coulter would not be caught dead carrying a briefcase.

He had a soul to catch.

Jake stumbled out of the bar at 3:00 p.m. He felt drunk, but not drunk enough; the morning's events still burned in his mind. Lighting a cigarette, he followed the crowded sidewalk to a quiet, residential street in the Murray Hill district, which consisted of town houses and brownstones. A craving gnawed at him, and a single word formed in his mind.

Cocaine.

Jesus, he wanted to get high. Perhaps he would drop in on his old pal, AK. At his current salary level, he could afford the best that Lester had to offer. Or maybe he would stick the kid up, just for old times' sake.

No.

He refused to slide back into that emotional sewer. He needed to keep his wits about him, and he grew angry at himself for drinking again. Taking a deep drag on his cigarette, he leaned against a black metal gate. He looked behind him, his eyes following the stone steps of the building to its steeple.

A church. Presbyterian, not that it mattered to him.

Sanctuary.

Aunt Rose had been Catholic, and she had forced Jake to attend St. Bartholomew's in Woodside until his high school graduation. Since then, he had only been in church once, to marry Sheryl. Casting his eyes upward to the storm clouds massing in the sky, he flicked his cigarette into the street. He stepped through the gateway and climbed the steps to the wooden doors. The scent of melted candle wax assailed him as he entered the vestibule and made his way up the aisle. Dull sunlight filtered through the stained-glass windows, and every footstep and rustle of clothing echoed beneath the arched ceiling. A dozen people sat scattered in the pews, their heads bowed in prayer. Jake sat down on a wooden bench halfway up the aisle and gazed at the giant cross behind the pulpit. He waited for an epiphany, but none came.

Ryan Coulter took the Number One local train downtown to the Spring Street stop and wandered up the incline of Houston Street. As he passed a skinny Hispanic man with a mustache and bandanna leaning against a cyclone fence, he felt the man's eyes on his leather.

"Where's your motorcycle?" the man said in a sarcastic tone.

Ryan faced the smiling man. "Parked outside your crack house." Neither Marc Gorman nor Byron would have been so bold. The man laughed, and Ryan continued up Houston until it intersected with Lafayette. He stopped outside a women's fashion boutique with a French name he could not pronounce, and he studied the feminine mannequins in the window. Tattoos and graffiti stood out on their Day-Glo-colored limbs. Bells signaled his arrival as he opened the door.

How cute, Ryan thought.

The door closed behind him and he looked around the small shop, which made the most of its limited space. No customers, just a chubby girl at the counter. He stepped around different mannequins to check out the racks of clothing, and they reached out to him with rigid fingers. An image of them pulling him down into an open grave flashed through his mind and he shook his head. Cupping one hand over a plastic breast, he laughed. The chubby girl, who had pink hair and wore a tie-dyed belly shirt, looked up at him with an annoyed expression.

"Can I help you?" Her tone had an irritating, judgmental quality to it.

"I doubt it," Ryan said. *Fucking dyke.* He caressed the cheek of an orange mannequin, then kissed its lips and wagged his tongue at it.

The girl moved around the counter, dressed in baggy

camouflage pants with a tiny cell phone on a silver chain clipped to her belt. "Maybe you should go to a men's store."

"That makes two of us. Maybe you should suck my dick."

The girl opened her mouth, but no sound came out, and Ryan saw a metal stud gleaming in her tongue.

"That's a start. Now all you have to do is get down on your knees."

Returning to her station, she picked up a phone. "Sheryl, I need you out here."

Weaving between the mannequins, Ryan smiled. He crouched and lifted up the long, flowing skirt on a blue figure posed like a ballerina. The patch between its legs had not been painted and the flesh-colored plastic stood out. From the corner of one eye, he glimpsed a woman in a black pantsuit join the salesgirl. Her hair had been longer in the photograph the Widow had provided.

"Guy's a real eighty-six," the dyke said.

Sheryl made straight for him as he continued to stare between the mannequin's legs.

"Go to Eighth Avenue if you want to get your jollies," she said. "We're not a peep show palace."

Ryan lowered the mannequin's skirt and rose to his feet. He looked into Sheryl's eyes, but she showed no sign of fear, her jaw set. Flaring his nostrils, he sniffed the air. "Maybe you should be. I'd pay to peep at you."

Sheryl offered him an icy smile. "Kelly, do you know

what we have here?" Kelly did not respond. "We have a real bad boy. An honest-to-God Johnny Rotten. He's so bad, he came into the shop just to intimidate us. Isn't that right, badass? You think you're scaring us?"

Ryan smiled. Kelly appeared to be frightened, but Sheryl seemed unimpressed. "I only want to scare you if that's what turns you on. Maybe the three of us should get together in that back room."

Sheryl held Ryan's gaze as she spoke to Kelly. "Call nine-one-one."

Ryan held out his hands. "Hey, that's not necessary. Be cool, I'm going. I was just trying to be friendly."

Sheryl's smile thinned. "Call nine-one-one anyway."

Kelly punched a number into the phone, and Ryan strutted to the door. "I'm outta here, ladies. But I'll see you around—*Sheryl.*" He opened the door and stepped outside.

Hurrying around the corner, he smiled. She was going to be good. He felt it in his bones.

Soon.

Jake sat smoking on a bench facing the East River, the FDR Drive behind him. Joggers, bicyclists, and dog walkers passed by him while Manhattan traffic snarled behind him. All he had to do was follow the asphalt path for ten blocks and he would reach Carl Schurz Park, not far from his apartment.

Sheryl's apartment.

Sheryl loved Carl Schurz Park. She liked to sunbathe there in the summer, read there in the fall, make snow angels there in the winter, and take long walks there in the spring. Standing on the viaduct overlooking the statue of Peter Pan, she enjoyed watching students in white Gi outfits train in Tae Kwon Do. She liked to circle Gracie Mansion and wonder aloud what the mayor was watching on television. And she liked to watch boats travel the river at night.

Sniffing the air, Jake smelled garbage.

There are dead people walking around this city. Talking. Pleading for their souls. Haunting the Tower.

He flicked his cigarette at the ground.

Corporate life was hell.

Ryan Coulter walked from one end of the block to the other, observing the apartment building with a sideways glance. He crossed the street and ordered a slice of pizza at a pizzeria on the corner of the next block. Pepperoni and mushroom. He carried the slice outside on a paper plate. From the corner, he saw the building just fine. He had gotten off the train around 5 p.m. and had circled the neighborhood. Folding his slice in half, he held it at an angle so that the excess oil spattered the white plate like blood drops. He would have that bitch's soul soon enough.

He enjoyed watching the life slip from his victims, enjoyed stealing their souls. It made him feel powerful and important, like God had created him for a reason.

Thunder rumbled in the distance, and he raised the slice to his mouth.

Sheryl left *La Petit Mort* shortly after 6 p.m. The air had ripened with electricity and she gazed up at the evening sky, sensing the drought's end. She hurried to Bleecker Street, where she caught the Uptown Number Six. Standing at a pole in the packed train, her body tensed up as an old man rubbed his hand against hers. She shot him an angry look and he backed off. As a cop's wife, she knew better than to give an inch to these perverts. They always backed down if you showed them some backbone, like that creepy punk in the store earlier. She wished she could have taken a cab home, but her budget did not allow for that. She had a good deal on her apartment, but Manhattan rent had reached ridiculous heights, and without Jake's income, she needed to watch her expenses. Of course, he would insist on chipping in, but she would refuse his offer. If only they had bought that house on Long Island—

Nothing would have changed. Jake would still have gotten himself into trouble, and now she would be taking the Long Island Rail home to an empty house instead of the subway to an empty apartment, and she would have a mortgage hanging over her head. She got off at Eighty-sixth Street, and on the ten-minute walk home she wondered how Jake was faring at his new job.

Darkness fell as she reached her building, and the wind intensified, causing her to shiver. Grateful that she had managed to beat the rain, she took out her keys and entered the lobby. After checking the empty mailbox, she started up the four flights of stairs. She did not know her neighbors—there had been a heavy turnover of tenants the last few years—but she knew what sounds to expect as she passed each door: a cat meowing, a dog barking, a canary singing, someone playing a flute. She had lived there for six years, three of them alone and three with Jake.

Reaching her apartment, she unlocked the front door. She turned on the overhead light as she stepped inside, then locked the door behind her and hung her coat in the closet. She went into the living room and flicked the light switch on the wall. The bulb in the overhead light blew out and her heart jumped. She frowned at the ceiling fixture. She hadn't needed to pull the stepladder out from beneath the bed since Jake had moved in with her. Her plants obscured the light coming from the windows of the building across the street, and she disliked the living room dark. Isolation crept over her. She missed Jake and had been uncomfortable living alone the past few days.

She pressed the PLAY button on the answering machine and entered the kitchen. At least the light worked in there. The messages played back as she crouched before the sink cabinet, punctuated by loud beeps. Opening the cabinet doors, she rummaged through cleaning chemicals and bug repellents for spare lightbulbs.

A click came over the speaker as she found the bulbs and removed one from a carton.

A second hang up followed as she closed the cabinet and stood up.

Then a third.

Staring at the machine, she rubbed the gooseflesh that had formed on her arms. *I wish Jake was here.*

And then, in the glass face of the microwave oven door, she saw color and movement, like a flag billowing in the wind. The silent reflection of a man sneaking up behind her. At first her mind refused to accept what her eyes witnessed. Then she heard a footstep on the linoleum and panic seized her. She spun around to face the intruder, the lightbulb slipping from her hand and exploding on the floor.

22

"It's just me," Jake said, raising his hands.

Holding one hand over her heart, Sheryl let the breath escape from her lungs. "What the hell are you doing here?"

"I didn't have anywhere else to go."

"You almost scared me to death!"

"I'm sorry. I just got here a few minutes ago and I lay down in the bedroom. I must have dozed off for a minute and the answering machine woke me."

"You stink like booze." She made no effort to hide the disapproval in her voice.

He offered a lame shrug.

"And you look like hell."

"You got that right."

Her tone softened. "How did you get that cut on your forehead?"

He touched the wound. "I fell down a dark hole."

She looked at the broken fragments of the lightbulb on the floor. "You're never going to change, Jake." She took a dustpan and a whisk broom from a tall cabinet and swept up the mess.

"I need help," Jake said.

She looked at him with an unreadable expression on her face.

"I need *you*."

"I really don't think this is the best time for that discussion." She dumped the fragments into a wastebasket beneath the sink.

"I really need to talk to you. Believe me, it's not what you think."

She put the broom and pan away and faced him, hands on her hips. "Fine. Let's talk about why you came in here without my permission."

He swallowed. "Can we at least sit down?"

Sighing, she nodded. "Of course."

They moved into the dark living room. Sheryl switched on the computer stand desk lamp and sat on the sofa. Jake peered out the window: people on the sidewalks had their umbrellas out and ready, but the onslaught had not yet commenced. He rotated a wand, closing the wooden blinds. Sitting beside Sheryl on the sofa, he wondered if it had really been only three days since they had sat in the same spot with his stash before them.

"I'm waiting."

He ran one hand through his dirty hair. "I don't know where to begin. I don't know how much to tell you or how much you'll believe. I'm not even sure how much I believe."

"What's going on?"

Hearing concern in her voice, he looked into her dark brown eyes. Did he dare tell her everything?

No. She'll never believe you.

"Did something happen at work?"

"You could say that."

"Did you get fired?"

He considered the question and shook his head. "No. I only wish that were the case. I may be stuck with that job until the day I die." He cackled. "Maybe even longer."

"What are you talking about?"

He took a deep breath and exhaled. "I stumbled onto something . . . incredible."

"Something you're not supposed to know?"

He nodded. "Tower International is conducting all kinds of genetic experiments that the public and the government know nothing about."

"And that surprises you? Watch the news sometime."

"They're creating new life forms. Flesh-and-blood weapons. Monsters."

A moment passed before she responded. "That sounds pretty far-fetched . . ."

Jake wrung his hands. "There's more. The Cipher

works for Old Nick."

"What are you talking about?"

"He's on their payroll. I guess that makes us colleagues. Maybe we can trade shop stories at the office Christmas party."

"Have you told Edgar this?"

"No. He wouldn't believe me. He couldn't."

She hesitated, speechless.

"I've seen things that no one could possibly believe without witnessing them with their own eyes."

"Do your bosses know what you've seen?"

"Oh, yeah—the old man spoke to me at length this morning."

"What did he say?"

"My soul is in jeopardy."

Sheryl sat in silence, as if wondering what to make of his story.

"Those two thugs I killed?"

She nodded, apprehension on her features.

"I saw them today. Right outside this building."

She raised her eyebrows. "Come again?"

"They're after me."

Her expression cooled. "Are you telling me you saw two ghosts?"

"Oh, I saw more than two."

"And do these ghosts also work for Old Nick?"

He paused. "I'm not sure." *Who else could they be working for?*

She stood, anger rising in her voice. "What are you on? Are you still just snorting coke, or have you started smoking crack?"

He stood as well. "Sheryl, please. I know what I just told you sounds crazy, but I swear to you, I haven't used anything."

"You've certainly been drinking."

"All right, so I got loaded after the most fucked-up day of my life. You'd have done the same thing if you went through what I did. But that's all I did. I'm clean, I tell you."

"Then you've lost your mind."

"I wish you were right. That would be a lot easier for me to accept. But I'm not crazy. I know what I've seen, what I've heard, and what I've experienced. Tower International is behind the Cipher, and they *are* making monsters."

Sheryl massaged her temples. "When did you last have a full night's sleep?"

"Three nights ago, but—"

"And when did you last eat?"

"I had some pretzels at the bar."

Pursing her lips, she nodded.

Jake saw that he had failed to reach her. "Listen to me. Please. I need a place to crash. Just for tonight, so I can get my head on straight and figure out my next move. I'll be out of here first thing in the morning, I swear."

She stared at him, indecision in her eyes.

"There's no one else I can turn to."

She sighed. "All right. I hope I don't regret this, but you can spend the night on the sofa. Go lie down in the bedroom for now and I'll fix dinner."

Closing his eyes, he bowed his head. "You believe me?"

"I didn't say that. But I want to talk to you after you've rested and sobered up."

Looking at her, he nodded. "I'm too exhausted to argue."

"Go lie down."

He started toward the bedroom, then turned back. "Thank you."

She said nothing.

"Wake me if the doorbell rings, and don't answer the phone." He went into the bedroom and closed the door. Peeling off his jacket, he slipped off his shoulder holster and laid his Glock on the bedside table. He collapsed onto the bed, burying his face in a pillow.

A tiny black speck moved up a great dune as the sun blazed down on a sea of sand.

That's me, Jake thought, as if watching himself on a movie screen.

He crawled on his hands and knees, parched and

exhausted in the afternoon heat. He suspected that he was dreaming, but the illusion seemed so real. Naked, his bright pink skin had started peeling. He clawed at the burning sand in agony, his knees raw.

Where am I? he wondered.

The last thing he remembered was falling into bed.

Is this hell?

No, not hell—someplace else. If the previous twenty-four hours had taught him anything, hell existed on Earth.

He reached the dune's peak and stood, staring across the vast sandscape. He raised his hand over his eyes, shielding them from the brutal sun.

Sand, as far as he could see.

He turned in a circle, scoping out his surroundings.

Sand, everywhere.

I'm screwed.

Not even Sheryl could save him from this.

Something glinted in the sand below him, at the bottom of the dune, reflecting light into his eyes.

Glass.

He stepped over the edge of the dune and slid down it, losing his balance halfway down. He rolled the rest of the way, sand tearing at his flesh until he stopped at the bottom. He spat sand out of his mouth and crawled over to the glass, his heart pounding. Using both hands, he dug out a bottle, its seal unbroken.

Good old Jim Beam.

Standing, he opened the bottle. Alcohol would only

dehydrate him further, but so what? This was a dream, after all. He raised the neck of the bottle to his cracked lips and tilted his head back, gulping the whiskey like water. The poison burned the inside of his mouth and the back of his throat, and he gagged. But his stomach felt great. Perhaps he would drink himself into a stupor and pass out, then die in his dream and never awaken. Better to burn out than to burn in hell.

But what about Sheryl?

He had reason to be optimistic on that front, even if the rest of his life had gone down the sewer. He wavered, his vision turning white for a moment. When his eyesight returned, something about his environment had changed.

The sand had turned gleaming white.

Salt?

Dropping the Jim Beam bottle, he fell to his knees and inspected the sparkling powder, touching it with one finger, tasting it. His tongue turned numb.

Cocaine.

Miles of it!

His eyes widened and before he knew it, he had scooped up a handful of coke and plunged his face into it, snorting it up both nostrils. Sheryl couldn't hold his dreams against him, could she?

He stood, waiting for the drug to kick in.

Nothing.

He should have known. Didn't this always happen on *The Twilight Zone?*

A droplet of blood landed in the coke between his feet. He ran his right hand beneath his nose and examined it. The blood had not come from him.

Thunder rolled across the desert, and he gazed up at the cloudless sky. He felt a raindrop splash his head, then another on his back. The drops felt warm, and others spattered the cocaine at his feet, turning it dark red.

Lightning flashed, and blood rained down on him.

He screamed.

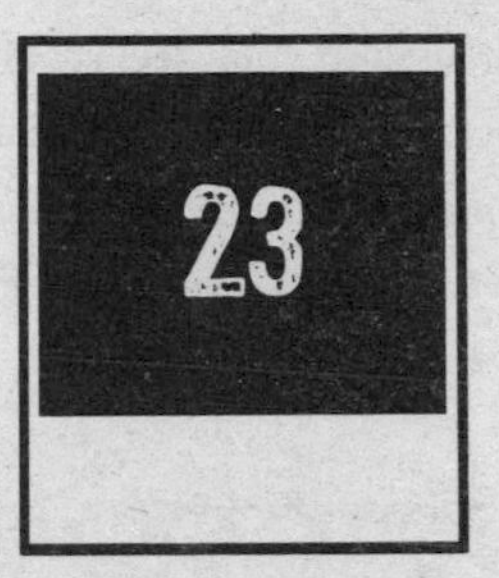

Thunder boomed over Jake's strangled cry as he sat up in the dark. He gasped for breath and for a moment he forgot his location. Rain and wind rattled the windows like machine-gun fire and lightning flashed nearby, illuminating the bedroom.

I've come home, he thought.

Thoughts and images tumbled in his mind, one on top of another, and the events of the preceding four days felt like aftershocks from his nightmare. Thunder shook the building, causing him to flinch.

Wiping sweat from his brow, he looked at the digital clock on the bedside table and swallowed. 9:11 p.m. He had been out for hours and felt worse now than he had before. He climbed out of bed with a groan, his head tingling, and staggered across the room. His limbs felt sluggish and he lurched from side to side. Closing his hands into fists, he willed his mind and body to awaken.

When he opened the bedroom door, the familiar aroma of Sheryl's cooking greeted him. He relieved himself in the bathroom, then followed the odors to the kitchen. He stopped in midstep when he heard whistling ahead of him. His chest swelled as he recognized the tune Sheryl had chosen: Van Morrison's "Have I Told You Lately That I Love You?"

Their song.

Moving just outside the kitchen, he gazed at Sheryl. She stood at the counter with her back to him, rolling ground beef into meatballs on a wooden cutting board. Her short hair gave way to her slender neck, which sloped down to her perfect shoulders. Steam rose from the large black pot on the stove, and the water inside it had almost boiled down. Starch rose to the surface and strands of spaghetti writhed like snakes in a crowded nest. Sheryl's whistling filled the kitchen and when she finished, she started over. In that moment, Jake sensed that everything would turn out all right.

"Sheryl?"

Her body jerked as she spun around, a startled cry escaping from her throat.

Damn it, Jake thought. "Sorry. I didn't mean to scare you again."

Taking a deep breath, she forced a smile to her lips. "That's okay. I'm fine. Why don't you go lie down for a while?"

"I just got up. The storm woke me."

"Storm?" She glanced at the window in the dark living room. "Oh, right."

"Look, I want to apologize again for barging in here like this. I know I should have waited until you got home, but it was an emergency."

Sheryl looked at the floor, then into his eyes. "Don't worry about it. You didn't do anything wrong. This is your home, too."

His heart clenched. "It is?"

She nodded. "Of course." A pause. "Do you believe in true love, Jake?"

Dèjá vu crept over him. "You know I do."

Her lips trembled. "So do I."

Jake debated how to react.

"I've made up my mind. I want to work things out. I want you to stay here with me."

He opened his mouth to speak, but the telephone rang. A sick feeling spread over him. Had his boss tracked him down? "Don't answer that."

A puzzled expression passed over her face. "Okay."

He went into the living room, his elation on hold. The ringing sounded shrill in the darkness. Regarding the phone with suspicion, he sat on the sofa and turned the caller ID box so that it faced him. Recognizing Edgar's cell phone number on the display screen, he lifted the receiver from its cradle. "Hello?"

"Jake?" Edgar's voice sounded strained, and Jake

heard rain falling in the background.

"Yeah, it's me. Sorry I haven't returned your calls, but things have been really crazy."

"Jake, I have to talk to you. Wait there, I'm coming right over."

"I need to see you, too, but I'm in the middle of something important right now."

In the kitchen, Sheryl started whistling again.

"Jake, this isn't a social call. Something terrible's happened that you need to know about."

Jake hesitated. "Go on."

"Not over the phone. I only called to see if you were home, since you haven't been answering your cell."

Jake lowered his voice. "Tell me now."

Edgar paused, then sighed. "Brace yourself. It's Sheryl."

Jake glanced toward the kitchen, his body turning rigid. He saw the roses he had bought arranged in a vase on the dining table, and his heart swelled. Sheryl's shadow moved along the wall behind them. "What about her?"

"I'm sorry as hell to be the one to tell you this . . ."

"Spit it out."

"She's dead. Murdered. It looks like the Cipher got her."

An invisible blow nearly knocked the phone from Jake's hands. "You're wrong. It must have been someone else. Sheryl's here with me now."

A long moment passed before Edgar answered.

"That's impossible. I'm standing in Carl Schurz Park staring at her corpse. Her purse is here and so is her ID."

Jake pictured the park, a few long blocks away. "I'll get back to you, Edgar."

"I'm on my way—"

Jake hung up and rose to his feet. Lightning flashed outside the windows as he approached the kitchen. Sheryl continued to whistle and his body shuddered. He stood at the kitchen's edge as she turned from the stove, an open jar of spaghetti sauce in one hand. Thunder rumbled and cracked.

"Who was it?" she said, setting the jar down.

He studied her face. It looked perfect. "Edgar."

"Oh. What did he want?"

"Never mind that. Did you go out while I was asleep?"

She hesitated, her mouth half-open. "Yes, I did. I needed to do some thinking."

"Where did you go?"

"To the park. You know I like to go there."

Jake grasped the edge of the archway, steadying himself. "In the rain?"

"It wasn't raining yet when I left, and I came home as soon as it started. What's the matter with you? Why are you giving me the third degree? I'm not one of your suspects."

He stepped forward. "Who are you?"

She backed against the counter. "You're scaring me."

"*What* are you?"

"You've been drinking."

"We've already established that." He seized her wrist and an electric current jolted him.

Grunting, Sheryl arched her back as electricity passed from her body into his. Her eyes darted to his hand on her wrist, fear spreading over her features. Then she looked back into his eyes. Her lips quivered and she spoke in a weak voice. "He hurt me, Jake."

Jake's vision blurred, hot tears rolling down his cheeks. *Oh, God, no.* "Sheryl . . ."

"He took my soul!"

Facial muscles twitching, Jake shook his head. "Bastards . . ."

Beams of light shot from her eyes and mouth, dissolving her beautiful face into a horrible mask. Ashes fell from her eye sockets like teardrops. Through his own tears, Jake saw light shooting out of her fingertips. Multiple colors coalesced as her flesh and clothing merged into psychedelic slop, steam rising from her pores. The light intensified, and Jake drew her close to him, hoping to somehow hold her together. His hands passed through her as they would through warm water. Her voice trailed off as the light faded and nothing remained of her.

Jake gaped at his outstretched hands, then sank to his knees, his entire body tingling. His chest constricting, he pounded the floor and wiped snot from his nostrils. "Sheryl . . ."

They had stolen her from him.

Forever.

And he had no one to blame but himself.

Stumbling into the bedroom, he pulled on his shoulder holster and snatched his jacket from the bed. He charged out of the apartment and fled down the stairs, weak in the knees. He would make them pay, but to do that, he needed to remain free, and Edgar would arrive any moment.

In the lobby, he threw open the vestibule door and jumped the steps to the landing. Rain pelted the front glass in a torrent, as if someone had aimed a fire hose at the building and turned the water pressure on full blast. He pulled the front door open and staggered outside, the wind blowing him sideways. As he fought his way into the street, headlights pinned him in their glare. He faced the oncoming vehicle like a trapped deer and the car screeched to a stop, knocking him to the wet pavement. Lying on his back, he stared at the black sky through the downpour. He heard doors open and close on both sides of the car, followed by two sets of footsteps rushing toward him.

Hands seized his arms and hauled him to his feet, and he stared in disbelief at Dread and Baldy as thunder cracked overhead. Baldy slugged him in his solar plexus, and he doubled over in pain.

Dread buried his left hand in Jake's hair, jerked his head back, and snatched Jake's Glock from its holster. Sneering, he waved the gun in Jake's face. "Remember us, pig?"

Jake could barely stand, and they had to support him between them. "Didn't I kill you once?"

"Someone wants to see you," Baldy said, snarling. "Get into the car."

Jake's head rolled back on his neck, his mouth catching raindrops on his tongue, and he saw the closed blinds of his apartment. The dead thugs dragged him to the car and threw him into the ruptured front seat. The car reeked of gasoline and rust. Dread got in on the passenger side, the car sinking from his weight, and jammed the Glock against Jake's ribs. Baldy slid behind the steering wheel and slammed his door. He shifted the car into gear and they surged forward through the driving rain.

Jake looked out the right side window and felt Dread shove the Glock harder against his ribs. "Don't try anything, piggy."

Jake sat still—then shot both hands out, seizing Baldy's right wrist and Dread's left wrist. He squeezed their flesh and waited for them to evaporate.

Nothing happened.

Baldy guffawed. Dread raised the Glock and brought it down on Jake's head, sending him spiraling into darkness.

Soaking wet, Marc felt like himself again as he entered his apartment and locked the door behind him. He slid the backpack from his shoulders and hung his motorcycle jacket in the closet. Climbing into the bathtub, he peeled off Ryan's wet clothes and hung them to dry on a towel rod; the rain had already washed the blood from them back at the park. He stepped before the sink and examined the scratches on his cheek.

Bitch got me good, he thought, fingering the five pink furrows in his face. None of his victims had managed to harm him before. He got back into the tub and ran the shower. Hot water stung the scratches, and he wished that he'd killed Sheryl before she'd had the chance to hurt him.

She'd been good, all right, just as he'd hoped. He hadn't been sure how to proceed when her husband had entered the building, and he'd debated snatching her from the vestibule when she arrived minutes later. He could have dragged her into the basement and sacrificed her there, but that would have been risky. He'd gone this far without getting caught or being seen by adhering to the letter of his plans once he'd selected his victims. He had slain Shannon Reynolds on impulse, without taking his usual preparations, and look at all the trouble that had caused him. Despite her reassurances, he knew the Widow had lost faith in him.

He had stood in the doorway of the building across the street, his black umbrella out, staring at his target's apartment window until the husband closed the blinds. He did not wish to invade the apartment with both of them there. The Widow had warned him to avoid the man, and she'd be furious if he screwed up again.

So he waited.

He could not believe his luck when Sheryl exited the building alone a short while later. He followed her to the park from a distance, watching as she passed beneath the streetlights, then closed in on her. She'd stood at the railing facing the river for nearly twenty minutes, even after the rain had started falling, while he observed her unseen from the empty dog run behind the trees. She opened an umbrella but the wind battered and twisted it, and she discarded it on the ground. She started back, but then the downpour drove her beneath the viaduct.

She hadn't expected anyone to follow her. Boy, had she looked surprised when Ryan appeared behind her. Then he blinded her with the camera flash and made his move. He didn't think she even saw the knife. A pity; he'd spent so much time searching for just the right one. She reached into her purse as he forced her to the ground, his body on top of her, crushing her scream beneath his weight as rain spattered the ground on either side of the viaduct. A dislodged can of pepper spray rolled from her hand and she clawed at his face. He guessed that she'd thought he intended to rape her, but he'd never do anything like that. Then he drew the knife across her throat twice, and her eyes opened wide and stayed that way as blood fountained out of the wounds. She had beautiful eyes.

He forced the oxygen mask over her face but she didn't even react to it. What a disappointment. Then he chanted as he'd been instructed, reciting the ancient verse in time with the inflation and deflation of the Soul Bag until she stopped breathing. He sealed the bag, stood, and slipped it into his backpack as her blood ran over the pavement. His erection pressed against the zipper of his jeans and he wanted to release himself right there, but waiting was a necessary part of the game. He looked around to ensure he hadn't left any evidence lying around, then took out his umbrella and made his way through the park.

Now, standing in the hot spray of his shower, he jerked on his penis until he ejaculated. His excitement sated, he put on his bathrobe, went to the telephone, and entered a number.

"I need to arrange a pickup," he said, eyeing the backpack.

Jake faded in and out of consciousness as Baldy steered the vehicle down the FDR Drive and onto Fifty-ninth Street. The *rat-a-tat-tatting* of the rain on the roof frazzled his nerves. The windshield wipers did little to improve visibility, and he barely saw the red taillights of the car ahead as it braked on the slippery surface. They took the Fifth-ninth Street Bridge into Queens, and he saw no way to catch the attention of the drivers around them. He considered seizing the steering wheel and crashing the car, but what purpose would that serve? He had already killed his captors once and that had not stopped them. Besides, he needed to stay alive to avenge Sheryl's murder.

Gripping the steering wheel in both hands, Baldy glanced at Jake. "Motherfucker," he said in a disgusted tone.

Dread leaned closer to Jake, who thought he smelled

lighter fluid on the dead man's breath. "Man, I'd love to snuff your ass right now."

Jake stared straight ahead. "So why don't you?"

Baldy shook his head. "Motherfucker!"

"We have orders to bring you in alive." Dread clenched his teeth. "If we disobey, he'll send us back. And we ain't ready for that."

Jake said nothing. Who would send them back? And back to where? Edgar was at his apartment by now, and he wondered what would have happened if his ex-partner had arrived as Dread and Baldy abducted him.

"*Motherfucker!*" Baldy drove his right elbow back into Jake's chest. Jake groaned and shut his eyes, rocking back and forth in the seat. He wanted to vomit.

Dread sniffed the air. "You stink of booze, man. You drunk? You high? You were lit when you took us out, weren't you? Pretty quick on that draw."

"It was self-defense," Jake said, opening his eyes again. "If you two hadn't been so fucked up, or if either one of you had been a better shot, things might have turned out differently. Maybe I'd be haunting your asses right now."

Baldy pounded on the steering wheel with both hands, frothing at the mouth. "MOTHERFUCKER!"

Jake flinched at the sound of the scream in the confined space but Dread just grinned. "Is that what you think we are? Ghosts? We ain't ghosts, man. We won't melt in your hands or in your mouth. Ghosts can't hurt the living, and believe me, we're gonna do a number on you."

Turning down a narrow Long Island City street, the car passed several abandoned brick buildings with shattered windows. Baldy parked along the deserted industrial stretch, and he and Dread yanked Jake out of the car. Rain spattered the pothole-strewn pavement, and somewhere behind them an elevated train rumbled on its tracks. Jake stumbled but his abductors held him upright and dragged him toward a deserted factory across the street. Bally kicked the steel door open and Jake guessed that the two dead men had been there before. They dragged him inside the cold, dark interior and slammed the door shut. The crash reverberated through the empty space, which reeked of printing ink and dead rats. Jake realized that he could disappear here and no one would ever find him. Dread and Baldy dragged him toward an open doorway thirty feet ahead, illuminated by flickering orange light.

Fire, Jake thought. *Maybe they're taking me to hell.*

They forced him through the doorway, and he scraped one hand on the rusty door. Halfway down a flight of metal steps, he looked over a thick railing at the dark, clammy space below. A gigantic, rusted-out water heater dominated the boiler room. When they reached the cracked cement floor, he saw a heavyset man with a greasy black comb-over and round spectacles sitting at a dilapidated rolltop desk. The man appeared to be in his late forties, and wore a drab green outfit and a miserable expression. He looked as if he belonged in the cellar.

Who the hell is this? Jake wondered.

The man did not react to their arrival, and Dread and Baldy ignored his presence. The flickering orange light came from the furnace, its steel door open so that flames licked out. Shivering, Jake appreciated the heat. Dread and Baldy threw him to the damp floor, covered with discolored mineral deposits. His face only inches from a corroded metal drain, he felt cold raindrops splashing the back of his neck.

Jake recognized the dark, faded splotches before him on the floor: bloodstains. Looking up, he saw more splotches on the dank walls, and heavy black chains with manacles dangled six feet above him. His eyes followed the chains up a shaft ten feet wide and twenty-five feet high, its crumbling brick walls patched with cement. The chains hung from pulleys fastened to a wooden beam in the shaft's ceiling, where rain fell between the blades of an industrial fan. Lightning flashed, illuminating the bloodstains, and Jake imagined he heard the echoes of tortured screams beneath the accompanying thunder. He had been brought to a human slaughterhouse.

Dread and Baldy raised his arms and yanked off his jacket, shoulder holster, and shirt. The garments absorbed brown water on the bloodstained floor. The dead men clamped the cold manacles around his wrists and moved to opposing brick walls, where the ends of the chains had been secured around protruding metal spikes. Grinning at each other, they freed the chains and hoisted Jake until his feet dangled two feet above the floor, his arms pulled apart at forty-five-degree angles. Then they fastened the chains to the spikes once more, and Jake groaned from the strain on his muscles. The falling rain kept him alert and the fire in the furnace blasted heat at him. Across the space, the fat man seemed to notice him for the first time with disinterested eyes.

"Comfortable, motherfucker?" Orange light outlined Baldy's features as his voice echoed in the shaft.

Dread examined the Glock. Pulling back its slide, he aimed the gun at Jake, who swallowed and waited. Dread squeezed the trigger and the gun barked. A single bullet ricocheted around the subterranean walls and Jake flinched, twisting his body on the chains. The dead men stood still and the bullet stopped whining. Baldy laughed hard, his chest heaving as he gripped his belly.

Shaking his head, Dread stepped closer to Jake. "I wish I could cap you. I've prayed for the chance to do you like you did us. Too bad that's not what he brought us back for." He nodded at the fat man, who stood up at his desk. "That little freak over there gets to take care of you. But you'll be dead soon enough and then you'll be on our turf."

As Baldy continued to laugh, the fat man opened a desk drawer from which he removed a black bag. Jake knew that bag contained bad news. The man removed a collapsed tripod, which he slung over his shoulder. He moved forward, stopping a dozen feet away from Jake. He extended the tripod's metal legs and locked them, then removed a digital camcorder and mounted it on the tripod's head. He flipped open the LCD screen, pressed the POWER button, and frowned.

"The batteries are dead," he said in a wheezing voice.

Dread rolled his eyes. "So are you, ya fat fuck. The Master didn't bring you back here to make one of your home videos. Just do what you're good at."

He's dead, too, Jake realized. And the camcorder appeared to be a recent model.

"I do my best work when the camera's running," the man said.

"Stop bitching and get busy," Baldy said.

The man studied Jake with a disappointed expression. "He's too old."

Chicken hawk, Jake thought; a child molester. The worst kind of predator.

"We wanna see this pig bleed," Baldy said. "Make him squeal."

The man returned to the desk and set the camera bag down.

Snuff flicks, Jake concluded. The abandoned facility must have been the man's makeshift studio when he had been alive, and the blood on the walls and floor belonged to his victims. Dread had been correct when he called the man a freak.

The fiend opened the rolltop, and Jake saw a canvas bundle inside. The man unrolled the canvas, and a half-dozen metal instruments gleamed in the darkness, secured by leather straps.

Oh, fuck.

Dread grinned. "You think we were bad? Clarence here was a real nasty piece of work. Used to videotape himself cutting up young boys and teenage girls. Liked to take his time and skin them alive. When they finally died, he dumped their bodies into that furnace and sold copies of the videos online. Cancer got him eight months ago and his crimes went unpunished—in this world. Doesn't say much for you pigs, does it?"

Jake concentrated on Clarence, who closed his right hand around the metal handle of a serrated blade six inches long and two inches wide. Clarence held the weapon before his face, inspecting it, and Jake saw that a metal guard covered with shiny spikes protected Clarence's fingers. Smiling with approval, Clarence picked up a second instrument with his other hand, this one with two narrow blades, spaced three inches apart, protruding from a wooden handle. Jake guessed the blades had been designed for gouging out eyeballs.

Crossing the space, Clarence stepped around the tripod and stood before Jake. The lenses of his glasses reflected the crackling furnace flames. "Don't tell me your name," he said. "I don't want to know who you are. It's more exciting that way."

Jake looked around the dungeon, searching for any possible means of escape.

"I was a janitor here back when this was a printing shop. After they closed it down, I used it for my own purposes."

Clarence raised his knife for Jake to see up close, waving it as a boy might a model airplane. The blade could cut Jake, slice him, dice him, and flay him.

"Now tell me: what does Nicholas Tower want with all those souls?"

Down to business, Jake thought. "I don't know what you're talking about." *Who are these guys working for?*

Clarence smiled. "Thank you."

Clarence stepped closer, the knife poised to strike, and Dread and Baldy grinned at each other with anticipation. Jake's body tensed up. Taking a deep breath as Clarence fell within his reach, he swung his legs up and scissor-kicked them, trapping Clarence's flabby neck between his left shin and his right calf. Gasping and wide-eyed, Clarence pounded on Jake's thighs. His glasses fell off and Jake saw bulging eyes with heavy lids. He knew that hesitating would give Clarence time to drive the weapons into his legs, so he thrashed to his right, snapping the dead man's neck with a sickening crack. Clarence's eyes rolled up in their sockets and his blades clattered on the floor. Jake thrashed to his left, but this time Clarence's neck made no sound. The body toppled to the floor and Jake lowered his legs.

Baldy shook his head in disbelief. "Motherfucker."

Jake swallowed. It had felt good to dispose of an

enemy as twisted as Clarence, and now he knew that the dead men could be slowed, possibly even stopped. Hearing a choking sound below him, he looked down to see if Clarence possessed some supernatural ability to reconstitute himself. Instead, Clarence's body burst into flames and the fat man wailed. Jake felt heat blasting up at him and he jerked his head back, looking away. His eyes teared up and the stench of burning hair and flesh permeated his nostrils. The flames reached as high as his sternum and he held still to keep his legs from swinging into the bonfire. He turned his head enough to see the flames cast twisted shadows on the cellar walls. The fire consumed Clarence, who struggled to move like a turtle on its back. Dread and Baldy launched themselves forward, panic in their eyes.

I'm next, Jake thought as they charged in his direction. Powerless to stop them, he feared they would burn him alive. Instead they stooped low, each seizing one of Clarence's flaming ankles, and dragged him back, even though it meant burning their hands. Clarence's screams faded into whimpers, his clawed fingers leaving scorched streaks on the cement floor. With pain etched on their faces, Dread and Baldy dropped his legs, which landed with soft thumps that sent burning embers flying in all directions. Gaping at their blistered palms, they licked their raw wounds like dogs.

Turning silent, Clarence stopped writhing. His still body crackled and popped, and oily black smoke rose from the flames and drifted up the shaft. Jake wanted to retch from the sickening smell. The air became dense and Dread and Baldy turned rigid, abandoning their wounds as their eyes grew wide. At the top of the stairs, a dead lightbulb flickered on and off, and Jake swallowed. To his left, an industrial valve rotated by itself and steam hissed from a wide pipe, causing him to flinch. Dread and Baldy retreated to the furnace's shadow, cowering.

A massive silhouette filled the doorway.

This is it, Jake thought, the hairs on the back of his neck standing up.

The Reaper stepped into the fiery light and moved down the steps with the focused energy of a great white shark prowling the ocean depths. Terror blossomed in Jake as he gazed at the pulsating muscles within the fearsome body coming for him. Pink light shone from the demon's throbbing brain, and Dread and Baldy dropped to their knees, bowing their heads.

"Master Cain!" they said in unison.

Staring at Jake, the Reaper ignored them.

Tears welled up in Jake's eyes. He had never experienced such intense fear in his life. *Master Cain?* So the Grim Reaper had a name. Sweat stung the cut in Jake's forehead and he shook his head. "Oh, Christ . . ."

The Reaper's brain turned bloodred. "NEVER MENTION THAT NAME IN MY PRESENCE AGAIN."

The booming voice echoed through the dungeon, and Jake's entire body trembled. Clenching his teeth, he pulled on the chains, which only caused the manacles to bite deeper into his wrists, and his body swayed in the falling rain. Seeing dried blood on the manacles, he understood the blind panic that drove animals to chew through their own limbs to escape from traps.

The Reaper stepped over the burning husk that had been Clarence, passing through the hungry flames without harm or signs of concern. "Do not struggle. There is no escaping your fate."

Jake allowed his weakened body to wilt. Facing the demon that had slain Laddock and Birch as if they were insects, he smelled fear in his own sweat. He possessed no hope of surviving this encounter, and he knew that he could only delay the inevitable. Still reeling from what Dread and Baldy had just called their master, he spoke with a cracking voice. "Cain—?"

The Reaper stood fifteen feet away, gazing at Clarence's camcorder. His brain had cooled to pink again and he turned to Jake. "I am the agent of my master's will."

Jake swallowed. *God Almighty.* Cain, the firstborn son of Adam and Eve, brother of Abel. The man who had invented the homicide game. The demon stood as still and silent as a statue, the glowing pupils in his eye sockets pulsing. Sweat burning his eyes, Jake studied the ancient monster before him. What could a biblical celebrity like Cain possibly want with a struggling atheist like him?

"Tell me what Nicholas Tower intends to do

WITH THE SOULS IN HIS POSSESSION."

Jake swallowed again, his throat aching. Every word that came from Cain's mouth made him shudder. "I have no idea. Really. I swear to—" He caught himself. "I only know that he claims to have them." *Please let him believe me.*

"I NEED YOUR ASSISTANCE."

Jake raised his eyebrows. "Really?"

"I MUST HAVE TOWER'S SOUL."

Delerium seized Jake. "'*Am I my brother's keeper?*'"

"NO, BUT YOU ARE HIS PROTECTOR."

Jake wiped his face on his left shoulder. "I quit that gig this morning, so don't let me stand in your way. If you want his soul, then just take it. He's all yours. You have my blessing."

"I DO NOT REQUIRE YOUR BLESSING OR YOUR PERMISSION. I MUST CLAIM TOWER'S SOUL ON MY MASTER'S BEHALF. THE ONLY THING STANDING IN MY WAY IS THE WOMAN. HER SPELLS HAVE MADE IT IMPOSSIBLE FOR ME AND MINE TO MATERIALIZE IN TOWER'S PRESENCE."

Spells? Jake thought, recalling the invisible force that had prevented Cain from reaching him in the Tower's lobby. *Kira's a witch!* Could she have cast a spell over him, too? That would explain his obsessive attraction to her. Twenty-four hours earlier he would have scoffed at the notion, but not now. The muscles in his arms stretched to their limits. "The security card in my pocket will give you all the access you need."

Cain shook his head. "TO UNDERMINE THE WOMAN'S SPELL, YOU MUST SUMMON ME TO THE TOWER WHILE IN THE OLD MAN'S PRESENCE."

Ah, shit. "I don't think I can do that . . ."

Interlacing the fingers of both hands, Cain cracked his knuckles. Each pop sounded like Clarence's neck had when it snapped, and Jake cringed. The demon turned toward Dread and Baldy as if he had just remembered some minor detail. Shaking his head, Baldy gnawed on his own fingers with such force that blood dripped from them.

"Master, please!" Dread said. "We did as you commanded. He's here in one piece. We barely touched him!" Spreading his arms wide, he realized that he still held Jake's Glock in his right hand. He dropped the gun on the floor as if holding it meant his destruction.

Cain's eyes flared and Dread and Baldy screamed. Bloody bullet holes appeared in their bodies where Jake had shot them and smoke billowed out of the wounds. They ignited into brilliant flames, and Jake smelled burning flesh once more as they cried out in agony. Blinded, they staggered around in desperation. With three pyres now burning, the cellar turned bright and hot. Collapsing at the same time, Dread and Baldy crawled toward their master.

"Mercy!" they cried. "Mercy . . ."

Cain focused on Jake as the minions threw themselves at his grisly feet and screamed. The flames grew higher, flanking the demon like pillars. "SOON YOU, TOO,

WILL SERVE MY MASTER."

Jake stared at the burning heaps writhing on the floor and shook his head. "Never."

"YOUR ACTIONS HAVE ALREADY DETERMINED YOUR FATE. HELP ME NOW WITH THIS SMALL MATTER, AND I PROMISE TO SHOW YOU MERCY WHEN YOUR TIME COMES."

Jake stared into the demon's indecipherable eyes. "No."

Raising his right hand, Cain made a fist. Pain shot through Jake's chest and an invisible force ripped a four-inch-wide strip of flesh from his collarbone to his waist. Jake screamed in agony, tears burning his eyes, and twisted his body on the chains. His screams merged with those of Dread and Baldy, forming a twisted chorus. He looked down at the gaping wound in the left side of his torso, and within the cavity he saw his bloody ribs. The strip of flesh remained connected to his waist and hung down to his left knee, pink side out. He stopped screaming and his sweat-soaked body sagged, his own odor offending him. Managing to raise his head, he mustered a weak half smile.

"YOU ARE A GLUTTON FOR PUNISHMENT. MY MASTER WILL BE PLEASED TO TORMENT YOU."

Cain opened and closed his fist again, tearing a matching strip of flesh from the right side of Jake's torso. His scream lasted longer this time, and he gazed up at the ceiling fan as he pulled on the chains. He twisted his body, which wilted along with his scream.

"YOU DO NOT HAVE TO SUFFER LIKE THIS. I CAN MAKE THE PAIN GO AWAY. ALL YOU HAVE TO DO IS AGREE TO HELP ME."

Barely conscious, Jake smiled again. Preferring death to this agony, he opened his mouth and a weak laugh came out.

The glowing blood in Cain's veins darkened. He opened and closed his fist, and a third strip of flesh ripped from Jake's torso, exposing his rib cage. Jake howled, unable to withstand any more pain. Staring at his own insides, he closed his eyes and sobbed. Dread and Baldy stopped screaming, but the flames dancing from their bodies continued to crackle. Jake's chest constricted, and his sobs turned into chuckles. Focusing on the pinpricks of light in Cain's eye sockets, he laughed in the demon's terrible face.

Cain stood seething, then bounded across the cellar with frightening speed. Jake's eyes widened and he jerked on the chains. Cain halted before Jake and punched his fist through Jake's ribs, shattering them like dried twigs. Arching his body, Jake threw his head back in a scream that only he heard. He felt Cain's hand groping around inside his chest, then close powerful fingers around his heart. Jake lowered his head, afraid to move or even breathe. Cain pulled his hand from Jake's torso and pieces of shattered ribs fell away and struck the floor. Blood dripped from the demon's hand, which clutched

Jake's heart. Jake gasped; his heart continued to beat, its arteries stretching to his chest cavity like spiderwebs.

"For the last time . . . will you help me?"

Cain's breath reeked of dead, rotting flesh and Jake swallowed bile. Jake heard a giggling sound and realized that it was coming from deep inside him. It would have been a simple matter for him to release his grip on reality and slip into madness. Biting down on his lip, he snapped back into awareness and felt the pieces of his mind settling into place once more. He could not take his eyes off his beating heart, and his voice turned hoarse and raspy. "How do you know . . . Old Nick . . . even . . . has . . . those souls?"

"We have followed the activities of the man you call the Cipher with great interest. He will make a fine addition to our realm."

"He murdered my wife tonight."

"Tower is building an impressive collection."

"If I agree to get you into the Tower, will you agree to set Sheryl's soul free?"

Blue flashes danced through Cain's brain like lightning bolts. His features twisted into a hideous imitation of a grin. "Certainly."

Jake tried to swallow again, but his mouth had turned cottony. "Then you've got a deal. How long will you give me to do the job?"

"Time is of the essence."

"What's the hurry?"

"TOWER HAS ALREADY EXCEEDED HIS LIFESPAN WITH THE AID OF EXPERIMENTAL DRUGS AND REPLICATED ORGANS. MY MASTER HAS GROWN IMPATIENT."

"Twenty-four hours?"

"AGREED."

Jake sighed. He could avenge Sheryl's death and appease Cain at the same time. Cain squeezed his heart, and Jake's eyes and mouth opened wide as his body went spastic. The heart ruptured in Cain's hand, and blood squirted out between the demon's fingers. Jake sucked in his breath. The manacles around his wrists snapped open, and he fell to his knees on the floor. The cellar grew dark again, filled with the sounds of Jake's labored breathing and the rain landing on the floor around him. Cain had disappeared with his minions, but Clarence's tripod and instruments remained and the flames in the furnace continued to burn. Jake sat back on the balls of his feet, his chest intact and seamless. He no longer felt any pain except in his wrists, where the manacles had bitten into his flesh, and he massaged them. Had Cain restored him, or had the demon simply been screwing with his mind all along? The air remained thick with foul-smelling smoke, and scorch marks covered the sooty floor. Jake looked at his watch: 10:02.

Twenty-four hours.

Whether by accident or by design, he found himself kneeling in the position of prayer.

Pushing the heavy steel door open, Jake staggered out of the factory and into the pouring rain. He had pulled on the tattered remains of his shirt, and his shoulder holster held the fabric together beneath his jacket. His clothes reeked of sweat, urine, and smoke, and he stood in the rain for a full minute, allowing the cold water to rinse the stench from them.

Cain, he thought, shaking his head. He believed in science and evolution, not fairy tales conceived by men who had thought the earth was flat. *The largest sea vessel in the world couldn't have transported two specimens of every living species on Earth, and the only burning bush Moses ever saw was between his wife's legs.* But if he could accept ghosts and Soul Catchers, why not heaven and hell, and the masters of each domain?

The car that Dread and Baldy had commandeered

remained parked across the street like a refugee from a scrap-metal yard. Before he could approach it, a figure clad in filthy rags stepped directly in his path, causing him to jump and suck in his breath. A gnarled face filled his vision, water dripping off the wild-eyed man's nose and whiskers. Where had the man come from? He remembered seeing no one in the deserted area. The EDP stared at Jake, who expected him to mutter something about losing his soul.

"Spare some change?"

Releasing his breath, Jake fished out his wallet and gave the derelict a fifty dollar bill. He limped toward the abandoned vehicle across the street, opened the driver's side door, and got in. Rain assaulted the car. No keys dangled from the ignition.

Cursing, Jake glanced in the rearview mirror. A pair of feminine eyes stared back at him. Screaming, he twisted around in his seat and saw Sheryl sitting behind him.

"Jesus!" Jake clutched his chest and gasped for air. The car had been empty when he got into it.

Sheryl sat perfectly still, staring straight at him and yet taking no notice of his reaction. "Do you believe in true love?"

Sighing, he nodded. "You know I do."

"So do I. And I love you. It's important to me that you know that."

His heart ached. "I love you, too."

She looked around the car's grimy interior. The

rainwater running down the windows obscured the view outside. "It's so hard to remember who I am. I feel incomplete, like I'm not all here. I come and I go." She touched her throat and, finding nothing wrong with it, lowered her hand. "I work as a costume designer on independent films. What do you do?"

She had spoken those words to him when they first met. Was he speaking to a memory? His chest convulsed and he swallowed to keep steady. He needed to be strong for her sake. "I'm a cop."

This caught her attention. "Oh, good. Then you can help me."

"I'll do anything for you."

Leaning closer, tears filled her eyes. "I don't know where I am. They've locked me up in some tower. You've got to set me free!"

As the tears rolled down her cheeks, Jake reached out to caress one side of her face. "I will, I promise." And before he could stop himself, he touched her flesh and it was her turn to scream. She dissolved before his eyes and beams of light shot shone through the car windows into the rainy night. When she had left him again, he pounded on the steering wheel and wept.

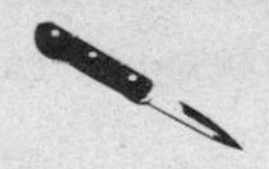

The rain had become a drizzle by the time Jake reached

the Tower, around 11:20 p.m. Two muscle-bound security guards stood in the private lobby, one Mediterranean-looking, the other Asian. Both men looked at Jake with suspicion as he approached the security station, his wet shoes squeaking on the gleaming floor, which showed no sign of Cain's attack that morning.

"Can I help you, sir?" the Mediterranean-looking man said. His badge identified him as Tataopoulis, Peter.

"I'm Helman."

Both men snapped to attention, but Tataopoulis said, "Uh, we still need to see your ID."

Jake took out his security card and held it out for Tatapoulis to read.

"Good evening, Mr. Helman. This is David Chan, and I'm—"

"I don't care who you are. I'm not interested in getting to know you. You're short-timers, understand? If you're smart and you want to stay alive, you'll quit now."

Both men stood speechless. Jake boarded an elevator and rode it to the sixtieth floor, where Graham sat behind his station with a grim expression on his face.

"Welcome back," Graham said in a flat voice, staring at Jake's clothing.

How much did Graham know? Jake liked him, but he could not afford to trust anyone in the company. "Pulling a double?"

Graham nodded. "I had no choice. I had to stay until you got back."

You're lucky I showed up at all, Jake thought.

The doors to Kira's office opened and she stepped out, a conceited expression on her face. Conscious of the Glock in his holster, Jake felt his blood boiling with rage. Cain had called her a witch; Jake could think of better names. *You sanctioned the hit, didn't you?*

"Mr. Tower's waiting for you in his quarters," she said.

Restraining his fury, Jake gestured at his ruined suit. "Do you mind if I shower and change my clothes first?"

"He wants to see you now," she said without inflection.

What choice did he have? Jaw clenched, he approached her doors.

"You didn't take my calls or respond to my messages," she said, taunting him.

"I lost the cell phone in all the excitement this morning." He wanted to strangle her with his bare hands.

They entered her office and she closed the doors. "Where's my security card?"

"I must have lost that, too."

"You'll find Nicholas is in the Soul Chamber's viewing room." She held out her hand and waited.

Staring into her eyes, he drew his Glock from its holster. It took every ounce of restraint he possessed to keep from pulling the trigger and blowing off her head. He placed the gun in her palm.

Kira arched one eyebrow. "Is there something you

want to say to me?"

"Not now," Jake said. "Later."

"Any time," she said, feigning sweetness.

Tower stood at the viewing room window as Jake approached him. The old man wore his security outfit again. Jake stopped midway to the window, a look of wonder spreading over his features. Inside the Soul Chamber, thirteen spheres of concentrated light streaked through the air in different directions, ricocheting off the walls. Each one the size of a bowling ball, they radiated different colors at alternating speeds, possibly communicating with each other. Halos of gold and silver reflected off the viewing window and Jake's heart fluttered. He had never seen anything so beautiful in his life, and he sensed the spheres' desperation to escape from their prison.

Souls.

Tower saw Jake's reflection in the glass. "You see them now, don't you, Jake?"

Jake nodded. After the horrors of the preceding twenty-four hours, he felt moved by the sight of the spheres, and his eyes filled with tears. "Yes," he said, choking up. *Sheryl's here. Which one is she?*

"A little faith makes all the difference in the world."

The intensity of the colors radiating from the spheres

softened as Jake moved closer to the glass. He felt connected to the Cipher's victims.

Tower turned to him and Jake saw that the bandage had been removed from the old man's rejuvenated left eye. "Sheryl's in there now. Do you understand what that means? I own your wife's soul. That makes me the most important man in your life, and the most important man in her afterlife. Fulfill your commitment to me and in time I'll free her."

Jake stared at Tower. He did not wish to discuss Sheryl with him. If he did, he might end up beating the old man to death. "I see your eye is better."

Tower grinned. "Like new."

"What are your plans for them?" He nodded at the chamber.

Tower's smile turned guarded. "You don't need to know that."

Jake's eyes followed the trajectories of the spheres. He found it impossible to identify Sheryl's energy.

"It was irresponsible of you to run out at the first sign of trouble like that," Tower said. "Graham had to dispose of those bodies all by himself. You didn't make a very good impression."

Jake pictured Laddock and Birch without their heads. "How will you explain their disappearances?"

"We've doctored security footage to prove that they left the building at the end of their shift. Why they never returned to work is beyond our understanding. We'll probably implicate the ACCL and RAGE."

Jake noticed a briefcase on the floor, beneath a hatch in the wall. *That's how they put them in there. How I'll let them out.* "It's no coincidence that you hired me for this job, is it?"

"I was impressed with how you handled yourself in that shoot-out. After all, nothing succeeds like excess. But I was more than a little intrigued when I learned that you were also one of the detectives hunting my Soul Catcher. When Kira told me of your resignation, I couldn't resist the temptation."

"This is some kind of game to you, isn't it?"

"I take my business very seriously, and my security needs are genuine. I'm afraid of dying, whether at the hands of those chromophobes or that demon."

"The Grim Reaper. Does he drop by often?" Jake suspected that Tower did not know the Reaper's true identity, which he had no intention of revealing.

"He's made several assaults on the building, but this is the first time he ever made it through the lobby, and the first time he's killed any of my employees."

"So what are we doing about it?"

"I know that security is your domain, but we employ rather unique methods where the Reaper is concerned, and Ms. Thorn has increased them. I anticipate no more trouble from the Reaper in the immediate future."

That's what you think, Jake thought, touching the viewing window with one hand. He could have summoned Cain right then, but he had to deal with the Cipher first.

"You've kept me up late waiting for you, and I'm tired. Good night."

Turning away from the spheres, Jake left the viewing room, pausing to glance at the cylindrical machine hooked up to the wall. A mechanical breathing sound came from inside it.

Something is alive in there.

Jake took a long, hot shower in his unit, images flashing through his mind: Sheryl standing in line outside the Film Forum; standing at the altar in her wedding gown; and lying in bed with a relaxed smile on her face after they had made love. He remembered her scent, her voice, her touch. Breaking down in tears, he slid down the porcelain wall to the tub. After composing himself, he shut off the water, changed his clothes, and fixed a frozen dinner in the microwave. Devouring the meal, he checked his personal cell phone for messages. Just as he'd expected, Edgar had called. Sighing, he turned on the CD player and pressed an auto-dial button as a Tom Waits song drifted over the speakers.

"Detective Hopkins," Edgar said halfway through the second ring.

"It's me," Jake said over the rock music.

"Where the hell are you?"

Jake looked around his unit. "I'd rather not say."

"You had no business taking off like that. You're in a shitload of trouble, buddy."

"I couldn't help it. There was no way I could stay in that apartment."

"You're in a bar, aren't you?"

Bingo. "Can you blame me?"

"Tell me where you are and I'll join you."

"Thanks, but I need to be alone right now."

"It doesn't work like that. I have to bring you in for questioning."

"It's after midnight, and I'm not exactly in the mood. I'll come in tomorrow morning at nine."

Edgar sighed. "All right. I hate to put you through this at all, but it's got to be done. Don't be late."

Jake massaged the bridge of his nose. "Where in the park did it happen?"

"Under that viaduct near Gracie Mansion."

Jake knew the viaduct well. "Thanks." Switching off the cell phone, he booted his computer. He keyed in several entries without success: *Cipher, Soul Catcher, Soul Searchers, Reaper, Grim Reaper,* and *Cain.* On a security monitor he saw Kira emerge from her office and speak to Cutler, who had relieved Graham in the security bay. She summoned an elevator and boarded it.

I still have her security card, he reminded himself. Glancing at the row of jewel cases on the shelf next to his computer monitor, he removed one and opened it. A blank disc gleamed inside the case. Rising from his chair, he hurried to the front door and opened it, scanning the empty corridor. He closed his door behind him, tiptoed to Kira's unit, and waved her card at the scanner on her door. He expected her to have changed her code, but the door unlocked and he slipped inside her lair for the first time.

It had stopped raining outside and enough moonlight shone through the raised blinds in the living room for Jake to see that the units shared identical floor plans despite Kira's position in the company. He took a flashlight he had found in his unit from his back pocket. After his experience in the subway tunnel, he never intended go anywhere without one again. The narrow beam pierced the darkness as he crossed the floor to the computer and sat down. He touched the mouse and jumped when the computer screen lit up. It had only been in "sleep" mode, and Kira had left her password logged on.

Beautiful.

He clicked the flashlight off and slid it back into his pocket, then glanced up at the security monitors: Cutler sat alone in the security bay. Jake accessed the personnel files on the computer. First, he checked his own. He raised his eyebrows at the sight of photos of him and Sheryl, and a detailed summary of his police record—quite a bit more information than his official file contained. He found no files for Kira or Tower, but he discovered one for Russel. Removing the blank CD from its jewel case, he inserted it into the burner and downloaded the file. He went to the menu and clicked on "Documents," where he found a file labeled "Project Afterlife." He downloaded that, too, but the large file took longer.

Glancing at the security monitors, he froze as Kira stepped off the elevator. Turning right, she entered the utility corridor. She must have been heading to the Control Room or the conference room.

Jake's fingers danced over the keyboard. He tried searching for some of the same keywords he had used on his own computer, with no results. Then he tried "Biogenetic" and a file opened. He sat staring at an assortment of horrifying, photo-realistic images: monsters of different shapes, sizes, and configurations; creatures with tentacles, fish lips, and scorpion stingers; beasts covered with fur, scales, and translucent membranes; things that walked, crawled, and swam. Had the company actually produced prototypes of these abominations? He recognized the creature from the globe in the Demonstration Room and clicked on its image. The screen filled with multiple angles of technical schematics of the creature, as if it were a machine instead of a living thing. The text appeared in white, over a blue background. He scanned the data, but the terminology proved too scientific for him to decipher. He scrolled down and his eyes settled on a bullet hit near the bottom of the screen: "HYGROSCOPIC SUSCEPTIBILITY—SODIUM." He mouthed the words as he read them. Closing the page, he downloaded the file.

Then he entered "Soul Catcher" and a new file opened up. The screen displayed three images of a man in his mid- to late twenties. Each photo looked different, yet they all resembled the police sketch of the Cipher. White text appeared beneath the photos, over a black background. The document included numerous medical records.

Jackpot, he thought. He tried to download the file, but an on-screen prompt informed him that his disc had run out of memory—the "Afterlife" file had been even larger than he had thought. He pressed the PRINT SCREEN button on the keyboard and removed the CD from the computer as pages unfurled into the tray of the laser printer. He put the CD back into its jewel case, his eyes rising to the monitors again. Kira had returned to the security bay, carrying one of the industrial drums he had seen in the back of the Demonstration Room. He waited to see if she would go to her office or her unit. She headed toward the glass door accessing the residential corridor.

Damn it! Only ten out of eighteen pages had emerged from the high speed printer. He counted off the seconds as two more pages slid into the tray. Kira should have been halfway down the corridor, and six pages remained to be printed. He gathered the pages that had printed so far and rolled them up as her shadow fell over the floor on the other side of the door. He switched off the monitor so the work area turned dark again. The scanner outside the door beeped as Kira manually entered her personal code into the keypad. Three pages remained to be printed.

Out of time!

He snatched another page and sprinted toward the closet door perpendicular to the front door. Behind him, another page slid into the tray.

The front doorknob turned.

He only managed to open the closet door halfway, just enough so that it would not bump against the front door. Turning sideways, he slipped into the closet, which smelled like a leather store. Falling against long black coats, he crouched among shoes and boots and pulled the door shut three-quarters of the way. A ray of light from the corridor slashed the darkness, and Kira's shadow stretched on the floor before him. He held his breath, sweat beading on his brows. Had she heard anything?

The overhead light came on and Kira's shadow vanished. Jake's heart nearly burst as the last page of the document slid into the tray. Kira passed the closet, oblivious to his presence. Thank God she had not gone outside, or she might have had a coat to hang up. The drum had a metal handle, like a can of paint, and she carried it around the corner. A moment later, he heard bathwater running.

What the hell—?

With the water running, he could slip out the front door without her hearing him. But that would mean leaving the pages in the printer tray and the Soul Catcher's file open on the computer. He pushed the door open and crept out of the closet, entering the lit unit. The living room's tasteful decor disappointed him; he had expected to see a broom and a cauldron, not an eclectic selection of artwork from around the world. He inched toward the computer station, which afforded him a view of the bathroom door; Kira had closed it except for a crack. Snatching the remaining pages from the tray, he switched the monitor back on and closed the file and the personnel program. He only hoped that the computer would go back to sleep before Kira emerged from the bathroom. As he turned from the station, his eyes settled on the bathroom door and curiosity arose in him.

Why had Kira taken the drum into the bathroom?

He crept down the hallway, grateful that the carpeting and running water covered any sounds he made, the jewel case clutched in his left hand and the Cipher's file in his right. If Kira opened the door, he would be unable to hide. Through the crack in the door, he saw her reflection in the vanity mirror, steam rising around her. She stripped off her bra and panties, but her sculpted body stirred no reaction in him. He didn't want to screw her; he wanted to kill her for the role she'd played in Sheryl's murder. She opened the medicine cabinet and he ducked back as the mirror swung in his direction. When he heard the cabinet latch shut, he returned to his peeping spot. Kira now held something that resembled a metal tong in her right hand.

She bent over, below his view, and he heard her pry off the drum's lid. Then he heard sloshing water, accompanied by vicious hissing. Kira stood up, the tong clutching a Biogen from the Demonstration Room. The foot-and-a-half-long creature hissed at her, its teeth slick with anticipatory slime, its bulbous red eyes blazing with hunger. Its body twitched like a powerful snake, curling around Kira's wrist in an effort to force her to release it.

Kira shushed the creature and stroked the top of its head with one finger. It snapped its jaws at her and she slid her hand behind its head. Its body released her wrist, its movements less violent, and it curled itself into concentric rings around her left breast, obscuring her nipple.

"That's better," she said with a smile.

Jake's stomach churned. Kira stepped over the edge of the tub, her foot slicing through the steaming water. She dipped out of view and he heard her settle into the bath. Crouching lower, he peered through the keyhole. Kira lay in the tub, her head against the tiled wall and her knees visible above the tub's edge. She held the tong between her legs. Jake could not see her hands or the Biogen, but he heard thrashing in the water. When Kira closed her eyes and moaned, he recognized the sound all too well. Clamping one hand over his mouth, he tasted bile climbing up the back of his throat. He staggered backward and fled the unit, crumpling the documents in his hand.

Jake awoke with a fever and a sore throat before his alarm went off at 7:30 a.m. He popped two aspirins and gargled with a glass of saltwater. After his shower he dressed in sneakers, blue jeans, and a black sweater. He checked local online news sites: Sheryl's murder had made the headlines, which announced that the Cipher had struck again. He concealed his Glock inside his three-quarter-length leather coat.

Back in black.

Graham looked up from his security station when Jake entered the security bay at 8:30.

"I'm taking a personal day," Jake said, turning in the walkie-talkie that Graham had given him upon leaving the Soul Chamber the previous night.

Looking surprised, Graham set the walkie-talkie into its charger. "Does Ms. Thorn know that?"

"There was a death in my family. According to the HR book, I'm entitled to a week's bereavement, but I'll be back this evening. If she wants to scold me, she can do it then."

Graham's eyes showed suspicious concern. "I'm sorry to hear that."

"Thank you. I need to check something in the Control Room before I leave."

Graham nodded. "Whatever you say."

When Jake stepped off the elevator in the private lobby, Tataopoulis and Chan looked at him with apprehension in their eyes.

"Good morning, Mr. Helman," Tataopoulis said.

"Still here, huh?"

"Mr. Graham's got us working nine-to-nine today," Chan said.

"Nine o'clock, huh? I guess you'll live."

They both looked relieved to hear him say so. Jake glanced at the front doors. Outside, the Soul Searchers stood staring up at the Tower.

"What the hell do they want?" Tatopoulis said.

"Don't worry," Jake said. "They're harmless enough and they'll leave soon."

"I don't like the way that one keeps looking at me,"

Chan said, nodding at Shannon.

"She's a handful," Jake said, retrieving a nightstick from beneath the security station. "If any of them get in here, use this." He slapped the stick down in the palm of his other hand. "That will get rid of 'em." He laid the stick across the top of the counter so they wouldn't forget it. Crossing the lobby to the front doors, he made eye contact with Shannon, who glared at him.

He heard Tataopoulis whisper to Chan, "Can you believe this guy? What a hard-ass."

Jake pushed a glass door open and stepped outside. Gray clouds loomed overhead. Shannon detached herself from the group and circled him like an animal.

"How are you?" Jake said under his breath. *As a Murder Police, I used to speak for the dead; now I speak to them.*

Shannon took a step back at the sound of his voice. "I need to find my soul."

"So do I," he said. As he turned around, another figure stepped before him: Sheryl. His heart skipped a beat and he stared into her eyes, waiting for her to speak. The windows to the soul.

At last she said, "I need my soul."

His heart sank.

"Mister—?"

Stepping around her, he hurried away with his back turned.

"I need my soul!"

Police vehicles lined the curb outside the Detective Bureau Manhattan on East Thirty-third Street. Jake's palms turned moist as he pulled the wooden door open and mounted the creaking, rubber-coated steps in the dark stairway. He bowed his head, hoping that neither of the uniformed officers descending would recognize him. He had been in this building day after day for three years, and now he entered it as an outsider. Stepping through the squad room's doorway, he pinpointed the locations of his former colleagues: Hoskins and Garcia stood at the watercooler; Kozey and Gardner sat speaking to L.T. in his office; Butler disappeared into the men's room with the morning papers; and Edgar sat at his desk, speaking on the phone and scribbling notes in a pad, his jacket draped over the back of his chair and his sleeves rolled up.

Jake saw copies of the police sketch of the Cipher everywhere. He approached his old desk, now covered with colorful knickknacks, framed photographs of what appeared to be a very large Hispanic family, and a nameplate that said DETECTIVE MARIA VASQUEZ. A brown leather jacket hung over the back of his former chair. Looking up at him, Edgar cut his call short and stood up. They embraced like brothers.

"I'm so sorry," Edgar said.

Closing his eyes, Jake felt his chest contract. Shut it

down, he told himself as they parted. The other detectives joined them, and one by one they shook Jake's hand and offered their condolences. Lieutenant Mauceri emerged from his office.

"I'm sorry about Sheryl, Jake."

"Thanks, L.T."

"We're doing everything we can."

Jake said nothing.

"If you need anyone to talk to, my door is still open for you."

"I appreciate that."

Mauceri returned to his office and closed his door.

Exactly, Jake thought. "Let's get this over with," he said to Edgar.

"Do you mind if we do this in the box?"

"No, let's go by the book." Jake preferred to be interviewed without an audience. He and Edgar crossed the squad room together.

Edgar opened the door to the interview room and Jake stepped inside. After working at the Tower, the squad room seemed small and confined, and this room felt like a closet. A vertical hot water pipe broke up the horizontal pattern of the cinder blocks, and a pretty woman with curly brown hair sat waiting for them at the interview table, a notepad before her. Jake recognized Detective Maria Vasquez from some of the photos on his old desk. She appeared to be in her late twenties, too young to have earned her gold shield through achievement, and he guessed that the brass had promoted her to meet some departmental quota. Special Homicide had lacked female detectives when he had been on the Job, and he knew he would have found Vasquez's presence distracting.

A digital camcorder on a tripod overlooking the table reminded Jake of Clarence's equipment in the boiler room. How many interviews had he conducted in this very room, and how many meals had he and Edgar consumed here? Too many to count. He approached the table as Edgar closed the door behind them, and Vasquez offered him a sympathetic smile.

"I'm Detective Vasquez."

"My replacement." Jake sat on the opposite side of the table for the first time.

"I'm sorry for your loss." She wore a purple sweater with a gold crucifix hanging from a chain around her neck.

Like Shannon, Jake thought, still feeling feverish. "Thank you."

"I'll try to make this as fast as I can."

Edgar sat beside Vasquez. "Why don't you take off your coat and stay a while?" he said to Jake.

Jake removed his coat, careful to keep his Glock hidden. He would have left the weapon back in his unit, but he feared that if he returned to retrieve it, Kira would find some excuse to prevent him from leaving again. And he had things to do.

Edgar folded his hands before him on the table. "Since I knew Sheryl, L.T. felt it would be better for

Maria to be the Primary on this. I agreed because I want to be as involved as possible, and if I'd refused, the case would have been assigned to another team."

Jake studied Vasquez. She had green eyes and honey-colored skin, unusual for a Latina. "Congratulations. Primary on your first big homicide case." *At Sheryl's expense.*

"Do you mind if we record this?" Vasquez said, ignoring his retort.

Without a lawyer present? "Go ahead." He wanted to appear cooperative.

Vasquez stood and switched on the camcorder. After checking the focus, she sat down again. "This is a preliminary interview with Helman, Jake; husband of Helman, Sheryl; homicide case number 77610. Attending detectives are Hopkins, Edgar, Detective Second Grade, and Vasquez, Maria, Detective First Grade, Special Homicide Task Force, Detective Bureau Manhattan." She recited the date. "Until recently, the subject was a detective with this Task Force and served as Detective Hopkins's ex-partner. He is aware of his rights and has not requested an attorney."

Jake lit a cigarette, and as he blew smoke over the detectives' heads, he stared at the reflective window on the far wall. He knew that Mauceri stood on the other side of the two-way mirror, observing the session. *Sanctimonious little prick.*

Vasquez composed herself. "Mr. Helman—"

"Call me Jake, Maria."

"You resigned from this department on Monday, November first."

He stared at her, waiting for a question. *Never volunteer information.*

"Can you tell me why?"

Jake tapped his cigarette against the ashtray. "Personal reasons."

"You killed two men on that day, didn't you?"

That's a matter of opinion. "I killed two perps in self-defense. IAB ruled it a righteous shoot."

"And earlier that same Monday you assisted on the Shannon Reynolds case?"

"That's right. Edgar was the Primary and I was the Second."

"And you were the Primary on two other murders attributed to the Cipher, weren't you?"

Jake nodded. "Edgar and I worked Luther Bass and Miguel Jerez together."

"So you investigated half of the Cipher's first six murders?"

"Half of the first six that we know about." He took a drag on the cigarette.

"That makes you an expert on his modus operandi, wouldn't you say?"

Exhaling smoke, he shrugged. "If I'd been an expert, we wouldn't be sitting here now."

"You're currently unemployed?"

"No, I have a job."

Edgar raised his eyebrows and Vasquez said, "Would you mind telling me what that is?"

"Sure. I'm the new director of security at the Tower."

Edgar and Vasquez glanced at each other, unable to mask their surprise.

"Since when?" Edgar said.

"I started there on Thursday." Jake took two business cards out of his wallet and handed them to Vasquez. "That top one is mine. The bottom one belongs to my supervisor, Kira Thorn."

Edgar stroked the ends of his mustache. "Did you already have this gig lined up when you resigned?"

Let him think so. "I'm not allowed to comment on that. I signed a confidentiality agreement."

Vasquez passed the cards to Edgar. "Did you work yesterday?"

"Yes."

"What time did you get home?"

"Six o'clock." No need for them to know that he and Sheryl had just separated.

"Did you see anyone hanging around your building?"

Just those two guys I already killed. "No."

"Where were you between 7:00 p.m. and 9:00 p.m.?"

"I was still home between 1900 and 2100 hours."

"Did you and Sheryl have an argument?"

Had any of the neighbors reported yelling in the apartment? "No."

"Why would she go to the park during a rainstorm?"

"That park was her favorite place to think. I'm guessing the storm hadn't started yet."

Vasquez made a note in her pad. "What do you think was on her mind?"

He swallowed. *Don't let her get to you.* "I have no idea."

"When did she leave the apartment?"

"I don't know. I was asleep."

"When did you wake up?"

Jake considered his options. "A little before Edgar called, around 2045 hours."

While Vasquez consulted her notes, Jake looked at Edgar, who shrugged.

"What did you do after he called?"

A tear formed in his eye and trickled down his cheek. He didn't care if they saw it. "I ran out of there as fast as I could."

"Why did you run? Did you do something wrong?"

Jake stabbed out his cigarette in the ashtray. "I didn't do anything wrong. I ran because I was upset, damn it. I'd just learned that my wife had been murdered and I had to get out of there."

She leaned forward. "Why not wait for Edgar and me to arrive?"

So she had seen Sheryl's corpse, too. "Because I didn't want to. I couldn't breathe."

"Where did you go?"

He sniffled and sighed. "To a bar."

"Which one?"

"I don't know, one I'd never been to before. It was pouring outside, and I was upset when I went in and tanked when I came out. Somewhere on the East Side, downtown from my apartment."

Her green eyes burrowed into him. "Where did you spend the night?"

"I crashed at my job." He knew that the security discs at the Tower could confirm this part of his story.

"Was Sheryl religious?"

So Vasquez shared his old theory about the Cipher's motive. *Good for her.* "She was Episcopalian—non-practicing."

"Is there anything else you can tell us that might help our investigation?"

"Unfortunately, no."

Vasquez stared at him, saying nothing. A prosecutor's trick: make the witness feel compelled to say something more, and usually he would.

Jack remained silent.

"This interview is concluded," Vasquez said, switching off the recorder.

Jake stood up. "Now what have you got for me?"

"You know we can't tell you anything at this stage," Vasquez said, removing a minidisc from the recorder.

He did know that, but he also knew that it would look suspicious if he didn't ask the question.

"The media publicized that you were after the Cipher

when you resigned," Edgar said, drawing a look of disapproval from Vasquez. "We're toying with the idea that he might have killed Sheryl to thumb his nose at the Department."

Jake turned to Vasquez. "Are you sure you don't think that an ex-cop killed his wife and tried to frame it on a serial killer?"

Vasquez blanched. "Your wife wasn't killed at home. The Cipher's other victims were."

"His other victims were alone."

"That's true," she said.

"Every possible theory has to be explored," Edgar said.

Jake pulled on his coat. "I wouldn't want it any other way. Did you toss my place?"

Edgar shrugged. "We had to. Your super locked up after we left."

Jake did not relish the idea of CSU going through his and Sheryl's belongings. "My work number is on that card and you know my cell." Edgar stood up and Jake raised one hand. "I know the way out."

Edgar offered his hand. "Let me know if I can help with anything, okay?"

Jake shook his hand. "Yeah, I'll be in touch." He winked at Vasquez. "You did fine." On his way out of the room, he gave the mirror a hard look.

Tower and Kira raced stationary bicycles in his private gymnasium. Digital projectors threw video footage of Central Park onto two wall screens before them, and digitally recorded bicyclists soared past them, encouraging them to pedal faster. Vents blew silent wind resistance at them, and counters in the left-hand corner of each screen tracked their speed, energy output, and calorie burn. Tower wore an expensive designer sweat suit and Kira wore form-fitting bicycle pants and a muscle shirt. Safety helmets completed the illusion.

"What time is your meeting with Seguera's people?" Tower said, feeling winded.

"Three o'clock." Kira pedaled faster and the images on her screen sped up.

"I want that contract signed," Tower said, trying to catch up to her.

"You'll have it."

"How does it feel to be this close to true power?"

She smiled, her legs pumping like pistons. "Stimulating."

He wiped sweat from his forehead on the back of one hand. "We have enough souls. Terminate the Catcher before he gets us into trouble."

"Done."

"You did a good job with him."

"Thank you."

"You know, when I was your age—" Tower stopped pedaling, a confused expression on his face. Then he clutched his chest and moaned. Kira twisted around on her seat as he toppled over.

"Nicholas!" Leaping from her bike, she tore off her helmet and threw it aside as she ran over to him. Kneeling beside him on the exercise mat, she rolled him over so that he faced the ceiling.

He looked dead.

"No!" Pinching his nose with her fingers, she leaned over and administered mouth-to-mouth resuscitation. She breathed into his mouth three times, then massaged his chest and repeated her actions.

After a minute of this, the old man coughed and looked at her with frightened eyes. He whispered something inaudible, and she flipped her hair back and pressed her right ear against his quivering lips.

"Soon . . ."

29

Jake parked his rental car, a black Jetta, on West Seventy-sixth Street, near West End Avenue, opposite the address listed in the Soul Catcher's file. Pulling on a knit ski cap and a pair of shades, he got out and plied the parking meter with quarters. He crossed the street, mounted the front steps of the granite building, and entered its vestibule. Scanning the apartment directory, he found what he wanted: Gorman, Marc, 609.

He studied the lobby: no doorman or security cameras, a welcome change. Returning to the Jetta, he checked out the other cars parked along the street. Sliding behind the wheel, he took out his cell phone and entered the number from Gorman's file.

On the third ring, a man with a remote-sounding voice answered. "Hello?"

Jake felt a chill, then a rush of anger. He shut the cell

phone off.

You motherfucker.

He glanced at his watch: 11:20 a.m. Just over ten hours remained before his rendezvous with the Reaper. He studied the building, his eyes settling on the sixth floor. After six months, he knew the Cipher's identity and location. He sat back in stakeout mode, popping a throat lozenge into his mouth and waiting.

The hydraulic lift lowered the platform into the life support unit. Standing on the platform, Kira clasped Tower's hand as the old man lay on his king-sized bed, eyes closed. Beneath the oxygen mask attached to his face, his lips trembled.

A tall man with thinning hair and a pensive expression stood waiting below them. He wore an expensive-looking suit with a stethoscope around his neck. A uniformed nurse stood beside him.

"Hurry," Kira said as the platform settled.

Dr. Kenneth Gavin stepped onto the platform. He examined Tower's eyes and checked his pulse, then unzipped the old man's sweat jacket and placed the stethoscope over his heart. While he listened to the heartbeat, the nurse wheeled medical equipment closer to the platform. Gavin's expression turned grave, and he spread the flaps of the sweat jacket apart, exposing the Anting-Anting in a nest of white hair on Tower's chest.

"Hook him up to the EKG," he told the nurse as he reached for the amulet.

"Leave that alone," Kira said.

Raising his eyebrows, Gavin left the amulet alone. The nurse affixed six sensors to Tower's chest in a circular pattern. Gavin helped her attach plastic clips to the sensors. The wires at the ends of the clips ran to the EKG machine, and he studied Tower's biorythms on a monitor.

"He needs to be airlifted to a hospital immediately," Gavin said.

"There's nothing in a hospital that Nicholas can't get right here," Kira said. "We've spent a fortune on your toys, Doctor. Now you can play with them."

"Mr. Tower's suffered a minor heart attack. That term is an oxymoron. He could recover completely or he could suffer another attack, which could cause even greater damage to his heart. We have the equipment here to monitor his condition, but we don't have the personnel to give him the care that he needs."

Kira stared at him. "Your colleagues will be here within the hour, and they're each bringing a nurse."

"This is insane."

"Your objection's been noted, but Nicholas is staying here. So are you."

"I don't want this man's death on my conscience."

Kira chuckled. "Nobility in the medical profession?

I doubt it. You're just worried that your meal ticket is about to expire."

Ready to argue, Gavin bit his tongue.

"Don't worry." Kira smiled. "I'm sure he'll outlive us all."

A man in his midtwenties left the building and Jake tilted his head forward, peering over the top of his sunglasses. After sitting in the Jetta for two hours, his back felt stiff. The man wore glasses and a dark gray coat over khaki slacks, his short dark hair parted at the side. He had a slender build and a delicate face. Jake studied the copy of the police sketch and the photos from Gorman's file, all of which he had taped to the dashboard, comparing them to the man heading up the block. Perp Fever spread through him, and he knew that he had found Sheryl's killer.

As Gorman rounded the far corner, Jake called upstairs again. No one answered. He got out of the car and locked the doors with a remote control.

How much time did he have?

He had no idea. Gorman could have stepped out for a newspaper, or he might be gone for hours. Jake loaded more quarters into the parking meter and crossed the street. He did not want a parking ticket to put him at this location on this particular afternoon. The wind picked up and he shivered.

Stepping into the vestibule once more, he took a pair of latex gloves from one pocket and pulled them on. For a moment, he felt like a cop again. Then he removed the lock-picking kit that he had borrowed from the Control Room and unlocked the front door within seconds. Sliding the kit back into his pocket, he crossed the lobby's checkered floor, his footsteps echoing. He boarded an old-fashioned elevator, which smelled like Chinese food, and pressed the sixth floor button. As the elevator rumbled upward, he took several deep breaths.

I might go to prison for this, he thought. *But that doesn't matter.*

He emerged into a long corridor lined with apartment doors, and stood still for a full minute, listening for sounds. Convinced that no tenants were about to exit their apartments, he crept toward the door marked 609. The sudden bark of a large-sounding dog on the other side of a door made him jump and reach for his Glock, but he relaxed as the unseen animal pawed at the metal separating them. Again he waited, and when no one shouted at the dog to be quiet, he proceeded.

Using a precision tool from the lock-picking kit, he undid both locks on Gorman's door, a turnkey and a dead bolt, and entered the warm apartment. As he closed the door behind him, a keypad on the wall to his right emitted an electronic whine, a red light on its face flashing. Returning the kit to his pocket, he keyed in the code listed in Gorman's file, disarming the device. If Gorman came home, he would know that someone had broken into the apartment, so Jake rearmed the alarm with the same code.

He unsnapped his coat, leaving the cap on his head to ensure that he left no stray hairs behind. At the far side of the deep living room, sunlight shone through tall windows with raised blinds. Jake crossed the room, his footsteps muffled by the carpet, and entered a white kitchen. Bracing himself, he opened the refrigerator and gazed at its contents: skim milk, orange juice, vegetables. No decapitated heads or severed limbs. He tried the upper freezer and found nothing but low-fat frozen dinners. Gorman worried about his figure. Closing the door, Jake searched the rest of the apartment.

He switched on the overhead light in the bedroom, a white room with basic luxuries that lacked personality. A packet of photographic printing paper lay on a computer desk, next to a monitor. If Gorman was a photographer, he had not put any of his work on display. Jake went through the drawers and tossed the mattress without any results.

Then he opened the closet door, squinting at the coffin-like space. Two separate rods, one above the other, displayed clothes on hangers. Sliding the hangers across the rods, he inspected the garments: a business suit; a security guard uniform; a priest's robes; surgical scrubs; a tuxedo; white kitchen garb; and a motorcycle outfit. On the floor of the closet, he spotted a black leather briefcase next to numerous shoes, sneakers, and boots. He picked up the briefcase and studied it. It looked identical to the one he had seen beneath the hatch in the Soul Chamber. Turning it over, he saw that no dust had accumulated on it. He shook the case and more than one object thudded inside it. The tabs had combination locks, but he lacked the patience to pick them.

Carrying the case into the living room, he set it down on the coffee table, then went into the kitchen and drew a long blade from a wooden butcher's block on the counter. He returned with the knife and sat on the sofa. Puncturing the surface of the briefcase with the tip of the knife, he carved an *X* into its lid from corner to corner. He set the knife down and tore the case apart with his hands, shredding cardboard. Turning the case upside down and shaking it, he dumped its contents atop the table. He felt along the inside of the case, making sure he had emptied it, then tossed it aside.

He examined an open package of latex gloves. Gorman had also been careful not to leave evidence behind at crime scenes. A digital camera fit in the palm of his hand. Next he picked up a stack of digital photo prints attached to a metal ring, a collection of photographs. His hand shook as he flipped through the shots. He did not know the identities of the people in the first six photos, but he had seen them as Soul Searchers outside the Tower. Each victim stood alone in a dark setting and each wore a terrified expression. These were Gorman's souvenirs, his keepsakes, the missing ingredients that he and Edgar had been unable to discover. The Cipher caught the souls of his victims for Old Nick, but he stole the images of their final moments for himself.

The remaining photographs showed people whose identities and apartments he knew: Abigail Williams, Luther Bass, Sung Yee, Miguel Jerez, Rachel Rosenthal, and Shannon Reynolds. The sense of dread he felt increased to an unbearable level as he reached the last image. But there was no photo of Sheryl.

That can't be, he thought. Then he shifted his eyes to the camera and picked it up again. He turned on the camera's power and its LCD screen lit up. Switching the screen to VIEW, he pressed an arrow button below the screen. Sheryl stared back at him. She stood petrified beneath the viaduct in Carl Schurz Park, wearing her black raincoat with her purse slung over her right shoulder. Jake saw the fear in her eyes. Why hadn't she used the pepper spray he had given her? A teardrop splashed the screen.

Stop it! There would be time to grieve later, he hoped. He switched off the power, reached into his coat pocket, took out a tissue, and wiped the tear from the screen. Then he carried the camera into the kitchen, where he opened the cupboard beneath the sink, removed a bottle of cleaning solution, and sprayed the back of the camera. He wiped the photo with a fresh tissue, stuck both tissues back into his pocket, put the cleaning solution away, and returned to the living room. He did not want to leave behind any genetic evidence of his visit; Edgar Hopkins had proven himself to be a very thorough Homicide detective.

Sitting on the sofa, Jake examined a bag of cleaning rags. Then he picked up a long knife and raised its deadly blade to the light. Rotating it with his fingers, he saw no trace of blood. Still, he knew that the Cipher had used this knife to kill Sheryl. He set it down and picked up the final item, a strange-looking oxygen mask with a clear vinyl bag attached to it. A twist-valve separated the mask from the bag.

He laid the items out across the table, forming a literal chain of evidence, and looked at his watch: 2:05. He had been inside the apartment for forty-five minutes. Leaning back against the sofa, he faced a flat screen TV mounted on the wall. The same model he had in his unit back at the Tower. He reached inside his coat and removed his Glock and a black metal cylinder. Screwing the silencer into the barrel of the gun, he stared at his reflection in the dark face of the TV.

Tower remained unconscious, but his breathing had returned to normal with the aid of additional oxygen. He wore a hospital gown, and a blanket had been pulled up over the lower half of his body. Kira stood beside him on the platform, surrounded by Gavin, two other doctors, and three nurses. An IV bottle fed a solution into his arm, and several pieces of medical equipment had been stacked on top of the platform.

"He's stabilized," Dr. Jonas said in a Haitian accent. The tall black man wore thick-rimmed glasses.

"He's in remarkable condition for a man his age," Dr. Maloski observed, the island of scalp on the crown of his head as pink as his cheeks.

Gavin said nothing, grateful to have someone else around to take Kira's heat.

"Yes, he is in remarkable condition," she said. "No thanks to you three wise men."

They stared at her with blank faces.

"When will he regain consciousness?"

Jonas shrugged. "'Where's Old—'" Catching himself in mid-speech, he changed his tone. "Who knows? But I don't recommend waking him. Rest is critical at this juncture."

"Is all of the equipment you need to care for him on the platform?"

Maloski nodded. "Yes, I believe so."

"Then I want him back in his room."

"I think that's a very bad idea," Gavin said. "If you won't let us transport him to a hospital, he should at least stay right where he is for the next twenty-four hours."

"I only want to raise the platform to the next level. You'll be observing him around the clock."

Before Gavin could argue his point further, a buzzer sounded and Kira pressed a button on an intercom mounted on the wall. "Yes?"

Graham's voice came out of the speaker: "Your guests have arrived."

"Have Russel show them to the conference room. I'll be right there."

"Copy that," Graham said.

Kira gestured to the doctors. "All aboard, gentlemen. This platform is going up."

The doctors looked down, making sure they stood on the platform.

"What about our nurses?" Jonas asked.

"We're going to a restricted area," Kira said. "There are three of you now. Surely one of you is capable of taking Nicholas's temperature?"

None of the doctors responded. Kira pressed a switch on the side of the bed and the hydraulic lift raised the platform toward the corresponding space in the ceiling. Looking displeased, Jonas kept silent. The platform raised into Tower's bedroom and came to a rest at its floor level. Kira stepped off the platform first as the doctors looked around the enormous room in wonder. A walk-in closet, sitting room, and bathroom extended from the walls facing the four-post bed in the enormous hexagonal-shaped room. An original Monet hung on one wall, overlooking a golden telephone.

"It's like Xanadu," Maloski said.

"You can take turns resting in the sitting room," Kira said, pointing at a set of double doors. "I have to attend a meeting now. While I'm gone, you'll be sealed inside this suite. If you need me, call Graham. I expect Mr. Tower to still be alive when I return."

Kira and Russel sat facing Fortaleza and Villanueva at the large conference room table as Fortaleza signed a stack of contracts. When he had finished, Kira separated the contracts into three shorter stacks and handed one stack to him.

"How soon can you begin production?" Fortaleza said.

"We need ten days to incorporate some new design elements that I'm sure you'll appreciate," Kira said. "After that, we can start producing seventy Biogens a week. You'll have your full order before Christmas."

"Excellent. You're positive shipping won't be a problem?"

Russel said, "Exportation has already been arranged."

Fortaleza smiled. "President Seguera will be most pleased."

Russel returned the smile. "That's what we're here for."

"Will it be possible for Mr. Villanueva and I to meet Mr. Tower before we return to our country?"

"I'm afraid not," Kira said. "Mr. Tower is feeling a little under the weather this afternoon."

"Nothing serious, I hope?"

She smiled. "Nothing that a little time won't cure."

Marc Gorman returned to his apartment at 4:30. Disarming the alarm, he switched on the living room's overhead light. He took off his coat and reached for the closet door. But as his fingers closed around the doorknob, the door burst open and he jumped back with a cry, dropping his coat on the floor. A man leaped out at him in a blur of motion, and the word cop flashed through Marc's mind. Before he had time to react, the intruder brought the grip of a handgun down on his head, sending waves of pain through his brain. The man stepped to one side of him and kicked him in the ribs, propelling him across the living room. Marc sprawled out on the floor, and his attacker shoved the barrel of a gun in his face.

"Get up," the man said.

Marc's glasses had fallen off, but he didn't really need

them. He had perfect vision. Looking up at his assailant, he recognized the man holding the gun. The man the Widow had warned him about when she had assigned him his last mission, the man she had called dangerous. The same man he had seen looking down from Sheryl Helman's apartment window shortly before Marc had killed her. Her husband. How had the cop learned his identity?

Gorman stared up at Jake with frightened eyes. Five pink lines striped his left cheek: fingernail scratches.

Good, Jake thought. Sheryl had given her attacker something to remember. "Get up."

Swallowing, Gorman got to his feet. He wore a short-sleeved polo shirt that revealed taut arms.

"Now turn around."

Gorman faced the windows, his back to Jake.

"Lower the blinds."

Gorman obeyed, darkening the room.

"Hands on your head."

Gorman folded his hands behind his head.

"Move into the kitchen."

Gorman hesitated.

Why did the cop want him to enter the kitchen? He kept nothing important there.

Helman shoved him with his left hand. *"Now."*

Marc moved forward, Helman close behind him. He heard the flip of a light switch and the overhead light came on, illuminating the ruptured remains of his briefcase on the counter by the stove.

"Turn around."

Stopping short of the counter, Marc turned. Helman gripped the gun in both hands now, aiming it at Marc's head.

"You're making a mistake," Marc said. "I've done nothing wrong."

"Bullshit. You've been a wrong number ever since you whacked your mother."

Shock spread through Marc's body, numbing his limbs. "What do you know about my mother?"

"I know that you strangled her with your bare hands."

Where had Helman gotten his information? "It was a mercy killing."

"Is that what you told yourself while you hacked her body to pieces and buried them under the swing set in your backyard?"

Marc said nothing. He had closed off the memories

of his mother's dismemberment years ago, at the Payne Institute. Now they came flooding back.

"You spent three years in an experimental institution owned by Tower International and now you're Old Nick's Soul Catcher."

Marc's eyes widened. Helman knew far too much about him. "I want a lawyer."

Helman shook his head. "You won't need one where you're going. But I bet there will be plenty of them there."

Marc stared at the gun's silencer, sweat forming on his brow. His left eye twitched.

"My name's Helman. Does that mean anything to you?"

Marc shook his head. "No. Should it?"

Releasing the gun with his left hand, Helman reached into his coat pocket and took out the oxygen mask with the vinyl bag attached to it. "Did you use this on my wife after you murdered her last night?"

A muscle leaped in Marc's cheek. "You have to arrest me."

Helman smiled, his expression remaining grim. "I'm not a cop. Not anymore, anyway. I turned in my badge days ago."

Shit, Marc thought. Why had the Widow put him in this situation?

"I work for Tower International now," Jake said. "Kira Thorn is my supervisor."

Gorman's jaw dropped open and he looked as if he had been slapped.

Good, Jake thought. He hurled the mask at Gorman's chest and it landed at his feet. Jake returned his left hand to the Glock's grip. "Pick it up."

Gorman stood frozen.

"I said, *pick it up.*"

Gorman crouched with his hands still locked behind his head.

"Just use one hand . . ."

Gorman removed his left hand from behind his head and picked up the bag. He stood, eyes on Jake.

"Breathe into it."

Gorman looked from the gun in Jake's hand to his eyes. Taking a deep breath, he held the oxygen mask over his mouth and nose and exhaled. The bag expanded with his expelled air, swelling like a small balloon. He inhaled and the bag deflated. He exhaled and it inflated again.

As Jake's finger tightened on the Glock's trigger, he noticed a spot of color on Gorman's neck, within the open collar of his shirt. An alarm went off in his head. "Put the bag down and take off your shirt."

Gorman stopped breathing, confusion clouding his

eyes. He removed the mask from his face and set it down on the counter behind him. He pulled his polo shirt over his head and dropped it onto the floor, then stood before Jake with his torso exposed.

Marc could not understand why the Widow had set him up, but there would be time to figure that out later. He would deal with her as he had his mother. But first he needed to teach this cashiered cop a lesson.

Jake felt the blood rushing from his head, and the muscles in his face twitched as outrage surged through him. Tattoos covered Gorman's shaved chest and a fresh bandage masked his left breast. The faces of the Soul Searchers stared back at him, perfect reproductions of the photos Gorman had taken before slaying them. Their terror had been woven into a tapestry of needlework and dyes, primarily black and green. Jake did not see Sheryl's face.

That's right, look at my body in awe. Look at the Needle Man's artwork in wonder. Gaze at the images of my handiwork. Fear my craft. I'll make you pay for hurting me. And then the Widow will be mine, body and soul.

"Take off that bandage," Jake said, his voice cracking.

Gorman did not move.

"Take off that goddamned bandage!"

Keeping his eyes on Helman, Marc felt along his chest for the bandage. Locating the edge of the white adhesive tape, he tore the bandage from his chest, revealing his most recent tattoo.

Sheryl had become part of Gorman's obscene collage, his blood visible on her features. Jake realized where Gorman had been for the last three hours: at a tattoo parlor. His hands shook and tears filled his eyes, obscuring his vision. His prey went out of focus.

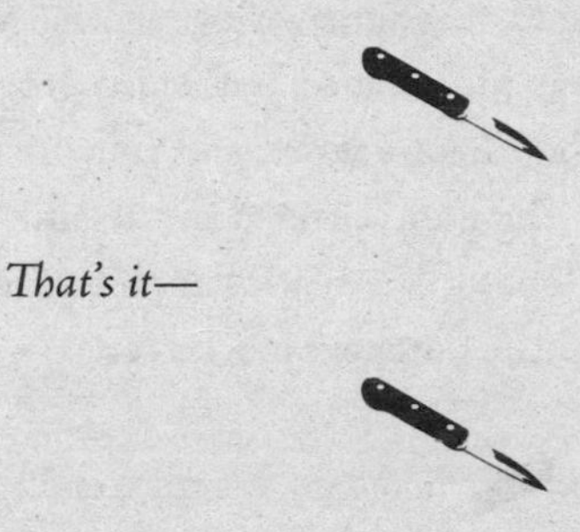

That's it—

Releasing the Glock with his left hand, Jake wiped the tears from his eyes. His right hand shook even more.

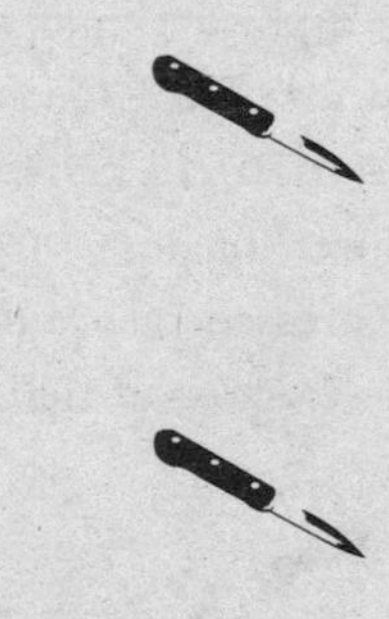

Now!

Feeling the floor shake, Jake saw Gorman charging at him, the briefcase in one hand. *No!*

Marc swung his briefcase at Helman's outstretched hand, knocking it aside, the gun firing at the wall. Helman tried to recover his balance, but Marc dropped the briefcase, seized the ex-cop's wrist, and smashed his hand on the counter. The gun clattered in the sink and Marc reached out for one of the black-handled kitchen knives protruding from the butcher's block . . .

Jake heard the sound of metal scraping wood, then saw Gorman swinging a paring knife with a four-inch blade at him in a decisive arc. He felt himself being jerked forward, and his eyes darted to the knife, buried to its hilt in the flap of his coat, over his heart. Opening the flap, he saw the knife's blade pressed flat against his sweater; it had missed his flesh by a fraction of an inch.

Marc jerked the knife straight up out of Helman's coat and plunged it down again. Face turning white, Helman raised his left hand in a defensive gesture.

Jake screamed as the short blade pierced his palm, then bit his lower lip as the metal emerged through the back of his hand. Pain blasted through his entire arm, and blood filled his latex glove.

Marc put both hands on the paring knife's handle and drove the blade into the wall like a nail, pinning Helman.

Blinding agony traveled Jake's body. He gritted his teeth, wide-eyed, as blood from his palm trickled around the blade and through the slashed glove. He thrashed from side to side, like a hooked fish, each movement increasing his pain. Gorman scooped up the oxygen mask with one hand and drew another knife from the butcher's block with the other: a carving knife with a long blade. With tears streaming down his face, Jake clutched the paring knife's handle and tried to pull the blade out of his hand. His pain doubled.

Sneering, Marc advanced on Helman. Too many emotions flowed through his mind: sadness, anger, betrayal.

Revenge.

He intended to watch Helman's life slip away as he had the others.

Jake pulled the knife free with a desperate cry, and blood spurted out of the hole in his hand. He swung the knife in a broad arc, forcing Gorman to step back.

Knife fight, he thought, glancing at his gun in the sink.

Marc swung the carving knife at Helman, its blade whistling through the air. It missed his quarry's face by inches. Rotating his wrist, he swung again, missing once more. To his surprise, Helman dropped the bloody carving knife on the floor.

Jake knew that he could not stab Gorman with a knife coated with his own blood because DNA tests would prove that he had been present at Gorman's death. Dropping the knife to the floor, he stepped so close to Gorman that the killer had no space in which to attack. Ignoring his pain—no, *feeding* on it—he closed his left hand around Gorman's right wrist and raised Gorman's arm at a forty-five-degree angle. Then he drove the flat of his right hand straight at Gorman's elbow, shattering it.

Dropping the carving knife, Marc screamed. He felt his legs being swept out from under him and he crashed to the floor with Helman on top of him, their faces only inches apart. He struggled to roll free of Helman's weight, but the pain in his broken arm proved too great. Then he saw Helman reach into the ruptured briefcase lying on the floor.

Jake drew Gorman's knife from the briefcase—

Not my sacrificial dagger!

—and drove it through one side of the killer's neck and out the other. Gorman's body quivered, his eyes widening. Rising to his feet with his hand still gripping the knife, Jake pulled the blade toward him, slicing through Gorman's throat, and hot blood gushed at him.

Baptize me, he thought.

Marc stared at Helman as his life flowed out of his open throat. His body tingled, hot liquid washing over him, and he could not move. Was this how his victims had felt? Turning away for a moment, Helman shoved the oxygen mask over Marc's face.

It doesn't matter. He doesn't know what he's doing. Doesn't know the incantation . . .

He tried to breathe, but failed.

My soul is safe.

Let's see how you like it, Jake thought as he held the oxygen mask over Gorman's face. *Give up the ghost.*

The plastic bag did not inflate.

He had killed the Cipher.

Standing tall, he looked at his Glock in the sink and the bullet hole in the wall. He'd have to dig the bullet out if he wanted to use the gun again. He looked at his blood-drenched clothes, and the spreading pool at his feet, then wrapped a dish towel around his injured hand.

He had a major cleanup ahead of him.

Darkness.

Floating, disembodied.

No tunnel of light.

Where's my mother?

A presence, bearing down on me.

Twin pinpricks of light stare at me like eyes.

A cold embrace envelops me.

I'm the Cipher!

Is that laughter?

The presence pulls me screaming toward an opening in starless space.

My soul . . .

The sky darkened as Jake crossed the street to the Jetta, his left hand bandaged with gauze he had found in the bathroom medicine cabinet. Holding his breath, he scanned the sidewalk for possible witnesses. At the east end of the block, a traffic cop in an orange rain slicker slipped a parking ticket beneath the windshield wiper of a blue Corvette. Jake unlocked the Jetta's doors with the remote control and slid behind the steering wheel. He closed the door and let out his breath, then jammed his keys into the ignition. He craved a cigarette, but he had to get away first. In the rear-view mirror, he saw the traffic cop making her way toward him, vehicle by vehicle.

I did it, he thought. *I killed the bastard who murdered Sheryl.* After three years of investigating premeditated homicides, he had committed one himself. *This wasn't murder,* he told himself. *It was an execution. Biblical justice.* He pulled into the street and proceeded to the west end of the block, careful not to exceed the speed limit. He stopped at the corner, his spine icing over as a police cruiser passed before him. His fingers tightened on the steering wheel, the pain in his left hand flaring up as blood seeped through the bandage.

As he drove through Central Park, his right leg shook on the gas pedal and the car sped up and slowed down. He followed Third Avenue, crowded at rush hour, to East End Avenue, where he parked the Jetta. As soon as he got out of the car, he lit a cigarette. The nicotine rush only made him shake more, and his knees wobbled as he crossed the street to Carl Schurz Park.

Tall gas lamps glowed as the sun set on the other side of the city. He passed a homeless man huddled on a bench and followed the winding, flagstone steps beneath rustling trees to the park's upper level. He flicked his cigarette at cement, then followed a narrow path to the viaduct near Gracie Mansion, where he had once worked a security detail. Torn crime scene tape fluttered in the wind as puddles of rainwater rippled. He entered the dark tunnel and looked around. The ground had been inspected and scrubbed, but bloodstains remained. He pictured Gorman's photo of Sheryl standing in this very spot, and he imagined her struggling with the Cipher, clawing at his face, her screams echoing.

Stop it.

The Cipher was dead; he had killed him.

But Sheryl was dead, too.

He thought he sensed her standing beside him, but when he turned around he faced empty air. His eyes teared up again.

Phantom pain.

Kira leaned over Tower, who appeared weak and frail, his breathing raspy. She removed the oxygen mask from his face and shook him with gentle fingers. His eyes fluttered open and she smiled down at him.

"What happened?" he asked in a strained voice.

"You've had a heart attack, but you're going to be fine."

He swallowed, pain etching his features. "Where are my damned doctors?"

"I sent them back down to Life Support so we could be alone. They were only getting in the way. It's all up to you now. How do you feel?"

"Helpless," he said in a whisper.

She touched his cheeks, then his forehead. "It's almost time. We can't wait much longer. You have to prepare yourself."

He gazed at her with unblinking eyes. "I'm frightened."

"I know you are."

"I don't want to die."

"You won't."

"You sound so sure."

"I am."

"Everything is so dark . . . so empty."

"Don't succumb to it. This is the most important deal of your life."

"I need strength . . ."

She smiled. "I know what you need." She removed a metal case from the bedside drawer, opened it, and withdrew a syringe and a tiny bottle of clear blue liquid labeled Deceleroxyn-21. She filled the syringe with the drug and squirted some out, expelling air bubbles. She waved the syringe at him with a seductive smile, then inserted the needle into his arm and pressed the plunger.

Old Nick shuddered and smiled.

Returning to the Jetta, Jake unlocked his door and sat behind the wheel. East End Avenue stretched before him, with the park on his left and tall condominiums on his right. Traffic had diminished. He glimpsed a flash of light in the windshield, as if an oncoming car had aimed its brights at him.

"Hello, Jake."

The voice came from beside him, inside the car. Jerking the door open, Jake exploded out of his seat. Pressed against the door with one foot on the street, he pulled his Glock from its holster and aimed it inside the car. A tall man with long, golden hair sat on the passenger side of the front seat. He wore a green- and tan-colored duster, and the brim of a white Stetson cowboy hat shaded his eyes.

The car was empty! Jake thought.

The stranger smiled, his teeth gleaming white. "Relax and get in. I'm not here to hurt you." His voice sounded like some musical instrument that Jake had never heard before, pure and soothing.

Jake gave him a skeptical look.

The man leaned across the seat, his features serene, and extended his right hand. "Try me." His voice echoed in Jake's brain.

Jake looked down at the hand before him, unadorned with jewelry. Shifting the Glock to his left hand, he grasped the stranger's hand. The man's skin felt soft and smooth, like an infant's.

"See? I didn't melt."

The man knew about the Soul Searchers. *Dread and Baldy didn't melt, either.*

"I'm no minion, thank you. Please get into the car. We have a lot to discuss in a short amount of time."

Jake scanned the neighborhood's deserted sidewalks, then eased into the front seat and closed the door. Gun still in hand, he faced his uninvited guest. "How did you get in here without me seeing you?"

The man removed his Stetson, and without the shade of its brim, his eyes glowed brilliant blue in the setting darkness. "I created a portal in my dimension that enabled me to materialize here. Does knowing that make you feel better?"

Twisting his body, Jake reached for the door handle again, but the man squeezed his shoulder and golden warmth spread through him like liquid sunshine. In that moment he felt calm and serene. Settling into his seat, he stared at his visitor with incredulous eyes. "Who are you?"

"Names are meaningless where I come from, but you can call me Abel."

Jake's heart skipped a beat. *No fucking way.* The world's first homicide victim. "I guess I met your brother yesterday."

Abel seemed unsurprised. "Flesh-and-blood relationships are irrelevant in the realms beyond this one."

Jake studied Abel's lips as they moved. The strange echo in his head preceded the spoken words by a split second. "You two don't exactly look alike. Different fathers?"

"Different energies." Intense white light emanated from within Abel, rendering his clothing invisible and his flesh transparent.

The light reminded Jake of the spheres in Tower's Soul Chamber, and the energy that had consumed Shannon and Sheryl. Shielding his eyes, he looked out his window. "That's a little conspicuous."

The shimmering light faded and a dark-skinned man with long black hair, a beard, and a mustache sat beside him, dressed in a white cloth resembling an oversized diaper. "How about this? We can shoot for historical accuracy."

Jake glanced around the outside of the car. "I wouldn't want to be pulled over with you looking like that, either."

In the blink of an eye, the blond cowboy had returned. "Whatever makes you comfortable."

Jake looked down at the white hat in Abel's hands. "So you're one of the good guys?"

Abel shrugged. "I like to think so."

"Are you my guardian angel?"

"More like an observer. In the Realm of Light, we take a strict vow of noninterference regarding this world."

Like the Federation on Star Trek, Jake thought.

"Exactly."

Jake's eyes widened. "You just read my mind!"

"Sorry, it's a habit. I didn't mean to invade your privacy." Abel looked out the windshield. "You have to return this car and report to the Tower."

Staring at Abel, Jake holstered his Glock, inserted the key into the ignition, and started the car's engine. "Your brother didn't read my mind. He tortured me to get what he wanted." Shifting the car into gear, he pulled out of the parking space. His left hand hurt too much to steer, so he rested it on his lap.

"My brother is the chief emissary for the Dark Realm. He's a being of negative energy, whereas I'm a being of positive energy. His abilities are limited by his lack of intellect and patience. He didn't read your thoughts because he's insensitive. He prefers torture and intimidation over understanding and negotiation."

Jake stopped at a red light. "He crushed the skulls of two of my men yesterday morning. That's not exactly my idea of noninterference."

"Those in the Dark Realm disregard the laws that we in the Realm of Light hold dear. But they have their own rules, and Cain can only claim souls that have already been tainted beyond repair."

Recalling the guards' military records, Jake made a left turn and steered the Jetta west, across town. "He said I'm going to hell. Does that mean he can claim my soul before I die?"

"It's his nature to lie. He just wanted to frighten you."

Just thinking about the industrial dungeon made Jake shudder. "He succeeded."

"The scales haven't tipped conclusively one way or the other regarding your ultimate destination, but your fate is questionable. That was nasty business you committed today, but there's still time to redeem yourself."

Jake shrugged. "'An eye for an eye', right? That's what the Old Testament preaches, anyway. The New Testament doesn't leave much room for justice."

Abel studied Jake. "Is justice important to you?"

"It's why I became a cop."

Abel aimed his eyes forward. "Gorman will spend

eternity in the Dark Realm. His suffering has already begun."

Jake considered this. "Good." He made another left turn and they circled the block. "So why are you honoring me with 'face time' when I'm knee-deep in all this shit? And why are you being so forthcoming with me? Right now I know more about the afterlife now than the pope does."

Abel spoke in a deliberate tone. "Every soul in the Realms of Light and Darkness began its journey here on Earth, which we call Eden. Think of yourself as a caterpillar waiting to evolve into a higher life form. The Realms have been at war since the creation of mankind. Each side's strength is determined by its energy level, or the number of souls that make it up. Since the dawn of man, the Light has held the Dark at bay. Now, a fierce battle is being fought that could turn the tide of the war in the Dark's favor."

"Sounds grim," Jake said.

"Apocalyptic, is more like it. The outcome of this battle may determine the fate of every soul in existence, on Earth and beyond. There's always been a delicate balance of power between the Realms, with the Light holding the edge. If that balance changes, the Dark will subject us all to eternal torment. The shift of power is occurring even as we speak, all because thirteen souls bound for the Realm of Light never reached their destination."

Jake gripped the steering wheel. "The Soul Chamber . . ."

"Tower's held some of these souls hostage for as long

as a year. They must be liberated. The potential for catastrophe increases with each passing hour. And you've just given the other side a new warrior."

A sick feeling grew in Jake's stomach. *The Cipher.* "So what are you doing about it?"

"The same defensive shield that prevents Cain from entering the Tower hinders my kind as well."

"Your brother wants me to get him into the Tower so that he can get his hands on the old man."

"The Dark needs reinforcements as badly as we do and Tower's soul is strong."

"When I break the spell for him, can you free all of those souls?"

"I already told you: we don't interfere."

Jake snorted. "It seems to me that the possible destruction of heaven warrants an exception to the rule."

"We must remain true to our ideals. If we weaken in our resolve, if we sell out our values, we'll be unable to withstand the onslaught of our enemies."

"Are you telling me that none of you higher-ups are 'positive' enough to sacrifice yourselves for the greater good? You're as hypocritical as some of the so-called holy men and political leaders in this world."

"And you're willing to damn your own soul by allying yourself with my brother to free Sheryl's soul."

"Some things are worth going to hell for."

"You'll only serve to strengthen the Dark."

"And you want me to serve you instead by doing your

dirty work."

"You wish to strike against Tower anyway."

Jake glanced sideways at the being. "Not if it means risking Sheryl's freedom."

"We're as concerned for her as you are. We just want you to realize that each of those souls is equally important in the grand scheme."

"And what are you offering me to risk my life?"

"Nothing. We don't barter. But you stand to lose as much as everyone else does. You just don't understand how severe your loss will be. In all likelihood, you'll be killed if you help us. But if you sacrifice yourself to free those souls, you might earn a place for yourself in the Realm of Light."

Jake pulled the Jetta over and double-parked it. "'Might?' That's it? If I die helping you, *I might get* a parking space on Cloud Nine, which may not even exist much longer? You're asking a lot."

"We have faith in you."

"Fat lot of good that will do me. I've been jammed up before, but this is the first time I've been caught between heaven and hell."

"That's what you think."

"No, this is what I think: if you can't help me, then I don't need you. And if I don't need you, I'm not risking my ass for your precious souls. I'm in this for Sheryl and Sheryl alone."

"Forgive me, but you don't know what you're saying."

"Oh, yes, I do. You're worthless to me, you understand? At least Cain offered me something in return for my trouble."

"He'll betray you. It's his nature."

"You're unbelievable, you know that? My mother died giving birth to me. My father blew his brains out. The aunt who raised me died from an 'accidental' overdose of antidepressants. The Cipher murdered Sheryl. Where were your people any of those times?"

"We've sworn—"

"I know, I know: 'a strict vow of noninterference.' What are you wasting my time for? I don't need this shit. I'll handle things my own way."

Abel stared at him. "If you don't mind my saying so, that hasn't worked out very well for you in the past."

"I've gotten smarter. Get out of the car."

Abel put on his Stetson and offered a friendly smile. "Good luck."

"Enjoy the show." Jake felt a warm tingling sensation in his head, and Abel disappeared without a trace, as if he had never been there.

Out of mind, out of sight.

After returning the Jetta to the rental agency, Jake ate at Dante's, an Italian restaurant on Second Avenue he and Sheryl had frequented. He ordered a bottle of their finest red wine, enjoyed a single glass before his dinner arrived, and set the bottle aside. He sipped a second glass with his dinner—linguini with red clam sauce—then took a cab downtown. His watch showed 7:48 when he reached the Tower, which appeared deserted. The protesters and all but two police officers had left, and now that the drought had ended, the illuminated fountains in front of the building rose five feet into the air. With just over two hours remaining before his deadline, Jake felt jittery as he glanced at the inky black sky.

Pulaski and an Indian guard named Badeseo guarded the private lobby. Jake had read Bada Badeseo's file, and he recalled that the man had been a cop in

Guyana. Graham sat at his security station on Sixty, exactly where Jake had left him eleven hours earlier. The exhausted-looking man nursed a cup of coffee, and his bulging eyes suggested that he had already consumed a gallon.

"Don't you ever go home?" Jake said as he entered the security bay.

Graham shook his head. "It's been a hectic day. The old man had some kind of medical emergency. His doctors have been going in and out since 10:30 this morning."

Jake raised his eyebrows. "Is he okay?" He needed Tower alive.

Graham shrugged. "As far as I know."

"Where's Kira?"

"Except for one meeting with Russel and some of his people, she's been with Old Nick all day."

"She give you any grief about me taking the day off?"

Shaking his head, Graham handed Jake a fresh walkie-talkie. "She didn't even seem surprised."

I'll bet, Jake thought, sliding the walkie-talkie into his coat pocket.

Graham set a new cell phone on top of the monitor nearest Jake. "This is for you."

Jake examined the device and pocketed it. "Thanks." He retrieved the framed photo of Sheryl from his office and went to his unit.

Dressed in silk pajamas, suede slippers, and a velvet robe, Tower sat in a wheelchair at his office desk, the Anting-Anting around his neck. He took a hit from his portable oxygen tank as he gazed at the monitors before him. "There goes Helman.".

Kira nodded. "I told you he'd be back. His wife is his greatest weakness."

"What time is it?"

"Almost eight o'clock."

"Is the Soul Catcher dead?"

"I'm sure everything's been taken care of."

He squeezed the Anting-Anting with gnarled fingers. "Take me to the Garden."

8:42 p.m.

Jake disinfected his swollen hand and changed its bandage. The bleeding had stopped, and he just hoped he had not suffered any nerve damage. He needed stitches on both sides of the hand, but that had to wait. He packed his clothes into his suitcase and lit a final cigarette.

8:57 p.m.

Yawning, Pulaski stretched at the security station console in the private lobby. Christ, he hated working weekends. He loved the overtime pay, but he had trouble dealing with the boredom factor. He stared at the monitors, their images as still as photographs. Occasionally he glanced out the doors, but the lack of traffic or pedestrians made him sleepy. Silence ruled the Tower.

"Why don't you let me sit down for a while?" Badeseo said from beside him. "I've been standing since we started."

"Fuck you. I've got seniority."

"Very good. One day I will have seniority, too."

"Don't count on it, Gunga Din."

Badeseo ignored the remark. Outside the glass doors, faces with blank stares appeared in the darkness, drifting closer. "We have visitors."

The Soul Searchers stepped before the glass doors and peered in at them.

Pulaski sat up straight. "Son of a bitch. What do these freaks want at this hour?"

9:02 p.m.

Jake stopped at the security bay station and Graham looked at his coat.

"You going out again?"

"No, I caught a chill yesterday and this AC is only making it worse."

Graham nodded. "Yeah, this place can be an icebox at times. Pulaski just called from downstairs. Our morning callers are paying us a nighttime visit."

Jake grunted. Maybe the Soul Searchers sensed something in the air. "Tell him to lock the doors." He did not want Sheryl's apparition anywhere near Cain.

"That's illegal while anyone's inside the building—fire hazard."

"I don't want any more trouble with those things, okay? Tell Pulaski to lock the doors and stand by them. If a building inspector or fire marshal shows up, he can unlock the doors before they give him any static."

"Okay," Graham said, reaching for his telephone.

Jake waved his card at the scanner for the utility corridor's glass door.

9:04 p.m.

Pulaski snatched the ringing telephone from its cradle. "Yeah?"

"Helman says to lock the doors," Graham said.

"Fuckin' A. I don't want these things getting anywhere near me. They might be radioactive or something."

"After you lock the doors, he wants you to stand by them in case an inspector comes along."

"Uh-huh. Maybe we should serve these things milk and cookies while we're at it." Pulaski hung up and turned to Badeseo. "Hey, Mowgli, the new boss man says to lock the front doors." He took a set of keys from a hook near the computer and tossed them into the air.

Badeseo caught the keys with one hand. "Then why don't you lock them?"

"Because I have seniority, you damned Ali Baba."

Badeseo offered an insincere smile. "It will be my pleasure, you damned redneck." He walked over to the glass doors, where the Soul Searchers stared at him with unblinking eyes. He found the right key, hunched over, and turned the locks at the bottom of each door frame. When he stood up, the faces continued to stare at him. "These are certainly pitiful wretches."

Pulaski grunted. "Then you should feel right at home with them. Stand there and unlock the doors if anyone who looks like a regular person shows up."

Sighing, Badeseo stared back at the strange-looking men and women.

9:06 p.m.

The security monitors glowed on Jake's face as he entered the Control Room. Many of them displayed empty cubicles on the corporate levels. One by one, he shut down the recorders, deleted their digital files, and erased the discs inside them.

9:09 p.m.

Kira pushed Tower in his wheelchair along the central path of his Garden of Eden. The overhead lights had dimmed, suggesting nighttime, and he held the oxygen mask in his lap, occasionally taking deep breaths from it.

"How are you feeling now?" Kira said.

"Better," Tower said. "Stronger. But—"

"What?"

He held out a shaking hand. "I feel like I've turned the final corner. The DCL-21 jump started my system, but it's saturating my blood. If our plan doesn't succeed, I'll never see the sun rise again."

Leaning over, she spoke into his ear. "It will work. It has to."

9:12 p.m.

Entering the dark conference room, Jake closed the door behind him and turned on his flashlight. Ignoring the spectacular view of the city, he strode to the Demonstration Room door and waved Kira's card at the scanner. The door unlocked and he stepped inside.

Cool air descended upon him from the ceiling, and he switched on the lights and closed the door, leaving it ajar just a crack. He crossed the humming room, gazing at the snakelike shadows that swam within the globe's murky green water. He placed his right hand on the curved glass, and one of the creatures dove toward it, flashing its teeth and hungry eyes at him. Jake stared at the face of the little monster. Was it his imagination, or did the creature resemble Tower? He left his hand on the glass and more Biogens appeared, all of them glaring at him as they tried to get at his flesh. He looked at the bottom of the globe, and in the sand he saw two human skulls and a pile of bones riddled with teeth marks.

Laddock and Birch, he thought.

The skeletons of the two security guards had been picked clean. Jake raised his eyes to the globe's top and saw a seam in the glass. Above it, an iron hook on a heavy chain hung from the ceiling. The top must have been removed, and the bodies lowered through it into the green liquid. He removed his hand from the cool glass and the creatures dispersed. Circling the globe's filtration system, he opened a metal lid and gazed down at clear water rushing through a metal trap. A wide faucet protruded from a device near the filter, over a round base with a blue button and a red button. Closing the lid, he wandered over to the metal drums stacked at the back of the room. He picked one up, shook it, and examined it. Three latches attached the lid, which had a three-inch valve on it, to the drum. Knocking on the lid, he heard a hollow echo inside. He carried the drum to the filter and set it down on the round base like a bowl on the turntable of a mixer, then rotated the base until the drum's valve aligned with the faucet: a perfect fit. He twisted the valve so that it adjoined the faucet and pressed the blue button.

The hum emanating from the globe's base grew louder and the green liquid whirled counterclockwise. The Biogens tried to swim against the powerful current, but their efforts proved useless: one by one, the filter sucked them toward its trap, and one of them disappeared. The faucet shook with a loud *shlurp!* and water gushed into the metal drum, accompanied by something solid. A moment later, Jake heard the creature shrieking, the horrible sound echoing inside the drum. He pressed the red button and the water in the globe stopped swirling. The Biogens resumed their swimming pattern. Closing the valve, he rotated the drum away from the faucet, which dripped green liquid. Swimming in a tight circle, the isolated creature bumped against the inside of the drum. Jake grabbed the metal handle with both hands and set the drum on the floor. He supposed it contained a gallon or so of mock seawater, enough to support the bloodthirsty creature for the immediate future.

Opening the filter's lid again, he removed a twenty-six-ounce container of kitchen salt from his coat pocket, compliments of the corporation. He pulled the tab on the container and poured the salt into the filter. A white cloud formed within the globe, and the Biogens swam away from it, their movements jerky. Jake shook the container, speeding the salt's flow until the creatures had no place to flee. Fissures opened in their bodies and trails of blood streaked the water. Jake slipped the empty container back into his coat pocket and watched the saltwater tear at the Biogens' flesh, dissolving it like Alka-Seltzer. Crablike legs burst through their sides and clawed at the glass surface. The creatures writhed in agony and exploded, their insides blooming outward. Oxygen bubbles rose to the top of the globe, and the cloudy water turned putrid brown.

9:41 p.m.

Entering the security bay, Jake set the drum on top of the security station and aimed his Glock at Graham's chest. Graham glanced at the gun and stiffened, his eyes registering alarm.

"I like you, Graham. Why don't you get lost?"

Graham swallowed. "I can't do that."

"Sure, you can. Take the night off. That's an order. And take Badeseo and that asshole Pulaski with you."

Graham rose to his feet. "You don't know what you're doing."

"Everyone keeps telling me that. You're all wrong. I know exactly what I'm doing. It's going down tonight. You understand? They killed my wife and there's going to be hell to pay."

Graham's eyes darted to the camera above the front door.

"Forget the cameras. Forget this job. Just get the hell out of here while you still have your soul. The Reaper will be here any minute, and this time he's going to have free run of the building. You don't want to get in his way."

Graham's eyes widened, and Jake saw the wheels in his head turning. Graham raced to the door and palmed the lock release.

"Graham?"

The bearded man looked at him. "I've copied all of Kira's personnel files. Whatever she had on you, I have, too. Forget I was even here tonight."

Graham nodded, then hurried to the elevators. Jake sat behind the station. He reached beneath the console, found a series of toggle switches, and flipped them up one by one. All of the doors around him unlocked in a staccato of metallic clicks. He stood, took the drum from the counter, and carried it to Kira's office doors, which opened with ease. As he crossed the threshold, the lights of midtown Manhattan beckoned beyond the windows. Turning to his right, Jake pressed his eye to the retina scanner and opened the anteroom door.

9:45 p.m.

Palming the anteroom's DNA scanner, Jake did not react as the needle pricked the back of his hand. The steel doors parted and he entered Tower's office. With his jaw set, he passed the miniature Tower and the monitors, then circled the gargantuan desk. Throwing open the doors leading to the atrium, he saw that the overhead lights had been dimmed to simulate nighttime. Lights glowed from beneath the waterfall and from behind bushes, and crickets chirped over invisible speakers. He headed toward the brick structure that housed the Soul Chamber. Pale yellow light spilled out from the open doorway onto the walkway.

Inside the building, with her back to Jake, Kira supported Tower at the viewing window. She held two thick documents with matching blue covers under her left arm. The old man wore a robe and pajamas, and Jake observed his profile: he appeared to have aged twenty years since the previous night, and he raised a portable oxygen mask to his face and took a hit. The spheres of light spun around the chamber, intensifying as Jake approached. The sudden flurry of activity caused Kira and Tower to turn around, and Jake saw that Tower wore his Philippine amulet in plain sight.

"Well, well," Jake said. "If it ain't Lady Macbeth and the Picture of Dorian Gray."

"There you are," Tower said with a weakened smile. "I wondered where you'd run off to."

Jake moved closer, the glow of the spheres on his face. "I had a few things to take care of."

Tower looked at the drum in Jake's bandaged hand. "Those Biogens were only prototypes, and would have perished soon anyway. You haven't impacted my deal with Seguera in the least."

Jake set the drum down on the floor. "Maybe so, but it felt good to kill something. I've heard that owners and pets start to resemble each other after a few years. The resemblance between you and these little monstrosities is downright genetic."

Tower's eyes twinkled. "We did incorporate some of my DNA into them. They're the closest things I have to offspring—other than Kira."

Jake glanced at Kira, who offered him a wicked smile. "I should have known." And then it occurred to him: when Kira had performed her disgusting act with the Biogen in her bathtub, she had actually been mating with a strain of her own species.

"I never met a woman who lived up to my expectations," Tower said, "so I had one created for me. Kira was grown from one of my cells. We didn't even need a whole rib."

"That's one way to fuck yourself."

Tower's smile faded, and he grasped Kira's hand with an arthritic claw. "We've never consummated our relationship, an unfortunate side effect of DCL-21. But our time is coming. Isn't it, my dear?"

Kira stared hard at Jake. "Yes, Daddy."

"She's the living embodiment of my fantasies," Tower said. "Surely you appreciated her abilities?"

Jake felt nauseous. Had he screwed Tower's daughter, or a younger, feminine version of the old man? "She was the best whore I've ever had."

Tower's face darkened, but Kira's smile remained unbroken.

"You used her to get at me," Jake said.

Tower's narrow lips tightened. "Kira's the fourth model in her lineage. She has a photographic memory, muscular dexterity, and intensified pheromones."

Jake recalled Kira's fragrance. Her genetically enhanced scent had aroused him, not her perfume or some magic spell.

"You couldn't help yourself," Tower said. "No one can resist her charms. And she craves me with every DNA strand in her body. I programmed her to desire what only I can give her: true power."

"What happened to her predecessors?"

Tower's silence spoke volumes.

Jake turned to Kira. "How does it feel knowing that you'll wind up on the scrap heap as soon as your sugar daddy here thinks up some new trick that you're unable to perform?"

Kira smirked. "I'm indispensable."

"I bet that's what all the trophy Biogens say."

Kira's smile faded. "I run Tower International."

"You're a witch."

She narrowed her eyes. "I did intern with a coven in Massachusetts, but the spells we use to shield the Tower were discovered through Nicholas's research project. No Wiccan has ever tapped into such power."

"She's irreplaceable." Tower said like a proud parent. "I intend for us to grow old together."

Jake gestured with his gun. "I'd say you're way ahead of her on that score."

"Put that gun away. If you shoot me now, your wife's soul will never see the light of heaven."

Jake maintained his grip on the Glock. "Thanks, but I think I'll hang onto it. It makes me feel better." He glanced sideways at Kira. "Besides, I could always shoot her."

Kira's eyes became slits. "I'll see your blood turn cold."

Jake smiled. "That's just pillow talk." He faced Tower. "You had the Cipher kill my wife to get me back here, and that solved another problem for you."

"My Soul Catcher. His carelessness made him a liability. Who better to take the fall for his execution than the vengeful spouse of one of his victims, an ex-cop who'd hunted him while still on the force?"

Jake cocked his head in Kira's direction. "You deliberately left your security card in my unit for me to find. That was the real purpose behind your late night visit."

"You weren't supposed to discover the Biogens," Kira

said. "We just wanted you to have access to my personal computer when the time came for you to learn the Soul Catcher's identity."

"You set us both up."

A satisfied look spread over Kira's features.

"Those tattoos on his body were as good as a signed confession."

"One can't be too obvious when dealing with the police," Tower said. "The original Soul Catchers had tattoos, too. Mayan symbols, representing the souls they'd absorbed. The more tattoos a priest had, the higher he rose in the sect. Kira merely encouraged our man to be as authentic as possible."

"What about Russel?"

"Bill's a capable man. He knows about the Biogens, of course, but not about my other endeavors."

"I read his file. His travel records over the last year correspond to incidents the media attributed to RAGE. But there is no RAGE, is there? You made them up to discredit the ACCL and paint yourself as a victim. Russel planted evidence that make them appear real."

Tower raised the oxygen mask to his face and took a hit.

"You say Russel doesn't know about your other projects, but some of the guards know about the Soul Searchers—"

Exhaling, Tower lowered the oxygen mask. "Why do you think I pay these Keystone Kops top dollar? Every man has his price—and every man becomes expendable eventually. Like Laddock and Birch. Hazard pay is an acceptable business expense."

Jake gazed through the viewing window at the spheres of light darting around the Soul Chamber like fireflies trapped in a jar. "What's in store for them?"

Tower took another hit of oxygen. "Let's just call them my insurance policy."

Jake looked at his watch. Though his left arm shook, he read the time: 9:58. Two minutes to spare. "You screwed up when you gave the order for that psycho to kill my wife." Turning in a small circle, he shouted at the ceiling: "Cain! *Come and get it!*"

9:59 p.m.

Tower turned to Kira with a look of excitement. "Cain? Of course! The first killer is the Reaper!"

"He had me snatched off the street for a little man-to-demon powwow yesterday," Jake said.

"I knew he would, but I didn't expect him to act so fast. That Soul Searcher's meltdown in the lobby triggered events ahead of schedule, and this heart attack of mine expedited the time table even more."

Jake narrowed his eyes. "You knew—?"

"I knew that the time would come when I'd need a Judas to betray me for thirty pieces of silver."

"You didn't need me to override this spell; you and Elvira here could have done it yourselves."

"But then I wouldn't have had the element of surprise on my side, and surprise is an essential factor in every negotiation."

Jake snorted. *Negotiation?*

The lights flickered and dimmed, and the air grew thick.

This is it.

A seam opened up in the air, three feet above the floor, like a tear in the middle of a piece of paper. Flames shot through it into the room, spread out, and coalesced into the shape of an immense man. The seam closed, the flames burned out, and Cain stretched his pulsating muscles as though he had just made a long car trip. The lights brightened again and the temperature rose. Anticipation filled Tower's eyes and Kira licked her lips. Inside the Soul Chamber, the spheres of light moved faster. Jake tightened his grip on the Glock.

"AT LAST," Cain said, staring down at Tower.

"Welcome to Tower International," Tower said between oxygen hits.

"OUR MEETING IS LONG OVERDUE. YOU HAVE PLAYED A GOOD GAME. YOU ARE THE FIRST HUMAN BEING TO EXTEND HIS LIFE FOR SO LONG BY UNNATURAL MEANS. YOU HAVE BROKEN NEW GROUND. THE FUTURE SHOULD PROVE INTERESTING. WE LOOK FORWARD TO IT."

"So do I," Tower said with a mischievous smile.

"YOU DON'T LOOK WELL, OLD MAN."

"I'll live."

"NOT LIKELY."

"Everything is negotiable."

Cain said nothing.

"We're both from old, respected families. I'm sure that we can find common ground for discussion."

"WE'LL HAVE ETERNITY FOR CONVERSATION."

"I prefer to conduct a dialogue here, in this world." Tower turned to Jake. "You're fired."

Jake waved the Glock in the air. "I think I'll stick around for the last act. A soul is at stake."

Tower turned back to Cain. "He's right, you know. A soul is at stake. Several, in fact."

"THIRTEEN."

"I'm glad to see that you follow current events." Tower swept his right arm toward the viewing window. "Take a look."

Jake stepped aside as Cain moved forward, and he felt tremendous heat on his face. Kira helped Tower step to the right side of the viewing window. Inside the chamber, the spheres ricocheted off the walls as Cain approached. The demon stopped six feet from the window and gazed at the trapped souls, their light shining on his hellish features.

"I possess something that even your Master doesn't," Tower said. "Innocent souls."

"THERE IS NO SUCH THING."

Tower shrugged. "Semantics. These souls were on their way up. Hell has never known such purity."

Jake watched Cain stand motionless, a bad feeling growing in the pit of his stomach.

"I CAN TAKE THEM ONCE I'VE CLAIMED YOUR SOUL."

"Who do you think you're talking to, a neophyte? I've done my research. I know some of the rules. These souls are in my possession. They belong to me. You could liberate them, but you could never take them back with you . . . unless I agree to give them to you."

Cain's face showed no sign of emotion. "WHAT DO YOU WANT IN RETURN?"

"That should be obvious."

"ETERNAL LIFE? NEVER."

"I thought as much. Sooner or later, every soul has to go one way or the other, doesn't it? And forever is a long time. With my resources, I just might achieve that on my own—if I had a little more time to continue my work."

"HOW MUCH MORE TIME?"

"A second lifetime should suffice."

"I'M LISTENING."

Tower smiled. Jake realized that he had underestimated the old man despite everything he knew about him. His finger tightened on the Glock's trigger.

"Ms. Thorn?" Tower nodded across the room.

Kira left Tower at the viewing window and crossed the room, glancing at Cain's lower region. She stopped at the giant metal cylinder and popped the machine's latches.

I knew it! Jake thought.

Kira raised the cylinder's lid like that of a casket. Bright light glowed inside it and she stepped back, revealing the horizontal body of a man. She gestured at the naked figure with a sweeping hand motion, like a hostess on a TV game show. The muscular man appeared to be twenty years old, and he must have been over six feet tall. His wrists and ankles had been clamped to the padded base that he laid upon, and he breathed with the machine's aid. Sensors attached to his temples and chest allowed the monitors on the wall to display his vital signs.

Jake stepped closer, peering at the face, and a shudder ran through him. Even with its eyes closed, the thing in the cylinder had Tower's features.

"I've had myself cloned several times for organ replacements," Tower said. "Adult models, grown in pods like this, not infants. You're looking at a vegetable. A shell waiting for a soul."

Cain turned from the clone to Tower. "WHAT ARE YOUR TERMS?"

He's going for the deal, Jake thought. Cain planned to betray him, too! His eyes turned to the hatch in the wall. He had to free Sheryl.

"I want a minimum of sixty years in that body," Tower said. "I want perfect motor function and health as Nicholas Tower Jr., whose DNA will prove that he's Old Nick's son. Tower Senior's documents will confirm that he provided for the care and education of his secret heir; there will be no contest in court. I wish to enjoy life without fear of pain, disease, or incarceration. I want to enjoy my beloved Kira's body to its fullest. There must be no *O. Henry* twist to spoil my plans."

Jake's mind reeled. What kind of diabolical brain hatched such schemes?

"I CAN TRANSFER YOUR MIND AND SOUL AS YOU WISH, AND WE WILL DO NOTHING TO UNDERMINE YOUR WISHES WHILE YOU INHABIT THAT BODY, BUT WE WILL PROVIDE YOU WITH NO ADDITIONAL PROTECTION. YOU WILL BE RESPONSIBLE FOR YOUR OWN HEALTH AND SAFETY, AS YOU ALWAYS HAVE BEEN."

Tower beamed. "Agreed. Then we have a deal in principle?"

Cain bowed his head and the light faded from his eyes, as if he were communicating with some unseen force. Jake tightened his grip on the Glock. Kira's breasts rose and fell, her eyes bright with excitement. Then Cain's eyes glowed again as he looked at Tower.

"AGREED."

Jake felt anger flushing through his body. He had been sold out by both of these monsters!

"Splendid," Tower said. "I hope you don't mind, but I've had Kira draw up some contracts for us to sign. It's best to cross our T's and dot our I's in an agreement as unique as this, don't you think?"

Cain said nothing.

Tower turned to Kira. "My dear—?"

Taking took one step forward, Kira dropped both copies of the contract on the floor, oblivious of everything in the room except for Cain. She grabbed the flaps of her blouse and pulled them apart, popping buttons and exposing her full breasts. She stepped into Cain's shadow and gazed up at his glowing pupils. "*Take me.*"

Tower's face collapsed like the infrastructure of a demolished building, and Jake blinked as Kira reached up and seized Cain's skull with both hands. Standing on her toes, she pulled his head down toward her face and kissed him on the mouth. Probing him with her tongue, she pressed her breasts against his muscular chest, then wrapped her left leg around his right leg and ground her pelvis against his enormous penis.

"I think you programmed her too well," Jake said to Tower, who watched his fantasy woman stroke Cain's penis with one hand.

Fanning the fingers of one hand over the back of Kira's head, Cain returned her kiss. Jake considered making a run for the wall hatch, but he knew that the demon would never allow him to reach it. Cain's black tongue moved into Kira's mouth, forcing her to open her jaws wider, her eyes filling with panic. He reached around her back with his right arm and lifted her off the floor. His tongue continued to slither into her mouth and down her throat like a great serpent, and Jake thought he saw spotted scales on its slimy surface. Kira beat at Cain's chest and tried to kick him, but he turned as solid and immovable as a statue. Her throat expanded, as if she had swallowed a whole squash, and her body shook. She went slack in Cain's arms and the serpent retreated back into his mouth. He released her body, which slumped against the cylinder's base, and she stared up at him with catatonic eyes.

"SHE HAS NO SOUL."

Swallowing, Tower fingered his amulet. "What did you do to her?"

"I GAVE HER WHAT SHE WANTED: A TASTE OF REAL POWER. SHE WAS TOO HUNGRY FOR HER OWN GOOD. YOU WERE SAYING—?"

Tower took a hit of oxygen and glanced at the discarded contracts on the floor. "I suppose we can dispense with the formality of a written contract." He cast a weary eye in Jake's direction. "A handshake's good enough for me, isn't it, Jake?"

Jake stared at the billionaire. *Can you read my mind?*

Cain cracked his knuckles and Tower cringed. "A HANDSHAKE, THEN." The demon extended his right hand.

Tower stared at the hand as if it carried the plague. Swallowing, he stepped forward, shifting the oxygen unit into his left hand . . .

Aiming the Glock in the direction of the old man's head, Jake squeezed the trigger. Tower flinched at the sound of the gunshot, and the viewing window ruptured into a spiderweb of cracks behind him. Cain jerked his head toward Jake. A moment passed before Tower realized that he had not been shot.

Jake had been tempted to put a bullet in the old man's head, but he wanted to avoid signing his handiwork if possible. Seizing the metal drum in both hands, he turned it sideways and popped two of the three latches securing its lid. He stepped to one side and hurled the drum at Tower with all of his strength.

Tower cried out as the drum struck his chest and propelled him through the weakened glass, which shattered. He disappeared over the window's edge, taking large shards of glass with him. The spheres of light scattered in different directions, like pool balls on a break. The drum rolled over Tower's head and struck the middle of the mosaic floor.

"No!" Cain bellowed.

The drum's lid popped off and green liquid sloshed out as it rolled rattling against one of the columns supporting the roof.

Jake and Cain rushed to the shattered viewing window and stared at Tower, who lay on the floor, his robe covered with broken glass and blood trickling from his mouth. Moaning, Tower rolled onto his chest and propped himself up on his elbows. Ahead of him, the Biogen emerged hissing from the drum and sped at him with hungry eyes, slithering like a powerful snake. Jake had not expected the creature to be so fast on land. Eyes widening, Tower groped for the Anting-Anting around his neck. He opened his mouth to scream, which allowed the Biogen to squirm past his jaws. The old man struggled to his feet, gagging on the creature's head. A high-pitched squeal escaped through his nostrils as the Biogen, feasting on his tongue, burrowed down his throat. He staggered toward the broken window, reaching out with his shaking right hand, still hoping to seal his devil's bargain.

Jake vaulted over the edge, kicking Tower in the chest with both feet, and Cain's fingers closed around empty air. Tower struck the floor and rolled to its center. He convulsed as the Biogen snaked inside him, the end of its tail disappearing through his mouth.

Stepping over the old man, Jake looked down. Tower stared up at him with hateful eyes, helpless as the Biogen chewed its way through his jerking body. Blood fountained out of his mouth and nose and the light faded from his eyes.

Cain stared at Jake, his fury palpable. The spheres of light formed a perfect circle around Jake and spun around him clockwise. He saw vague impressions of distorted faces within them, crying out for freedom. He stared through the ring of light at Cain, who shook with anger. Then he lifted his gaze to the stained-glass skylight.

Cain leapt over the window ledge with blinding speed. The spheres rose in perfect formation above Jake, escaping the approaching demon's reach. Aiming his gun at the skylight as Cain bore down on him like a mad bull, Jake squeezed the trigger and kept it depressed, the gunshots sounding like firecrackers. The stained glass above him exploded, shards raining down. He stopped firing and dove free of the downpour, rolled across the mosaic floor, and came up crouching behind a column. Falling glass sliced Tower's body and the Biogen inside it to ribbons and shattered on the floor before Cain.

One by one, the spheres streaked up and out of the Tower, comet tails trailing them, and vanished into the night sky. Jake felt his chest contract: a single sphere remained behind. It circled the chamber, dodging Cain's outstretched hand as the demon tried to snag it.

Sheryl!

Jake rose to his feet and the sphere streaked straight at him. He spread his arms apart in a welcoming gesture, the Glock dangling in his right hand. The sphere struck his chest dead center and entered his body. He felt himself absorbing Sheryl's energy, and for an instant he felt closer to her than ever before, every nerve in his body tingling with her purity. He saw Cain charging at him again, but he did not care; having achieved his goal, he stood ready to die.

A single thought pressed itself on his mind: *I love you, Jake.*

The sphere emerged from his back and Cain skidded to a stop before him, shrouding him in shadow. Sheryl's soul spiraled toward the ceiling and disappeared into the night. His body still tingling, Jake felt tears in his eyes.

Cain pulled his arms back and thrust his hands into Jake's chest, his forearms disappearing into Jake's body. The triumphant grin on his face faded, replaced by a look of bewilderment.

Standing toe to toe with the demon, Jake felt no pain

or discomfort. Looking over his shoulder, he saw Cain's hands protruding from his back, grasping at empty air. Cain roared, filling Jake's nostrils with putrid-smelling breath. The demon took a single step back, pulling his arms free of Jake's chest and opening and closing his fingers. Jake patted his torso, which showed no signs of mutilation. A brilliant white light filled the Soul Chamber, solidifying into a familiar human figure in a cowboy outfit.

"Hello, brother."

Jake felt relieved to see Abel again. Cain's pupils pulsed red and steam rose from his body.

"STAY OUT OF THIS! YOU ARE NOT PERMITTED TO INTERFERE."

Abel looked around the Soul Chamber and at Tower's tattered corpse. "Oh, I'm just observing. But Jake's beyond your reach now. His wife's spirit has cleansed his soul."

Cain stepped past Jake and punched Abel in the face with ferocious power. Abel collapsed onto the floor with his Stetson beside him, his nose having disintegrated in a soft explosion of blood. Jake watched wide-eyed as Cain straddled Abel, seizing his brother's head in both hands, and drove his thumbs into Abel's eyeballs, rupturing them. Abel screamed and Cain smashed his head on the floor over and over.

Jake stepped back as blood spread across the mosaic tiles. Abel turned still and silent, but Cain continued to smash his head on the floor, crushing his skull like a giant eggshell. A flash of white light made Jake close his eyes, and when he opened them again Abel had disappeared, along with the Stetson and his blood. Cain balled his empty hands into fists and stood facing Jake once more.

Holy fucking shit! Jake thought, swallowing.

Cain's shaking body pulsated red light, like a volcano poised to erupt. Turning toward the bloody shreds of Tower's corpse, he reached out to it with the fingers of his left hand spread wide apart. Black light pulsed within the gory heap on the floor and a dark sphere rose from the carnage. Gray and black and bloody, like a malignant tumor, it floated toward Cain, drawn to him. Jake thought he saw Tower's face screaming within the sphere before the demon's body absorbed it. Cain trembled for an instant, like a junkie receiving a fix.

Jake could not help flinching when Cain thrust a finger in his face.

"WE WILL MEET AGAIN." Flames burst from inside his body, enveloping him. Jake felt tremendous heat on his face. The flames burned out, as if a gas line had been shut off, and Cain disappeared, leaving behind the faint smell of sulfur.

Jake stood shaking for a moment, then crossed the Soul Chamber and hopped over the window ledge into the viewing room. Stepping before Kira, he pressed the barrel of the Glock against her forehead and squeezed the trigger. He heard an empty-sounding click. Kira's mouth opened and she drooled a long strand of saliva. *Fuck it,* he thought, lowering the empty gun.

He studied Tower's clone, which continued breathing inside the cylinder. Did it have a soul? Cain had said that Kira did not. Had he spoken literally? How would the world fare in the hands of a Nicholas Tower with no soul, even a corrupt one? Closing the lid, he fastened its latches and disconnected the life support equipment. A flat line appeared on one of the monitors. He glanced at his watch: 10:20 p.m. He decided to take one last walk in the Garden of Eden.

35

Jake's sneakers squeaked on the polished floor as he carried his luggage through the deserted lobby. Pulaski and Badeseo had followed Graham's lead, and the Soul Searchers had disappeared. Exiting through the only unlocked door, he stepped outside. The cold night air refreshed him as he walked to the East River, where he tossed his Glock and its silencer. He felt he'd covered his tracks pretty well, but he'd still shot up the Soul Chamber. At Twenty-third Street, he hailed a taxi.

He checked into the Lexington—not his old room—and remembered to hang the DO NOT DISTURB sign outside the door. He unpacked clothes for the next day, then took a long, hot shower before falling asleep in the king-sized bed.

The next morning, he awoke with a start. Sunlight streamed into the room, and he did not recall any dreams or nightmares. He did feel a pang of disappointment: he had hoped that Sheryl would visit him one more time.

I'm alive, thanks to her.

His muscles ached, his body bruised from his numerous encounters.

Purchasing the Sunday newspapers at a corner newsstand, he felt no desire to buy cigarettes; perhaps Sheryl had purged him of his addictions once and for all. He scanned the papers over breakfast in a coffee shop but found nothing in them about Old Nick, Tower International, or the Cipher.

It was Sunday, and he turned off his cell phone and rested.

On Monday morning, he checked out of the Lexington, bought the papers, and took a taxi uptown. He did not want to remain in the apartment without Sheryl, but it would have to do for the time being. The front pages of the *Daily News* and the *New York Post* featured photographs of Marc Gorman. "REVENGE," announced the News, with the tag, "Police Believe Murder Victim Was the Cipher." "EXECUTION OF A SERIAL KILLER," declared the *Post*.

Skimming the articles, Jake learned that Gorman's downstairs neighbor had complained to the building's super when blood had seeped through her kitchen ceiling.

The super had let himself into Gorman's apartment and discovered his body, as well as "undisclosed evidence leading police to believe Gorman was the serial slayer known as the Cipher."

Both papers featured two-page pictorial spreads on the life and times of Nicholas Tower, a.k.a. Old Nick, who had died of a heart attack on Saturday night while in the care of his personal physician, Dr. Kenneth Gavin. Photos showed Tower before he had become a recluse, and his personal monument, the Tower. His body had been cremated, according to Gavin, "to protect Mr. Tower's impressive legacy from ghoulish paparazzi hoping to exploit his death." The articles pointed to Tower's aggressive advances in the genetics field as his major contribution to humanity, and speculated that he might have lived longer if the FDA had approved the sale of DCL-21. Neither paper mentioned Laddock or Birch, the skeletal remains in the tank, the dead clone, or Kira Thorn's mental collapse. Folding the papers, Jake paid the taxi driver and got out.

He felt strange carrying his luggage upstairs, and even stranger entering the apartment. Edgar had left a business card taped to the front door, with Sunday's date on it. Setting his bags down, Jake looked around. CSU had taken care to leave everything as he had left it. Opening the living room blinds, he felt Sheryl's presence all around him. He picked up a water bottle and sprayed her hanging plants. The petals had started falling from the roses he had given her.

The LED light on the answering machine flashed

nonstop. He decided to listen to the messages later, and carried his bags to the bedroom, stopping in the doorway. The bed in the dark room seemed like a grave calling out to him, and he decided to sleep on the sofa.

He called Edgar two hours later.

"Where have you been?" Edgar said. "I left half a dozen messages."

"I crashed at a hotel and turned my cell phone off. Thanks for cleaning up in here."

"Don't mention it. Vasquez helped. Did you read today's papers?"

"Yeah, I saw them."

"The evidence in Gorman's apartment confirms he was the Cipher, and his DNA matches some skin samples we found under Sheryl's fingernails. She must have put up a fight. Someone did the world a favor." He paused. "Your supervisor already told us you were at the Tower all day on Saturday after you left the station, so you won't have to come in for questioning."

Jake's heart skipped a beat. "My supervisor?"

"That Thorn woman. We called her first thing this morning, and she came in and gave us a statement. You're not even a suspect."

Did he detect a trace of sarcasm in Edgar's voice?

Jake felt his stomach tightening. It had not taken Kira long to recover from Cain's kiss, and she had cleared Jake of Gorman's murder, even though Tower had intended for him to take the fall for it all along.

"I won't keep you," Edgar said. "I just wanted you to know that you don't have to worry about this. Let me know about the funeral arrangements, okay?"

"Yeah." Dreading making the necessary calls, he hung up the phone and massaged his temples. *I should have finished her off with my bare hands,* he thought. *But then I wouldn't have this alibi.*

He went over to the liquor cabinet and opened its door.

When the doorbell rang an hour later, he knew that Kira had come for him. Stepping out of the bathroom, he buzzed her into the building, then unlocked the door and stood in the hall. The sounds of Mozart filled the apartment, one of Sheryl's CDs. Unarmed, he wished that he had held onto his Glock just a little longer. Footsteps rose from below and fear crawled up his spine.

It ends here, he thought. A shadow stretched across the stairway wall and Kira came into view, wearing a long black leather coat belted at the waist. She had never looked more beautiful, and Jake felt sick to his stomach.

She stepped before him, her hands deep in her pockets, the familiar half smile on her lips.

"Hello, Jake."

Just like that. "You look better than you did the last time I saw you."

She tilted her head to one side. "You mean when you pressed your gun against my forehead and pulled the trigger?"

Stay cool. "Yeah, that time."

"I feel better, too. And I have a proposition for you."

"I'm in mourning. Get yourself another private dick."

She held her smile. "Nicholas named me as his sole beneficiary in case he died before completing his deal with the Reaper. I'm a multibillionaire now, and I'm officially the president of Tower International."

Jake snorted. "Congratulations. You fucked hard for it."

"Why don't you let me in and hear me out?"

Staring into her crocodile eyes, he felt only loathing. "All right." *Better here than in some dark alley.* He stepped back, and as she glided past him, he caught a whiff of her scent. Muscles tensing, he closed the door and locked it. He joined Kira in the living room, keeping a safe distance between them.

She surveyed the room without turning her head. "What a quaint apartment."

"Make your pitch." He disliked her judging Sheryl

in any way.

She faced him. "I'd like you to come back to the Tower as my DS. With Graham and Pulaski in hiding, I'm short on qualified staff."

"What about Russel? He was qualified enough to help you cover up everything that went down Saturday night."

She seemed amused. "Bill left for the Philippines this morning. Besides, he despises office work."

"I know the feeling."

She stepped closer to him. "Come on, Jake. Everything will be legit this time. No demons, no ghosts, no witchcraft."

"How about Biogens?"

"We have to honor our contract with President Seguera, and we'll continue to develop different life forms for research purposes, but I plan to focus our resources on genetic medicines. I want to rid the world of the diseases that still plague us."

"You and Miss America. What happens when your hair turns gray and those magnificent tits of yours start to sag? How legitimate will your goals be then? It's in your genes to fear old age and death, and I doubt your libido will tolerate those DCL-21 side effects."

Her smile cooled. "I'll cross that bridge when I come to it, darling."

"You'll cross it without me."

She removed her hands from her pockets, the fingers of her hands extended like talons. "I hoped you'd say something like that."

"That's why you covered up for me with the police, isn't it? If I went to prison for killing the Cipher, you couldn't exact your revenge on me in person. You're too 'hands-on' to let Russel cap me for you."

"While I admit to being disappointed that you ruined Nicholas's plan, I wouldn't exactly say that I'm out for revenge. He knew the chances he was taking, and he lived longer than he should have. I was willing to betray him myself to be with Cain. You just know too much for my own good." She unbuttoned her coat and allowed it to slip to the floor around her ankles. She stood naked before him, her nipples hard. "I came here to eat you."

Stepping back, Jake drew a knife from beneath his sweater, flipped it into the air, and caught its blade, poised to throw it.

Kira stepped out of her high heels. "I've wanted to do this ever since we fucked." Closing her hands into fists, she gritted her teeth until her face turned scarlet. "Nicholas's DNA wasn't the only genetic material used to create me." She raised her fists to her face, her elbows level with her shoulders. Concentrating, she clenched her teeth. Her face turned red and her upper body shook. Then a milky substance squirted out of her sides, two inches beneath her armpits. Ribs snapped inside her body and one slimy appendage burst through her flesh on each side of her torso.

Jake watched the appendages unfold into fully developed arms with articulated hands. More pseudo-milk squirted out of her sides, and two more arms escaped from the confines of her torso, below the second pair. She interlaced the fingers on her four new hands, their nails unpainted, and cracked twenty fresh knuckles. With little mass remaining between her breasts and her hips, her midsection appeared insect-like, and Jake shuddered to imagine her skeletal structure.

"If Nicholas was my father," she said, "then my mother was a black widow. It's in my nature to devour my mate." All six of her arms stretched their muscles, readying for action. "That's why Daddy destroyed my sisters. He wanted the ultimate bodyguard and the ultimate lay in one perfect body, but the combination presented certain complications."

Jake stood gaping. *I can't believe I fucked that!* He recalled the spider tattoo on her back. It must have been some kind of identification tag. Cocking his right arm and aiming for her heart, he threw the knife. Kira twisted her body to one side and the blade sank into her left shoulder. She pulled it out with one hand and ran her tongue over the blade, which she then tossed aside. Her breasts rose and fell, her face slick with perspiration.

"I mailed copies of your files to the Justice Department," Jake said. "I'm afraid you're president of a sinking Tower."

Kira's breathing turned ragged with anger. "You . . . little . . . *amoeba!*"

Jake spun on one heel and ran, certain that if he managed to escape through the front door she would catch him on the stairs. He wanted to duck into the bathroom, but his instincts told him that she would seize him as he made the turn. Sprinting straight into the bedroom, he gripped the door with both hands. Kira charged at him in a perfect cartwheel, her six hands and two feet rotating her body head over heels in his direction. He waited until she rolled through the doorway, then slammed the door on her and stepped back. The door burst open and she came out of the cartwheel on top of him. She wrapped her legs around his neck and her momentum drove them onto the bed. Jake lay on his back with Kira's pubis in his face. Straddling him, she reached back with two hands, pinning his ankles to the bed. Two more hands held his wrists down, and two remained free.

Jake gritted his teeth as she cut off his oxygen. He strained against her arms, her strength too great for him. He tried to bridge up on his neck, and she laughed at him. Her scent penetrated his flesh, her pheromones overpowering his senses, and he felt himself turning hard despite the intense fear that he felt. She reached back with one of her free hands and rubbed his crotch.

"Come on, Jake. Fuck me again. I want to taste your fear when I swallow you."

Jake laced the fingers of his hands together and pounded his doubled fists between her breasts, directly over her heart. The blow sent a shock wave of pain through his left hand. Kira grunted in surprise, pain distorting her face, and fell off him. Rolling off the bed, she toppled to the floor, all six of her hands landing palms down on the rug. She shook her head as Jake leapt off the bed. His footsteps hammered the floor, sending vibrations through the wood to her.

Turning in the doorway, out of breath and heart racing, Jake was unprepared for what he saw next. Kira crawled across the floor at an incredible speed, her arms raising her body above the floor and her legs pumping behind her for velocity. Her face a mask of rage, she gnashed her teeth.

Jake pulled the bedroom door shut behind him and ran into the bathroom. Slamming the door shut and pressing his body against it, he pushed the doorknob's feeble lock. Facing the drawn shower curtain, he wondered if he could escape through the small, translucent window behind it. He heard the bedroom door crash open, followed by what sounded like several children running over the carpet. Kira's body thudded against the lower part of the bathroom door. Her fists pounded on the wood behind his knees and rose to a point behind his head as she stood up. He scanned the bathroom for anything he could use as a weapon.

One of Kira's fists burst through the door on his right and clawed at his face. He twisted his head away and shoved her hand to one side. Another fist smashed through the wood on the opposite side of his head and seized him in a choke hold. Biting her forearm, he tasted blood, and she released him with a strangled cry. When a third fist smashed through the wood, he knew that he was fighting a losing battle. Reaching down, he grasped the wooden handle of the toilet plunger, twisted it free of its rubber cup, and stepped away from the door, facing it with his back to the shower curtain.

Using all of her hands, Kira tore the door apart, then charged through its jagged frame at Jake, who swung the handle at her like a baseball bat. The handle struck her face and she cried out as blood flew from her nostrils. Snaring his wrist with one hand, she wrenched the handle from his grasp with another. She backhanded him and he retaliated with a punch that dislodged her jaw.

Kira threw the wooden handle on the floor like a gauntlet and pummeled Jake with all six of her fists. He tried to box her, which felt like fighting three people at the same time with only one good hand. Her fists rained down on him, striking his head, his chest, his arms, and his stomach. He saw a blur of motion, with Kira's leering face the eye of the storm. He collapsed and two of her hands seized his upper arms, holding him upright. Then he felt himself being lifted off the floor. Two hands grabbed him beneath his armpits, and two more clutched his waist.

Kira pulled him toward her, and she kissed him on the mouth, jamming her tongue into it. He clamped his teeth shut, denying her entry. She laughed at him, but with her jaw hanging at an askew angle, she sounded more like a fighting alley cat. Rotating his body, she turned him upside down. Her mouth nipped at his crotch, making him grateful that he wore denim. Two of her hands gripped his throat and she forced his head into the toilet bowl. Realizing that she intended to drown him, he seized the bowl's rim with both hands and held his head above water. His vision blurred and he started to lose consciousness. He squeezed the toilet bowl hard, sending a shock wave of pain through his left hand that revived him. Kira came into focus again, sneering at him. Out of the corner of his right eye, he glimpsed the drawn shower curtain behind her. Bringing his right knee to his chest, he set his foot on what remained of Kira's abdomen and kicked out with all of his remaining strength. Kira cried out, her fingernails raking his neck as she flew backward. Her calves struck the edge of the tub, and she fell back into the vinyl curtain. Three of her arms flailed for the curtain rod but fell short. Her head smashed against the tiled wall behind the curtain, and she dropped ass-first into the water that Jake had run before her arrival. Her legs dangled over the tub's metal rim, and for a moment she looked confused. Then her eyes went wild and she sucked in her breath.

Jake stood up, massaging his neck.

The bathwater fizzed.

Kira looked down at the bubbling water, her face filled with fear as she clawed at the tub's edge. The water churned, foamed, and turned pink. Jake watched the remainder of Kira's midsection dissolve.

"Help me!" she said in a strangled voice, her jaw moving in an unnatural manner.

He kicked over the wastebasket and empty liquor bottles clattered on the tiled floor. Jim Beam, Johnny Walker, Smirnoff's, and Black Velvet—all of his old favorites. Seeing the bottles, Kira's eyes bulged in their sockets.

"Tower told me he'd built an Achilles' heel into all of his Biogens. With those snake things, it was salt, to prevent them from escaping the Philippines by sea. I knew that wasn't practical for a corporate biped like you, but I remembered you telling me that you don't drink because you're allergic to alcohol, so I made you a special cocktail."

Kira clung to the tub's edge with four hands, the remaining two pressed against the back wall for support as she tried to lift herself out of the water. Discarding the empty wastebasket, Jake raised his right foot and stomped on each of the hands before him. Kira held fast as pustules appeared on her flesh, pus erupting from them. She screamed as her torso separated from her hips. She resembled an insect as her upper body came free of the water.

She had a desperate yet determined expression on her face, as if she believed she could survive without the lower half of her body, which had almost completely dissolved. Jake grabbed the curtain rod with both hands and kicked her face, hard. What remained of Kira splashed into the bath, submerged in pink, foamy liquid. The curtain fell back into place and Jake jerked it open. When Kira rose to the surface, her eyelids, nose, lips, and nipples had dissolved, revealing cartilage, muscles, and bones. Her hair had become a sheen of dark slime clinging to her head and neck, and she stared at Jake with pleading eyes.

"Help meeeeee . . ." Her hands clawed at the air until her elbows dissolved, and then her forearms toppled into the water, where her fingers trembled.

"I'll help you," Jake said. "Just like you helped Sheryl."

Kira read the look in his eyes. Her body convulsed, and she opened her mouth wider than Jake had thought possible. He expected a forked tongue to dart out at him. Instead, a dark gray substance shot past his head, striking the mirror of the medicine cabinet behind him. The substance stank like vomit and congealed into a thick, gooey line extending from Kira's mouth to the mirror.

A spiderweb!

The mirror snapped open and slammed against the tiled wall, and Kira's upper body rose from the water as she sucked the web back into her mouth. Jake retrieved the toilet plunger handle and swung it at her as if she were a piñata. The web snapped and she splashed back into the tub. He climbed in after her, straddling her, and drove the handle between her dissolving breasts, forcing her trunk to the tub's bottom. The churning water splashed his face. Kira's eyes exploded in their sockets and her jaw separated, her tongue disappearing in a burst of bubbles.

Jake reached over the side of the tub, grabbed her dangling legs, and pulled them in. Feeling no sympathy for her, he only wished that he had more booze and a larger tub. Within minutes, nothing remained of Nicholas Tower's progeny. Jake sat on the tub's edge, his jeans soaked to his thighs. Blood soaked his bandage, but he did not care. Opening the drain, he watched the slimy water recede.

EPILOGUE

Jake laid Sheryl to rest five days later, after the autopsy on her had been performed. Her funeral took place in a cemetery located off the Long Island Expressway in Queens. Cops called that stretch of the LIE the Cemetery Expressway because so many boneyards occupied the land around it. The Manhattan skyline overlooked the gravestones, and the sun broke through the clouds, golden rays splitting the sky. Jake thought it a glorious sight, more impressive than anything Nicholas Tower could have concocted in the Tower.

Detectives from Special Homicide attended the service, as well as members of the Street Narcotics Apprehension Program. The priest who had married Jake and Sheryl performed this ceremony as well, and Jake's former colleagues served as pallbearers. None of the mourners seemed to notice the man with the mirrored sunglasses and long blond ponytail standing at the back of the crowd.

After the casket had been lowered into the ground, Jake tossed one dozen dead roses down onto it. If anyone found that peculiar, they kept it to themselves. As the mourners dispersed, Edgar and Vasquez joined Jake, and Edgar handed him a thick envelope.

"We took up a collection at the station. I hope this helps with the expenses."

Jake felt too touched to refuse the donation. "Thanks. Tell everyone I appreciate it."

"Are you going to be okay?"

"Yeah, I'll get through this somehow. It may sound corny, but at least I know she's in a better place."

"Good for you," Vasquez said.

Jake smiled. "Thanks for coming."

"No problem." She looked at Edgar.

"Well, I guess we'd better get back to the shop," Edgar said. "The Cipher may be dead, but we've still got plenty of customers to catch, including one very popular vigilante." He held out his hand. "See you around?"

"Count on it." Jake shook his hand. "I've decided to get my PI license."

Edgar laughed. "Oh, boy. Jake Helman, Private Investigator. I guess we will be bumping into each other."

Vasquez smiled. "Take care of yourself, Jake."

The Homicide detectives crossed the manicured lawn to their unmarked police car.

"They make a good team."

Jake looked at Abel. "Yeah, I guess they do. You look well."

Abel shrugged. "It helps when you can control your appearance."

"When you two go at it, you go all-out."

"It's always been that way."

"How goes the war?"

Abel gazed at the sun. "We won a major battle, thanks to those liberated souls."

Jake's voice turned somber. "How is she?"

"I shouldn't be telling you this, but I guess we owe you that much. She's looking over your shoulder right now."

Turning around, Jake only saw gravestones gleaming in the sunlight.

"You can't see her. But if you do ascend to the Realm of Light, you'll be closer to her than you ever were here on Earth."

Jake raised his eyebrows. "'If'—?"

"You might have a long life ahead of you. Are you sure you can walk the straight and narrow?"

Jake grunted. "Maybe I'm too down-to-earth for heaven."

"Don't sell yourself short. You did well. Sheryl and the others are free because of you."

Jake squinted as wind blew in his face. "Will I see you again?"

Abel shrugged. "'Where's Old Nick?'"

Jake stared at his companion for a moment, debating whether or not the superior being had made a joke. Then he laughed and Abel joined him.

They both knew where Old Nick was.

Medallion
M
PRESS

twitter

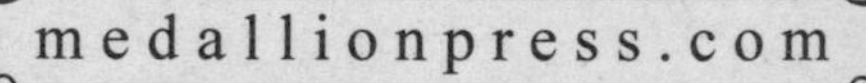
medallionpress.com